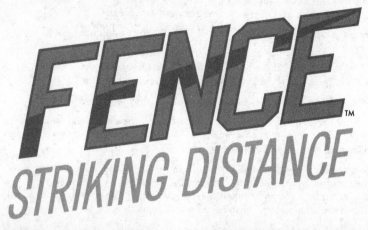

An original novel by
Sarah Rees Brennan
Based on the Fence comics created by
C.S. Pacat and Johanna The Mad

Little, Brown and Company
New York Boston

Cover design by Ching N. Chan. Cover illustration by Johanna The Mad.

Little, Brown and Company
Hachette Book Group
1290 Avenue of the Americas, New York, NY 10104
Visit us at LBYR.com

First Edition: September 2020

Little, Brown and Company is a division of Hachette Book Group, Inc.
The Little, Brown name and logo are trademarks of Hachette Book Group, Inc.

The publisher is not responsible for websites (or their content) that are not owned by the publisher.

Library of Congress Cataloging-in-Publication Data
Names: Brennan, Sarah Rees, author. | Pacat, C.S. Fence. | Johanna The Mad, illustrator.
Title: Fence: striking distance : an original novel / by Sarah Rees Brennan ; based on the Fence comics created by C.S. Pacat and Johanna The Mad.
Other titles: Striking distance
Description: First edition. | New York : Little, Brown and Company, 2020. | Audience: Ages 14+. | Summary: "The boys of Kings Row are assigned a course of team building exercises to deepen their bonds. It takes a shoplifting scandal, a couple of moonlit forest strolls, and a whole lot of introspection for the team to realize they are stronger together than they could ever be apart."—Provided by publisher.
Identifiers: LCCN 2020005647 | ISBN 9780316456678 (paperback) | ISBN 9780316456661 (ebook) | ISBN 9780316456685 (ebook other)
Subjects: CYAC: Interpersonal relations—Fiction. | Boarding schools—Fiction. | Schools—Fiction. | Fencing—Fiction. | Gays—Fiction.
Classification: LCC PZ7.B751645 Fen 2020 | DDC [Fic]—dc23
LC record available at https://lccn.loc.gov/2020005647

ISBNs: 978-0-316-45667-8 (pbk.), 978-0-316-45666-1 (ebook)

Printed in the United States of America

LSC-C

10 9 8 7 6 5 4 3 2 1

For C.S. Pacat and Johanna The Mad,

who built the school together.

Go team!

From: coachwiththemost@kingsrow.com

To: ermentrudewilliams@tmail.com

Re: you don't call, you don't write, you only fence . . .

Hey Ermie,

I'm sorry I haven't written in a while. Every time I start an email, a kid runs into my office with an emotional crisis and a sword.

You're right; it feels strange that I'm here and not back home. Of course I want to live closer to you. I miss you all the time. You're my big sister! I want to meet up for coffee every weekend and help you train Bruno not to eat the potted plants.

But I see something at this school that I haven't seen in fifteen years of coaching.

You'd love Connecticut if you visited. Kings Row is on a hundred acres, with woods you can get lost in and a lake the boys are strictly forbidden to go near. All the buildings are rambling redbricks from the 1800s, and they still teach Latin. The school was established a century ago to teach boys how to be "proper young gentlemen." Which meant those young gentlemen, as a natural part of their education, learning the blade.

Trouble is, their team has never won a state fencing championship. It's been decades since they even got close—decades of boys with dreams, chasing gold they could never win.

But something is different this year.

Yeah, this team is rough. They've never fenced together before, and some of them are complete newcomers to the sport. Our captain, Harvard Lee, is solid—he has a heart of gold and is the kind of kid who shoulders everyone's burdens. But his best friend is the school flirt, Aiden Kane. You may recall him from the times I have screamed into your ear, "Don't talk to me about Aiden Kane!" Do you know how many boys I've seen absolutely wipe out because they're heartbroken over him?

And then there are the freshmen. Nicholas Cox is a kid who's had no formal training. He sticks out at this school like a sore thumb. The kids around here don't know what to do with his undercut hair or his lower-class slang. At the other extreme, there's Seiji Katayama, the perfect fencer. He's lived and breathed nothing but the sword since he was five years old. He and Nicholas couldn't be more different, and when they're in a room it's like a cat and a dog forced into a bath together. But on the *piste* . . .

. . . On the *piste,* they have potential. They all do.

So I'm not coming home. I'm staying at Kings Row, because this year we're going to win the state championship. I want to see these boys pull together and become a true team. I know they can do it.

They're good kids. Even Aiden.

And I have a plan to prove it. . . .

SEND

1 AIDEN

"**Y**ou're here early."

Coach Williams scowled at the sight of Aiden and Harvard. She seemed preoccupied, apparently finishing up an email.

"If I'm not wanted, I can go," drawled Aiden, sauntering through the office. "I don't wish to be here at all, never mind early. I was on my way to a romantic rendezvous after class when my cruel roommate seized me by the collar and dragged me here against my will."

Coach's office was small as far as rooms in Kings Row went, and cozy in a neglected-paperwork way. The office walls, the color of institutional cream, were covered with photos from fencing glory days. One was entirely dominated by a poster of a saber that Aiden thought might be Coach Williams's celebrity crush. Coach, still in bright red-and-white

athletic wear, looked uncomfortable sitting at a desk. She'd clearly rather be standing in the gym ordering the team to do suicide drills and win state championships.

And Aiden would rather be making out! Yet here they were. It was impossible to get what you truly wanted in this life.

Aiden chose one of the chairs in front of the desk, and commenced lounging insouciantly. He looked toward Harvard and made a lazy gesture to the chair beside him.

"Great job dragging Aiden against his will, Harvard," Coach praised her captain.

Harvard gave her a thumbs-up. "No problem, Coach."

Aiden kicked him in the ankle for his wanton cruelty. Harvard grinned. After a moment, Aiden let himself grin back.

"I thought this was a team meeting," Aiden remarked. "Are we so punctual the others aren't here yet? I am deeply shamed."

He glanced around in anticipation of seeing the door open. The team was a bit of a mess this year, but they were an entertaining mess. Aiden was mildly surprised they weren't here already. He expected Nicholas the scholarship kid to be late. Nicholas didn't really know how to handle himself at Kings Row, any more than Kings Row knew how to handle his awful haircut and worse style. However, brawny Eugene was congenitally enthusiastic, and Aiden doubted Seiji Katayama had ever been late for anything. Seiji, their baby fencing genius, took life far too seriously.

Aiden shrugged. The important member of the team was here with him.

Unquestionably, Harvard was Aiden's favorite. Even if he did insist on dragging Aiden away from his life of careless playboy ease. Aiden tried to be very dedicated to his life of careless playboy ease.

When Aiden gave Harvard an approving glance for being the best captain, Harvard avoided his eyes. Aiden had known Harvard since they were five. Harvard was marvelous in many ways, but he was not skilled at deception.

"What's going on, Coach?" Aiden asked with sudden dark suspicion.

"Aiden, Aiden, Aiden," said Coach. "Can I direct your attention to this? All will be explained, in the fullness of time."

She was pointing to her bulletin board, which included a list of phrases such as *What's going on, Coach?* Anyone who said, or made reference to, any of the bulletin-board phrases had to do two hundred suicides. In their gym, Coach had a whole wall crowded with things people weren't allowed to say to her. One was *Aiden dumped me*. It made Aiden very proud.

"I already talked to the rest of the team this morning," said Coach Williams.

"Before class?" Aiden wrinkled his nose. "You made the poor little freshmen get up at some barbaric hour?"

"Seiji gets up at four every morning for fencing practice."

Even their coach seemed slightly horrified to report this.

"Seiji's life is so tragic," said Aiden. "I hope I never catch work ethic from him."

Harvard smacked Aiden affectionately on the back of the head.

"Wow, I wish you could. We're listening, Coach!"

Outside the picture window set high in the wall was a late September afternoon, even the trees golden with promise. The idea of Aiden's evening shone before him, all starlight and making out. Aiden didn't know why Harvard insisted on blighting Aiden's life by being a team player.

Coach raised an eyebrow at Harvard. "And why are *you* cluttering up my office and interrupting my writing to my sister to see if Bruno has stopped eating plants?"

"Is that a pet?" asked Harvard with real interest.

"You'd think," said Coach. "Actually, Bruno is my nephew. My sister's dog, Antoinette, started munching on the geraniums, then the baby started copying her. Any other questions?"

There was the obvious question: *Why would anyone name a dog Antoinette and a kid Bruno?*

"Can I see a picture of your nephew?" asked Harvard.

Coach, won over by Harvard's dangerous sincerity, softened and showed Harvard a picture on her phone. Harvard got out of his chair to take the phone and coo over the kid.

"Aw, Coach, he's so cute and little!"

Aiden sneaked a glance over at Harvard's glowing face, and

then smiled to himself. Harvard really got a kick out of kids. He also secretly collected videos of kittens and puppies being friends.

Suddenly, Coach slammed her hand down on the desk. Harvard laid Coach's phone down discreetly beside it.

"The reason I wanted to talk to the whole team in turn was to say you all have to do better," said Coach. "You hardly ever practice, Aiden. Nicholas choked during tryouts. Eugene choked against MLC. Seiji choked in his tryout against *you*."

Aiden snickered.

"I know I should do better," murmured Harvard. "I've been letting everyone down as captain."

Aiden stopped snickering and lifted his eyes to heaven. There was another picture of a saber taped to the ceiling.

"No, you haven't!" Aiden snapped. "You're an angel of a captain, and everyone is thrilled you're here."

"I do have a bone to pick with you, Captain. But stop lurking and go," said Coach. "I will speak with you in private later. For now, leave Aiden to me."

Harvard winced and nodded. Aiden sat bolt upright.

"Why would Harvard leave me?"

He found Coach's smile frankly sinister. "I asked him to bring you because I want to talk to you alone."

"It would be wrong to bring me to this place and desert me," said Aiden, but Harvard was already making for the door. He cast an apologetic look over his shoulder at Aiden as he went, but Aiden was not appeased. "You're betraying me like this? I can't believe it. I thought you loved me!"

"I do love you, buddy," said Harvard. "But I am betraying you, yeah. Coach's orders. Captain's gotta do what a captain's gotta do."

He waved goodbye and gave Aiden a mischievous grin. Since Harvard was a traitor, Aiden didn't wave back and only half returned the grin.

The door closed after Harvard, and the room seemed instantly darker. Aiden leaned back in his chair and sulked. Insouciantly, of course.

Coach was staring at him from across the desk. She'd steepled her fingers. Maybe she hadn't got the memo that only evil masterminds steepled their fingers.

"Aiden, Aiden, Aiden."

"Coach, Coach, Coach," Aiden responded.

"Are you aware we won our first team victory against a rival school last week?"

"Sure am," said Aiden. "Many congratulations."

"But you weren't actually at the match to help us win, or even to cheer your teammates on to victory?"

"Sure wasn't," said Aiden. "Many apologies. I had plans that couldn't be put off. They were ridiculously good-looking plans."

Coach seemed unimpressed by this information. Aiden was getting the feeling she might be a tiny bit annoyed with him.

"Kings Row has never won the state championship," Coach announced. "Do you know when we last reached the finals?"

"In the Jurassic period?" Aiden hazarded.

Coach didn't laugh. Harvard would have. As ever when Harvard wasn't there, Aiden wished he was.

"Kings Row reached the finals in 1979 but ultimately didn't win, despite having Robert Coste—a legend who went on to win Olympic gold. Why do you think we didn't win that year?"

Aiden shrugged. "Robert Coste had food poisoning?"

Coach regarded Aiden sternly.

"He was distracted by someone hot?" Aiden guessed. Coach's stern aspect only increased. "I don't know. Give me a clue."

It was interesting Coach should bring up Robert Coste, Kings Row's most famous alumnus. Robert Coste hadn't sent his son to his alma mater. Jesse Coste had gone to Exton, the better, shinier school where he was now the star of a better, shinier fencing team. And Jesse's former partner, Seiji Katayama, had thrown it all away to come to Kings Row for reasons nobody understood.

Aiden could probably work them out, but he didn't care that much.

He'd once needled Seiji about Jesse Coste, in order to throw off Seiji and win a match. It had worked. There were no hard feelings on Aiden's side, but Aiden suspected Seiji held it against him. That was why the phrase "sore loser" existed. Losers were the ones who got hurt.

Coach tilted her head to scrutinize Aiden in a way he found unsettling. Mellow afternoon light caught the silver glints starting in Coach's hair.

"Kings Row didn't win, because one genius fencer is not enough to win a team match," said Coach. "If we want to win the state championships, we have to be the best team we can be. Right now, we're hardly a team at all. I've been seriously thinking our teamwork could use a little, oh, work. *Aiden!*"

Her snarling his name might've made lesser men flinch, but Aiden maintained his lounge unperturbed.

"How many times did you attend our matches last year?"

"To tell you the truth, I never bothered to count. . . ."

He clearly saw the moment when Coach considered throwing a lamp at his artfully disheveled head. "Zero times, Aiden. That's how many. Zero times."

"Now that you mention it," Aiden murmured, "that does sound right."

Coach leaned both her elbows on her desk, ever more intent. "This has to change. If we establish stronger bonds as a team, nobody will skip matches *or* try to win them on their own. For the next few weeks, I've decided we must focus on teamwork."

Aiden nodded politely. He didn't see why Coach was telling him this, since it couldn't possibly apply to Aiden. When it came to participation, Aiden simply refused to participate.

Coach expanded on her demented scheme.

"We're going to do bonding exercises. I'm asking every one of you to write essays on your childhoods, which will be shared with your teammates so you can get to know one another better. I'm going to send you on expeditions. I want you to do trust falls.

At the end of the team bonding sessions, we can have a team bonfire."

Aiden gave the door Harvard had disappeared through a wistful glance. He'd been abandoned in this office, alone with a madwoman who wanted him to bond with freshmen instead of racking up dates.

"I have somebody waiting for me, you know," he reminded Coach reproachfully. "Somebody hot."

Coach snorted. "Who?"

"Well, I don't remember his name at this time," Aiden admitted, "but I'm sure he's distraught."

"Shame," said Coach. "What do you have to say about these training exercises?"

Aiden leaned back farther in his chair, his slouch going from insouciant to insolent. He understood now that Coach had Seiji on the team, she'd gone wild with ambition to win the state championship. Aiden wished her luck. This didn't mean he was going to put forth actual effort.

"Quick note on those: I won't be doing them."

The corner of Coach's mouth kicked up. "You think you're getting out of this that easily, huh?"

"I really do. Don't hate me because I'm beautiful and indolent," said Aiden. "I mean...I guess you *can*, but I won't care. See: indolent."

Coach's eyes narrowed. "I'll drop you from the team."

Aiden refused to show weakness.

"Easy come, easy go. Replace me with Eugene. Then burst into tears every time you imagine me in his place."

"I'll try to be strong." Coach's voice was dry. "Run along, Aiden."

Weird. Aiden had been pretty sure she was bluffing. He felt a pang at the thought of losing fencing, sharper than he would've thought. He couldn't help remembering the early days of fencing lessons, when he started to move in a way that was graceful rather than awkward. Fencing had taught him a new way of existing in the world. Fencing wasn't a person. Aiden hadn't thought he could ever lose fencing.

Harvard was in all his memories of fencing, as he was in every memory that mattered, his face luminous and his voice warm as he said, *We'll be on the same team, always.*

With fervor that surprised him, Aiden wanted to ask Coach to reconsider, but he couldn't let her win. He gave her a lazy salute, then ran his saluting hand through his long hair, which he usually kept in a ponytail.

"It's been real, Coach."

He was at the door when Coach said: "I'll also be replacing you as Harvard's roommate. With Eugene."

The whole world went still, and Aiden with it.

Aiden froze with his hand on the doorknob. "Excuse me. What?"

"It will be an opportunity for Harvard and Eugene to bond as teammates!" said Coach. "Like Seiji and Nicholas. They're roommates, and lately I think they've been connecting."

Aiden turned and snarled: "I found Seiji and Nicholas trying to murder each other in a supply closet last week!"

"I'm sure that was part of the bonding process," Coach said airily. "Well, ta-ta, Aiden!" She wiggled her fingers at him. "It's been real."

Aiden's vision blurred as he tried not to panic. The posters on the walls swam before him. He felt surrounded by fuzzy, dancing swords. That was naturally unsettling.

"Don't worry," Coach added. "I'm positive you can find some other boy to be your roommate."

"I don't *want* another roommate!"

Aiden paused, taking a deep breath. He was shouting. He didn't let himself shout. It wasn't cool. The ring of his own voice echoed in his ears like the remembered sound of people having fights downstairs. The kind of fights that ended in somebody leaving forever.

"Don't you?" Coach shrugged. "Guess you'll be participating in these exercises."

Coach's smile was smug. She was doing this on purpose. The detached part of Aiden, lounging in the back of his own mind, admired her play. It was important to know your opponent's weak points.

"If you try making me do trust falls with Nicholas, Seiji, or Eugene, goodbye team!" warned Aiden. "There will be fatalities."

"Fair enough," said Coach, benevolent in victory. "I'm a reasonable woman. I'm prepared to compromise. If you swear to me you will attend every match we have this year, *and* if you write an essay about your childhood to share with the team next week, *and* if you attend the sessions and the team bonfire, then you can stay. On the team. With your roommate. Deal?"

Aiden's soul writhed like a fish on a hook. He didn't want to participate in team bonding or let Coach win. He didn't want to write an essay on the awful, pathetic times of his childhood. He tried to think of a way to keep his dignity.

The office's picture window showed leaves golden as falling stars before Aiden's eyes. Clear as though the window were a photograph, Aiden could see his first day at Kings Row, walking on the smooth green grass of the quad under the oak trees. He could feel again the swift, hard beat of his heart as he worked up the nerve to ask Harvard a question. Aiden's father had suggested bigger, even more elite schools, but Harvard had picked this rambling redbrick place of deep woods and narrow lanes, and he wanted Aiden to be his roommate. Aiden loved Kings Row, as he loved fencing, because Harvard had chosen it for them.

His room at Kings Row was home. He wouldn't give it up.

"Deal or no deal?" After a pause, Coach called out, "Harvard! I'm going to need you to get Eugene."

"Fine!" Aiden snapped. "Deal."

Coach was smiling. Aiden wasn't.

It was Aiden's policy not to care much about anyone or anything. If Aiden knew one thing for sure, he knew that the person who cared more always lost.

This time, Aiden had lost.

2 HARVARD

Harvard was worried about his team. Most of all, he was worried about Aiden.

Harvard always worried the most about Aiden, but right now he had new reasons. Harvard was standing in the hall, leaning against the ebony paneling and listening to the muffled sound of voices behind the door, Aiden's easy cadence unmistakable. But then Aiden had gone quiet. Aiden hardly ever went quiet. When he did, it was a very bad sign. Harvard wondered if he should go back inside.

Just then, the rest of the team showed up and distracted him. Seiji was leading the charge, heading for Coach's door like a guided missile in a crisply ironed uniform.

"I wish to speak to Coach further about this absurd team bonding idea. It has been haunting me all day," said Seiji, just as Nicholas Cox checked Seiji's stride by grabbing on to his sleeve. "Release me, Nicholas!"

"Nope," Nicholas said.

He and Seiji were like that sometimes. Nicholas grinned while Seiji glared, and Eugene tried to creep up behind Harvard so he could listen at the door. Eugene was a big guy. His sneaking was not subtle.

"Seiji, Coach Williams is talking to Aiden right now," Harvard said, trying to calm the constantly troubled waters between their star fencer and their scholarship kid. "You'll have to come back tomorrow."

Seiji's almost-black eyes narrowed. "Captain, it's insanity to be wasting time forming human connections when we should be fencing."

Harvard liked Seiji, but he was very intense. He intimidated many of the other students at Kings Row. He didn't appear to intimidate Nicholas significantly, though.

Nicholas rolled his eyes. "Team bonding is gonna be cool. You just don't wanna do it because it means talking to people."

"Exactly," said Seiji. "I'm not temperamentally suited to bonding, and I won't do it."

Harvard tried to speak reasonably, as was his job as captain. He also made a gesture to Nicholas to tuck in his shirt. As usual, Nicholas was breaking every rule of the dress code.

"Coach thinks this is our best shot at winning the state

championship. We've never even come close to the finals, not since Robert Coste was a student. When we go up against Exton, we have to be the best team we can be if we're going to have any chance of beating them."

At the mention of Robert Coste, both Seiji and Nicholas jolted as though electrified. Harvard wasn't sure why Nicholas would care about Robert Coste. Maybe he was being sympathetic to his roommate. That was nice. Harvard gave him an encouraging nod.

"Oh, I'm going to beat Exton," said Seiji, his voice deadly calm. "Tomorrow I will explain to the coach that I can do it on my own."

"Wow, Seiji. You need me. I'm your *rival*," Nicholas muttered.

"You're not my rival," Seiji muttered back. "You're very bad."

"Let's not insult our teammates, guys," said Harvard.

Seiji blinked, finally breaking his intense gaze. "I didn't mean to be insulting, Nicholas. What I meant was, your fencing is very bad."

"Really?" said Nicholas. *"Really?"*

He started to shove Seiji, who turned and walked away down the corridor. Nicholas followed Seiji so he could continue shoving him.

Normally, Harvard would've sent two boys who fought as much as Nicholas and Seiji to their dorm, but since Nicholas and Seiji shared a room, that seemed like telling them to go kill each other in private.

Harvard realized Eugene had his ear pressed up against the door of Coach's office, and intervened hastily to pull him away.

"Whoa, bro," said Eugene. "Captain, bro. Do you wanna know what Coach just said to Aiden?"

"No, I don't," Harvard told him sternly, "because eavesdropping is wrong."

Whatever Eugene had overheard, it would be all over the school by nightfall. Harvard opened his mouth to order Eugene not to gossip about Aiden's business.

The door to Coach's office swung wide. Harvard pushed Eugene immediately out of the way.

Aiden didn't glance at Harvard, or anyone else, as he stormed, white-faced, out of Coach's office—and not, Harvard noticed, in the direction of one of his usual make-out spots. He would've chased after Aiden if he didn't have to meet with Coach next. Harvard had responsibilities. He couldn't just run off and do whatever he wanted.

That was Aiden's job.

Still, the glimpse he'd got of Aiden's green eyes set in a face gone salt-white stayed with him, even after the echo of Aiden's steps down the hall had faded away. Maybe Harvard could quickly go check on him.

Coach rapped on her desk. "Captain! Come inside."

Harvard hesitated a moment.

"When I get impatient, I have this irresistible urge to order captains to do five hundred suicides," threatened Coach.

Harvard did as he was told, and closed the door of the office behind him.

Coach studied him as he sat.

"What are you looking so thoughtful about, Harvard?"

"Aiden," said Harvard honestly.

"You're thinking about Aiden?" said Coach.

"Well, I'm thinking about all my teammates, really," said Harvard. "The team is in some, uh, disarray. Seiji and Nicholas were fighting about Seiji not wanting to do team bonding, and Aiden seemed . . . upset."

"You shock me," said Coach. "On all counts."

Harvard decided there was nothing to worry about, because he and Coach would put their heads together and work this out. Coach Williams was the best coach Harvard had ever had, and Harvard thought they made a pretty good pair. His mom thought she was awesome, too. Coach wore her hair in a natural cloud like Mom's youngest and coolest sister, Harvard's favorite aunt, though Harvard's auntie wore gold beads woven through her curls. Harvard couldn't imagine Coach doing that. Coach was too no-nonsense for beads.

"I'm really glad we're doing these bonding exercises, Coach.

It's a great idea, and I'm behind you one hundred and ten percent. Nicholas seems excited about team bonding, too. I know he doesn't seem like a people person, but I think he's what my Meemee would call a rough diamond."

"His technique is certainly rough," said Coach, but she said it with a forgiving smile.

Harvard suspected Coach had a soft spot for the new kid. Harvard liked Nicholas, too.

"Oh, but Seiji's technique is very smooth; they can learn from each other," Harvard said eagerly. "Maybe Meemee would call Seiji an overly polished diamond? You know how diamonds are created by coal under immense pressure? Maybe that's Seiji's problem. He's a diamond who puts himself under too much pressure, like he believes he's still coal."

He checked to see what Coach thought about this theory. Coach was frowning, kicked back in her chair, the way she did when she was mentally working her way through a new strategy.

"Diamonds aren't actually created from coal. Some diamonds are created by asteroid strikes," said Coach.

"Really?"

Coach winked. "Trust me, I'm a teacher. Sometimes you have to take drastic action to get shining results."

Harvard was silent. He saw what Coach meant, but he was slightly worried about what the equivalent of an asteroid strike would do to his team.

"What are your thoughts about Aiden?" Coach asked.

Harvard said it simply: "Aiden's the best."

Coach didn't look convinced, but she would see. Harvard had faith.

Eager to help, Harvard proposed, "I was thinking—maybe we could start by drawing up a points system."

Coach shook her head.

"You think we should play it looser and more relaxed? You could be right. Okay, let's lay out the beginning stages of the plan. You know, loosely."

Another head shake.

"Maybe a graph?" said Harvard, questing.

"Sometimes I worry...," Coach started.

"About Aiden? I'll talk to him."

"Don't you get tired of talking to Aiden?" asked Coach.

"No, never."

"I suppose you're used to it." Coach suppressed a shudder. "Friends for ten years and all that."

"Twelve." They hadn't gone a day without talking since they'd first met.

More recently, this meant Aiden would text Harvard messages at random hours, such as *In Swiss chalet, kidnapped by heir to Swiss banking fortune.* Harvard would wake in a panic at the notification, and then grin, texting back *Should I alert the authorities?* When Aiden replied *In the morning,* Harvard could go back to sleep, knowing Aiden was safe somewhere in the world.

It was nicer during the semester, when Aiden was always nearby. Then it was how they'd planned, ever since they were kids. They'd looked into other schools, but Harvard liked the idea of this small, lovely place where he could learn everybody's name. He'd been able to picture their future here ever since their first day walking around Kings Row, discussing how they would be roommates, teammates, and go to the fair in town every year. Aiden had swung around the stone pillars standing on each end of the quad and laughed. The sound was as bright as the spill of sunlight through the oak leaves, and Harvard had known they would be happy at Kings Row.

During the semester, it all went exactly according to plan.

Well. Almost.

"One day we'll hire a bunch of nuns to sing 'How Do You Solve a Problem Like Aiden?' and maybe we'll receive an answer," said Coach. "Besides him, don't you get tired of running around after the team, solving their problems?"

"Um," said Harvard. "No? I'm the captain."

"You did it before you were captain, though."

Coach seemed to be in a funny mood.

"I was happy to help," said Harvard. "And I was hoping to be chosen as captain. Which I was. Thanks, Coach! So, it's all good. Except I'm not really following you here. . . . If you're not worried about Aiden, is it Seiji or Nicholas?"

"I'm worried about you," said Coach.

"Me?" Harvard repeated, shocked. "But I'm—"

"All good?"

Coach raised a single eyebrow.

"Well . . . ," Harvard said. "Yeah. What's this got to do with team bonding?"

"I'm glad you asked. Your special personal assignment is to remember there's a *me* in team," Coach told him.

Harvard blinked.

"Do you realize the only person on the team you're not tenderly concerned about is you?"

"Oh right! I get it now. I could definitely get some more practice in," Harvard suggested. "I'll ask Seiji or Aiden—"

Coach held up a hand. Harvard felt seven years old again, confused and at a loss. The only thing he could be certain of was there must be something he could do to fix this and please her, but he couldn't think what.

"No. Don't think about fencing. Think about yourself."

"Coach," Harvard said helplessly, "I'm fine."

"Yes," said Coach. "But are you happy?"

"Well, of—"

"Don't answer me right away," said Coach. "Think about it. When was the last time you did something purely for yourself? Go on a date or something."

Harvard's head snapped back so hard Coach's cool sword posters blurred in his vision.

"A date!" said Harvard. "What do you mean?"

"You know, the sweet fruit that's a staple food in the Middle

East." Coach rolled her eyes. "I mean an outing, its intent entertainment and romance. You're Aiden's best friend. Surely you've become familiar with the concept of a date by osmosis? I'd understand if you didn't know what a *second* date was...."

She trailed off. Harvard must have looked slightly traumatized.

More gently, Coach said, "If you don't have any interest in romance, that's more than okay. It was just a suggestion. You don't have to date. You can get ice cream or play a video game."

"I do!" exclaimed Harvard. "Uh, that wasn't an 'I do' to playing video games, though I do occasionally. With my little cousin. Some of those games are very violent. Never mind that," he added hastily. "I mean—I do have an interest in romance. Dating. I mean, I always thought it might just—happen...."

"Did you believe a date might fall out of a tree?" asked Coach. "Again, you may be thinking of the fruit."

Harvard met many wonderful people and tended to get along with them pretty well. He'd had the hazy thought, now and then, that one day he'd meet someone great and feel what was described as a *coup de foudre*: a strike of lightning. Or a *coup de maître*: a masterstroke, someone delivering a strike that was both utterly recognizable and irresistible. He'd thought he would meet someone, and they would make sense to him in the same way fencing did. He'd want to be around them all the time.

That hadn't happened so far. Harvard hadn't worried about it. His mother said it was best to wait to get serious, and Harvard knew himself well enough to be aware he tended to get serious about everything. He'd probably meet someone in college. They'd get married and adopt a totally great dog. It would be…

All good, Coach's voice said in his mind, cynically.

He'd been silent for too long, he realized. Coach was giving him a keen look, sympathetic but still uncomfortable to receive. Her eyes were searching for an answer he'd just realized he didn't have.

"So that's your teamwork assignment," said Coach gently. "Go think about yourself."

And dating, apparently. Harvard nodded and left the coach's office, somewhat dazed.

There was always so much other stuff to do. He didn't want to let anybody down. Like he'd told Coach, he was fine, and he wanted to make sure everybody else was fine, too. He wasn't lonely. He had Aiden.

Usually.

He climbed the stairs, dark paneling on all sides. The stairs seemed narrower than normal today.

Maybe another reason Harvard hadn't tried dating was Aiden. Romantic stuff came so easily to his best friend. When they went into the city, Aiden was constantly approached by admirers and modeling agency scouts. All Aiden had to do was smile at people, and they fell in love. Aiden had his own devoted fan club, a group of boys Aiden had nicknamed the Bons, who came to every fencing match. Trying to date with Aiden around would be like learning to play a keyboard around the world's foremost concert pianist.

When Aiden was busy with a guy—which, in recent years, happened more and more—Harvard had his team, his family, and other friends. Kally and Tanner were good guys. Kings Row was a great place. Someone always needed help with fencing or homework. Harvard led a very full life.

Yes, Coach had said. *But are you happy?*

Harvard walked slowly down the hall to his dormitory, lost in thought.

When he opened the door, he found his roommate hunched over his laptop like a vexed cat brooding over an unsatisfactory dead mouse. His green eyes flashed with displeasure at being interrupted.

"Hey," said Harvard. "You seemed off earlier. You okay? Want to talk?"

"I need quiet!" Aiden snapped.

"I'll take that as a no."

Harvard gazed around. Something else was weird, besides his uncharacteristically cranky roommate. Their room was festooned with piles of flowers and chocolates. Aiden's bed was covered in roses and ribbons and cake, as if an unscrupulous thief had robbed a wedding and abandoned their loot.

Harvard was used to such displays on Aiden's birthday and Valentine's Day, but both were months away.

"Where'd all this come from?" Harvard asked.

"All what?" Aiden made an impatient gesture with his finger, and then glanced around the room. "I don't know. Some people wandered in with some stuff, I guess? There have been many interruptions during the past hour. Including you."

The room really did remind Harvard of Valentine's Day. Every Valentine's Day, Aiden got such a deluge of cards and gifts that Harvard feared they might drown in candy waterfalls and storms of lace-edged cardboard hearts. Harvard had never received a valentine himself. Except from Aiden when they were little, in a cute, platonic way. But Aiden hadn't given him one for years.

Harvard wandered uneasily over to his own bed, skirting around the suspicious lumps under the blanket of petals on the floor. His bed was also covered in presents. (Their beds were pushed together, and gifts seemed to have flooded in from Aiden's side.) He made out several fruit baskets, but he couldn't see his pillow, and he knew a pineapple wouldn't be a good substitute. A pineapple pillow did not promise restful slumber.

He poked at the heap, wondering if there was any way he could shift the presents around so he could sleep comfortably tonight. The pile of offerings tilted like the Leaning Tower of Pisa, then a flood of chocolates splashed onto the floor. Harvard let out a squawk.

"Aiden!" said Harvard. "My bed's a disaster!"

"Great," murmured Aiden.

Harvard was receiving the impression Aiden wasn't really listening.

Against his better judgment, Harvard peered at the note affixed to the largest fruit basket. It was a square of white cardboard reading, *Heard you might need a new roommate, Aiden!* A note on a box of chocolates wrapped with a dusky crimson ribbon read *Call me ~~lover~~ roomie.*

"Huh," said Harvard.

He thought again of their first day seeing Kings Row, when he'd asked Aiden to be roommates. Aiden had been talking excitedly about the harvest festival in town. Harvard had looked forward to going with him.

Only he hadn't. Aiden had gone with a date instead. People said the Kingstone Fair was a guaranteed great date. Harvard had never actually been to the fair.

"Are you...in the market for another roommate?" Harvard asked.

"Don't bother me with absurd questions," said Aiden.

Harvard didn't really think Aiden was. Of course, he'd seen Aiden cast off people with a shrug, as if they didn't matter, all the time...but Harvard was different.

About twenty guys had sobbed on Harvard's shoulder saying they'd thought *they* were different, wailing over Aiden while Harvard patted them on the back. But obviously, that was...not the same.

This was probably just a misunderstanding.

But...if Aiden did want a new roommate, who would Harvard room with? He got along well with everybody and didn't have anyone specific to ask. Just as he usually didn't have anyone specific to hang out with while Aiden was busy on his dates.

"Coach made some suggestions to me just now," Harvard said tentatively. "About the team bonding exercise."

"Yeah, yeah, go on a picnic, make a graph. Do whatever you like," snapped Aiden, crunching up another piece of paper. "Leave me alone."

"If that's what you want."

Harvard retreated from Aiden's mood and the gift apocalypse occurring in his room. He went into the hall to get a breath of air. Once he did, a basic strategy formed in his mind.

It was pretty clear what Harvard's next step should be. He took out his phone and called the person he knew would help, no matter what his problem was.

He smiled as soon as he heard her voice on the other end of the line. "Hey, Mom. Just called to say I love you. And, uh...do any of your friends have a daughter my age? Who might be interested in going on a date? With me?"

3 AIDEN

I believe you should start as you mean to go on, so I was born gorgeous, Aiden wrote.

So what if it was a lie? Aiden was literally being blackmailed to write this. Two wrongs gave Aiden the right to do anything he chose.

He looked distractedly about the room—it seemed as though there was more stuff in here than usual—in search of inspiration for his great work of fiction. Their shadowed bedroom floor stretched on like gray desert until it met the forbidding mahogany door Harvard had closed behind him. Aiden wanted to crawl under the beds he and Harvard had pushed together in the center of the room and hide there.

Actually, Aiden hadn't been a prepossessing child. He was born premature, so his first baby pictures were of him looking like a shriveled

hairless hamster in a plastic cage in the NICU. Even when he was out of the hospital, Aiden stayed shrimpy and spindly.

I had an oppressive childhood in many ways. "Stop doting on me, Mother, I have things to do," I would be forced to tell her. "Go to the country club; those charity galas won't organize themselves."

Maybe if he'd been a cuter baby, his mother would've stuck around. She was a model; she was always poised for the next great photo op. But by the time Aiden was cute, he'd looked too old to be a good accessory, and she didn't want the world identifying her as the mother of a teenager. She'd had other kids later—adorable, curly-haired tots with some soccer player in Spain—and taken glossy photographs with them. He'd seen them smiling perfect-family smiles at him from a magazine.

When Aiden was younger, he'd told himself he remembered his mother leaving, the sounds of shouts and thrown gifts and the screech of a sports car in the driveway. The truth is, Aiden was too young when she'd left. He couldn't possibly remember her leaving. He was remembering other women leaving, long after his mother.

His dad hadn't had any other kids. When he had Aiden, he'd discovered he didn't find fatherhood amusing. What his dad did find entertaining, and worth collecting, was women. Kids were boring because you had to keep them, but you could always find a brand-new shiny romance if you had enough money to pay for it.

It didn't really matter that Aiden couldn't actually recall his mother leaving. They all left in a similar way. His dad's women were all the same.

Aiden had believed one of them was different. Once. A long time ago.

When he was five, his father had taken up with a Brazilian singer foolish enough to believe faking a maternal instinct would please his dad. Aiden used to follow his father's girlfriends around the house, allured by the glitter of their jewelry and the scent of their perfume and the sense that something exciting and glamorous was happening. The Brazilian one used to take his hand when he chased after her, slow her step, and tell him stories as she did her eye makeup. She used to hug him and say, "Aiden, you're so cute." (Total lie. But he was a little kid back then, so what did he know?) When she and his father got engaged, she showed him the ring, told him they were going to be a family, and asked if she could adopt him. She told him she wanted to be his mother, and could she? Aiden said yes with all his heart.

His dad had married eight women so far. He didn't marry that one. She left more quietly than most, but she left. There was no screaming, no screech of a car in the driveway, only her engagement ring left gleaming in the shadows of their big cold house. She didn't even bother to say goodbye.

Whatever. She was only one of many. Aiden didn't even remember her name now, and he was never fooled again.

Aiden had cried every night for two months after she'd left. Then he'd started school and met Harvard.

Hadn't Harvard been around, just now? Aiden could've sworn

he'd come in. Aiden was occupied wrestling with writing and trying not to dwell on Coach's hideous threat.

Mostly, Aiden found it both useful and amusing to know other people's weak points. Eugene's was the fear of letting people down. Seiji's weak point was his former fencing partner, Jesse Coste. Aiden had used that weak point to needle Seiji and beat him in their tournament. Seiji was a better fencer than Aiden. Seiji should've won. Aiden had proved what his father always said was true: Caring was for losers.

Everyone had a weak point. Harvard did, as well. Aiden couldn't bear to think about it, because Aiden couldn't bear to think about hurting him.

Harvard was *Aiden's* weak point. Coach knew his secret. She knew it would work when she'd threatened to separate them, after even the threat of being removed from the fencing team hadn't been effective. Aiden had clearly been a lot more obvious and pathetic than he'd realized.

Aiden found himself chewing on a fingernail, stopped, and scowled at himself. What was he doing? He wasn't a beast of the field.

Where has Harvard wandered off to? Aiden wondered. It wasn't like him to not be here when Aiden wished for him. Perhaps he'd gone to find someone to deal with this mess.

Aiden swiveled in his chair as he took in the full extent of the situation. Their room was a vortex of paper hearts and flowers and chocolate boxes. It looked as though someone had eaten

Valentine's Day and thrown up everywhere. Aiden didn't even like Valentine's Day.

He squinted at his own bed with sudden outrage. He leaped up and began to toss garbage onto the floor until a way was cleared and he could rescue his stuffed bear from the wreckage. Aiden pulled his bear free and began to pick out the cream-cheese frosting matted in his fur. What had possessed some idiot to put red velvet cupcakes spelling out U R SEXY on Aiden's bed? Aiden already knew he was sexy. There was no need to assault a helpless stuffed animal.

He carried his bear back to the desk with him, and typed: *On my first day of school, I met my best friend, Harvard.*

Simple as that, the first true thing Aiden had written.

Aiden's clearest memory of early childhood was his first day of kindergarten.

Some of the other kids had cried. Aiden hadn't. Crying was better done alone. It felt much worse to cry when there were people around and see them not care. Aiden hadn't been around other kids much, and hadn't known exactly what to do with them, but they were more interesting than the toys. Aiden had toys at home. He'd hung back and watched the crying, the teacher trying to calm the riot, and the kid who was trying to help the teacher.

Harvard had been the tallest kid there—and the kindest. He'd gone to every crying kid and told them this was a big change, but he knew they would be brave. He'd had a stuffed bear under his arm and when a tiny girl couldn't stop sobbing, he'd pretended the bear was giving her a kiss, bumping the little plastic nose against her tearstained cheek. He'd given the girl a smile, warm as the sun, and she'd been helpless to do anything but smile back.

Harvard was the biggest person in any room, even when he was small.

Aiden had followed him around, trailing so close that when Harvard stopped unexpectedly, Aiden walked right into him. Harvard turned, looked down at Aiden's face, and came immediately to a beautiful but entirely wrong conclusion.

"Oh hey," were Harvard's first words to Aiden. "If you like the bear so much, you can have it."

He'd placed his teddy bear in Aiden's arms, and then patted Aiden on the shoulder. Aiden had reflexively clutched the bear and stared up in panic at this marvelous boy. He'd tried frantically to think of some way to keep the warm, steady light of Harvard's attention, and found himself frozen with fear by the impossible magnitude of his ambition. He'd known, he'd *known*, that Harvard would turn away.

Harvard hadn't. He'd kept looking at Aiden, then for no good reason at all thrown an arm around Aiden's skinny shoulders.

"I'm Harvard," he'd said. "What's your name?"

"Aiden," Aiden had squeaked.

"You stay by me, Aiden," Harvard had told him.

Aiden always had.

He'd kept the bear, too. Good thing he had, since it couldn't run off and desert him like everyone else.

The door opened, and Harvard returned, sliding his phone into his pocket and looking just—not the same as when they were kids, but essentially the same. Mature and responsible for his age, no matter what that age was. Aiden relaxed fractionally. In a world of blackmail and inexplicable cupcakes, Harvard made sense.

"Where did you go?" Aiden demanded. "Why did you go?"

"You told me to leave you alone," Harvard answered. "So I went out."

Aiden held up the hand that wasn't holding his bear in protest. "That's a very strange interpretation of my words."

Leave me alone obviously didn't mean *Go away and* actually *leave me all alone.* It meant *Your supportive presence is always welcome, but please don't talk to me about the fencing team right now.* Harvard had heartlessly and senselessly abandoned Aiden in his time of greatest need.

Since Harvard had come back, Aiden was prepared to be forgiving.

"Can't believe we were abandoned like this," Aiden told his bear loudly. "You're my only friend now, Harvard Paw."

He used the bear's little paw to hit Harvard in the arm as punishment for his crimes.

Harvard rolled his eyes. "I stepped out for ten minutes and called my mom."

"Okay, you're off the hook," said Aiden. "Please explain life's mysteries to me. Is there a reason my bed is covered in cake? Are the students of Kings Row doing a reenactment of the French Revolution?"

Perhaps the entire school had got high on paint fumes today.

"Marie Antoinette didn't actually say 'Let them eat cake' about the starving peasants," Harvard said conscientiously. "That was just something people said to feel okay about cutting off her head. You can't trust surface reports of history."

"Can't trust much in this life," drawled Aiden. "Can you unravel the cake mystery?"

"My bed is covered in gifts for you," said Harvard slowly. "Gifts that, since they are on *my* bed, I am keeping."

Aiden fussed with Harvard Paw, who still had remnants of frosting on him. "Sure, sure."

He always let Harvard eat the Valentine's Day chocolates Aiden got, partly to make his best friend happy. Partly out of guilt.

"There are notes everywhere from random students asking you to consider them as your new roommate," Harvard continued, a strange note in his voice.

Aiden hugged his bear to his chest and recalled he deserved to be showered in sympathy. "Right! You won't believe the horror of the day I'm having! Coach *threatened* me."

No sympathy was forthcoming. The world remained unjust.

Harvard was frowning at him. "What are you talking about?"

Aiden made a face. "Coach said that if I didn't do this

imbecilic team bonding exercise, she'd make me switch rooms. Now I have to write an essay."

"Oh," said Harvard. "Yeah, that's…about what I thought must've happened. So that's what you're doing."

Sympathy was forthcoming at last—Harvard was off his game today—when Harvard slung his arm around Aiden's shoulders and tugged him close. It was the same old gesture, though Harvard's arms were far bigger and stronger now, and Aiden's shoulders thankfully less skinny. Aiden let himself lean in.

Harvard's face was clear now, free of whatever had been preoccupying him. He was even smiling a little. "Aw. Would you miss me?"

Aiden elbowed Harvard in the ribs. "Hardly. But imagine the hideous consequences if I had to switch rooms. Either I have to put up with some miscreant like Nicholas Cox, or my roommate falls in love with me, and you know what happens next. Scenes. Tears. Unreasonable demands like 'Why can't you remember my name?' Besides, it would disrupt my elaborate scheme to kill you and have the only single room in Kings Row. Imagine the trouble I could get into with my own room! I couldn't let anyone get in the way of that."

Harvard shrugged comfortably. "Yeah, yeah."

"You should be on your knees," said Aiden. "Thanking me. If I wasn't writing this essay, you'd have to room with Eugene."

"I like Eugene," contributed Harvard.

"More than me?"

"What do you think, idiot?" asked Harvard fondly.

He gave Aiden's shoulders a last squeeze and let him go. Aiden's side where Harvard had been was now colder than Aiden preferred. Aiden flicked a last bit of frosting from Harvard Paw's ear.

"How's everything at home?"

"Good," said Harvard. "Mom's setting me up on a date."

That surprised an uneasy laugh out of Aiden. "What put that wild idea into her head? Don't worry, I'll handle—"

"*I* put the idea into her head," Harvard said mildly. "Coach suggested I should try dating."

Wow—how was Harvard dating in any way relevant to team bonding? This was nonsense. It was beginning to seem more and more as if Coach Williams was on a campaign to ruin Aiden's life! What had Aiden ever done to her, other than add a touch of class to the fencing team and, admittedly, never show up for matches?

Ruining Aiden's life still seemed like an overreaction.

"I'll talk to Coach," Aiden suggested. "This lunacy can't continue. She's high on victory and maybe paint fumes."

"Aiden," said Harvard. "I want to."

Since *when*?

Harvard had never been interested in dating before. Aiden should know. He'd been there the whole time.

Every year, when they were younger, Aiden used to timidly proffer a Valentine's Day card. Every year, his heart pounding so hard he thought his ribs would be smashed to dust, he'd think this time Harvard would understand. Harvard had always put his arm around Aiden's neck and said, "Aw, thanks, buddy." Harvard had never talked about wanting to date anybody.

To this day, Aiden got rid of Harvard's other valentines. Harvard didn't want to be bothered with valentines. His mind was on schoolwork and friendship and family and fencing. Aiden was doing him a favor.

And Aiden was doing himself a favor, putting those days of hope and humiliation far behind them.

Very occasionally, Aiden thought about maybe trying something, hinting, seeing if Harvard might be open to the possibility of dating. Every time, he remembered how he used to act around Harvard, and he wished to die of shame.

He couldn't endure ever being that pathetically transparent again. Bad enough that Coach knew and could use that knowledge anytime she wanted.

Only now, everything Aiden was certain of had turned out to be wrong.

"You on a date." Aiden tried to put the words together in a way that wasn't horrifying. "You dating."

"Yeah, dating. The thing you do practically every night?" Harvard reminded him.

Obviously, Aiden had to clarify his meaning.

"*You're* going on a date?"

"Yeah, I am," Harvard said, with uncharacteristic sharpness. "You're not the only one who gets to date, Aiden!"

Aiden shook his head, lost for words. Harvard had stranded

them both in unfamiliar territory. *Aiden* was always the one with sharp retorts. Harvard never got impatient with Aiden.

"Mom says this girl is really nice," Harvard added.

"A girl?" Aiden said. "Oh."

He'd thought...no. Obviously not. That had just been Aiden, seeing what he wanted to see. Harvard had never shown interest in anyone, because he was sensible and waiting until he felt ready to date.

Which, apparently, he did now.

Harvard was beginning to look suspicious. "Why are you being weird about this?"

"No reason!" Aiden responded, fast as a snake. "Just surprised! Aw, my little Harvard. They grow up so fast. I'm tired of trying to write my essay. What do you say you and I go have a practice bout?"

He patted Harvard's head, the texture of Harvard's close-cropped hair pleasantly soft under his palm. Then Aiden stepped back and put down his bear.

Harvard agreed with gratified surprise, as Aiden had known he would. Usually, Harvard was the one who had to bug Aiden to practice. It wasn't that Aiden didn't *want* to fence, but he liked when Harvard fussed.

They ran together down the broad back staircases, past the study halls that Aiden, for one, never entered, then across the evening-gray lawn toward the *salle*. It was dark and echoing in the gym before Harvard flipped on the lights and the floor stretched out in front of them, suddenly golden wood rather than shadows. Aiden put on his fencing mask with some relief, protected from the world and Harvard's gaze by the beehive mesh of metal. They lowered and extended their blades, mirroring each other's movements.

After that, Aiden broke pattern and twirled his épée, playing around. He caught the flash of Harvard's white teeth through the mesh of his own mask. Harvard let the weight of the world rest on his shoulders. It was Aiden's job to help him have some fun.

Harvard dipped the point of his blade twice, inviting attack, but Aiden didn't take the bait, so Harvard moved back a little.

Aiden followed, beginning to step. In that split second of opening, Harvard's épée flashed suddenly into attack.

It was so unexpected, Aiden wavered and let his point drop slightly as his grip on his épée went unsteady.

"*Arrêt*," Harvard murmured instantly. "What was that? Have you hurt yourself?"

"I was just thinking about writing my essay," Aiden admitted. "I think I'm allergic to doing things I don't want to do."

Arrêt. The term meant *stop*, putting an end to any fencing bout. Harvard always said it, never seemed to feel embarrassed about his ready surrender. He would always surrender rather than risk hurting Aiden.

Harvard wouldn't give up in a real match—that would be letting down the team. But whenever they were practicing, all Aiden had to do was show a moment of vulnerability and Harvard would throw down both his weapon and his guard, unconcerned with protecting himself. Only concerned with Aiden.

That was just who Harvard was. That was why he was the only person Aiden was close to. He could allow Harvard within striking distance, because Harvard would never hurt anybody.

All those years ago, little-kid Harvard had felt sorry for little-kid Aiden. That was understandable. Little-kid Aiden was a sorry specimen. Harvard had never got out of the habit of feeling bad for him. If Aiden—his best friend—asked Harvard not to go out on a date with some random girl, Harvard wouldn't do it.

Only Aiden couldn't ask him.

If this was something Harvard actually wanted, something that would make him happy, Aiden couldn't stand in the way.

There was a Greek legend about a hooded figure named Nemesis that pursued a man, slowly but surely coming closer to him. When Nemesis reached him, he would be destroyed. Aiden had always been uneasily aware of the shadow of the future, coming for him. They couldn't always live together at Kings Row. They wouldn't always be on the same fencing team.

One day, Harvard would leave. Like everybody else.

Aiden had been living on borrowed time for more than half his life. The most he could hope for was that someone would call a brief halt to inexorable progress, and he could avoid being hurt for a little longer.

"Are you *really* going on a date?" Aiden asked as casually as possible. Still hoping against hope that this might be a joke.

"Yeah." Harvard sounded tired. "I really am."

4 NICHOLAS

The walls in Kings Row were very smooth.

Maybe that was a weird thing to notice. Every room in Nicholas's new school had some feature that struck him as unbelievably luxurious, but the walls were literally all around. Since that was, like, the point of walls.

In any of his old schools, or the many apartments he and Mom had lived in, the walls had always been in rough shape. Wallpaper so old it was worn away, strips torn off or damaged by water so that the paper turned a mottled brown and peeled off by itself like a rotten sentient banana. Or just cracked drywall, the usual scuffs or dents from a door-knob slamming into a wall too hard or a plate being thrown. Nicholas had figured that was how walls were. Nicholas had never thought about it much, until he came to Kings Row and woke to see a stretch of perfect white wall gleaming in the morning light beside his bed every morning. Every morning, the wall made him think: *Where the hell am I?*

He didn't belong here. But it was nice, and he wanted to stay.

On the other side of Nicholas's bed was a blue shower curtain, patterned with ducks, to separate his and Seiji's halves of the room. Seiji had put it up for privacy, and because Seiji couldn't deal with the sight of Nicholas's face or the mess on Nicholas's floor early in the morning. Even with the curtain, this room was the biggest Nicholas had ever slept in. Nicholas had figured the curtain was a good idea at the time. That was when he and Seiji hadn't been getting along. But now—though they were still rivals—they'd recently agreed to be friends.

When they'd first met, Nicholas thought Seiji was the worst person and the best fencer he'd ever met. He hadn't been able to get Seiji out of his head. All he'd been able to think about was getting into Kings Row and beating Seiji someday. Then they'd both come to Kings Row, been forced to be roommates, and Nicholas had got to know Seiji better. He still wanted to crush Seiji on the *piste,* but Nicholas thought being friends was going to be awesome.

Buddies probably didn't need a strict separation of personal space. When Nicholas saved Seiji a seat on the team bus, Seiji didn't mind when Nicholas's stuff or limbs went everywhere. Well, Seiji sighed and snapped at him a lot, but Nicholas was pretty sure that was just part of their thing.

Nicholas pulled aside the curtain and peered out at the orderly part of the room. Seiji, already wearing his ironed-looking blue pajamas, was sitting on his bed with a book on his lap. Even propped up against a pillow, Seiji had weirdly excellent posture, as though someone had trained him by making him balance a book on his head. Or possibly his posture came from being super good at fencing. Seiji's face was intent—he was very focused in everything he did—on his book. He had a little bedside lamp with a twisty neck that cast a tiny gold pool of light on the side of his face and the open collar of his pajamas. The moonlight was a silver outline around his black hair. Seiji, Nicholas's new friend.

Nicholas had never had friends before Kings Row. He and Mom were always getting evicted. Finding new cheap places around the city meant switching school districts. It was tough to make friends when you were always on the move.

Here at Kings Row, for the first time in his life, Nicholas got to keep people around. He had his first friend, Bobby, who was little and vivid and as wild about fencing as Nicholas was himself. And now he had Seiji, too.

Seiji lifted his almost-black eyes from the page. "Nicholas. Stay on your side of the room. Do *not* move the curtain."

"Um, yeah," said Nicholas. "Right. That's the way we still do things, obviously."

Seiji nodded with unconcealed impatience. Nicholas walked into Seiji's side of the room.

"Nicholas! That is the exact opposite of what I said to do."

"Yeah, totally." Nicholas wandered over to Seiji's bookshelf. "I thought maybe I could borrow some of your books to help when I'm writing my essay about childhood. You've gotta let me! Because we're teammates, and we're bonding."

They had to write these essays, but Nicholas wasn't awesome with words. The only thing he'd ever been good at was fencing. Fencing words were used to describe conversation all the time—*parry, riposte*—so he should be able to figure out language eventually. Other fencers could do it: Seiji spoke really well, using words that stung Nicholas or sliced into him like real swords (*I'm so far ahead of you, I'm surprised you can see me at all,* Seiji had told Nicholas the first time they met, and that burn made Nicholas try getting into Kings Row.). It wasn't just Seiji: Coach Williams spoke, and the world shifted in Nicholas's mind. Their captain, Harvard, knew exactly when to reassure and when to command. Aiden never shut the hell up.

And one look at Jesse Coste and you knew he'd never wanted for anything in his life, including the right word at the right time.

So, Nicholas could do it, too. He was good at fencing—not great, but someday he was gonna be great. And he wasn't good with words, but someday he could be.

Nicholas read the titles on the spines of Seiji's books. Seiji had lots of books about interesting stuff, like the rules of fencing, the history of fencing, and famous fencers.

Seiji breathed out hard through his nose. "There's no need to go through my things. We have a school *library.*"

"I knew that."

Nicholas hadn't known that.

"Of course, their section about fencing is utterly inadequate," mused Seiji.

"Well, there you go," said Nicholas. "It's inadequate. Nothing I can do about that, Seiji!"

Utterly was a fancy way of saying *totally*, he was pretty sure. Nicholas didn't see what was wrong with just saying *totally*, but he made a private note to write *utterly* in his essay. *The way I grew up was utterly fine.* Yep, that sounded good.

"I still don't want to do team bonding," Seiji muttered.

"That's great news, Seiji."

A look that wanted to be startled began on Seiji's face, and then was sternly repressed.

"Team bonding lessons are part of fencing," Nicholas explained. "When you suck at team bonding, I'll beat you. So will Harvard."

Seiji closed his book.

"And Eugene!" Nicholas continued triumphantly.

Seiji's eye twitched.

"It'll just be you and Aiden, coming in dead last at team bonding, and Aiden doesn't even attend matches," Nicholas said with scorn. "Embarrassing for you. Don't worry; I guess you can still be my rival. Even if you suck at team bonding."

"I'm going to crush you at team bonding!" Seiji snapped.

"That's the spirit!" said Nicholas. "See? We're bonding already."

Seiji's books were lined up in an orderly fashion like soldiers.

Some of his possessions were lined up in front of them, as though they were guarding his library.

"Don't disarrange the books."

"Oh, are they arranged in some special way?"

"...Alphabetically?"

"Weird," said Nicholas.

There was a book called *The Twenty-Six Commandments of Irish Dueling*. That sounded cool. Nicholas reached for it, but Seiji's books were packed together so tightly he actually had to force the book out. The bookcase rocked, and a watch in a little case tumbled from the top shelf and hit the floor. A different book fell down and struck Nicholas's foot. Nicholas, hopping in wild dismay, stepped on the watch. The plastic case cracked. When Nicholas hastily removed his foot, he saw that the watch inside the case had cracked, too.

The whole disaster took about five seconds.

Seiji sounded calmly pleased to be proven right. "I knew you would do something like this."

"Um," said Nicholas. "Oops. Sorry. I'll pay for that! Or I'll get it fixed or something!"

Seiji sighed dismissively, opening his book back up. "All right."

That made Nicholas feel much worse.

There were plenty of guys at Kings Row who would've got very nasty about Nicholas daring to touch, let alone break, their stuff. Seiji wasn't like that.

Seiji's words might cut, but he didn't say them to cut. Seiji wasn't Aiden, whom Nicholas never paid attention to. When Aiden spoke, all Nicholas heard was: *Blah, blah, blah, I'm a snotty rich kid who talks too much.* Nicholas had never seen Seiji get any pleasure out of being cruel. That was what made Seiji's words cut deep. Nicholas knew Seiji meant what he said.

"I'm real sorry."

Seiji waved a hand, not looking up from his book. "It's fine."

Nicholas put the broken watch in his pocket, searching through his mind a little frantically for something that could make this better. The times Seiji and he got along best—well, the only times they got along at all—were when they were fencing or training.

"Wanna come train with me?"

"No, I can't help you right now. I'm staying here so I can perfect my essay about my childhood," said Seiji. "As I intend to excel at team bonding."

Nicholas wondered if he should point out that staying here by himself and *not* coming to train with a teammate was the total opposite of team bonding, but he'd already asked Seiji to come with and Seiji had turned him down. Why should he help out Seiji? It would be really funny when Coach told Seiji he sucked.

"Not gonna happen, Seiji," he said instead.

"I will decimate you at team bonding!"

Nicholas waved a hand over his shoulder as he left. "No way."

He took a detour on his way to the *salle*, as he usually did, to the cabinet full of trophies and photos of famous former students. He headed right for the plaque Kings Row had won during the match that got them into the finals for the 1979 state championship.

Even the glass of the cabinet glistened, clear and clean. Nicholas's breath fogged up the glass, making a little blurry patch of imperfection.

Nicholas was the only thing in this school that was in rough shape. Even the lawns here seemed made of smooth green velvet.

Hey, Nicholas thought as he looked up at Robert Coste's face in the old photo under the glass, shining with victorious happiness and almost as young as Nicholas was now. Even to himself, he didn't dare think *Hey, Dad.*

But that was what Robert Coste was. Robert Coste had had a fling with Nicholas's mom and left her before either of them knew Nicholas was on the way.

Robert Coste was his dad. One of the greatest fencers of his generation. Of all time. Surely there was something of him in Nicholas. Surely that was why he'd loved fencing so much, from the very start when he'd hassled Coach Joe into teaching him.

I'm doing okay, Nicholas thought, telling his dad stuff about his day the way he'd heard other kids say stuff about their day on the phone to their parents. *Coach had an awesome idea about team bonding. I think I'm going to rock at it! Seiji is not gonna rock at it.*

He'd studied this picture of Robert Coste carefully, time and time again, since he'd started going to Kings Row. Robert was tall and blond and polished, like a trophy made into a person. Nicholas didn't look anything like him. Jesse Coste, the guy with the name and the training, had gotten the face as well. But fencing mattered more than faces.

Nicholas was so absorbed in staring at Robert Coste that he didn't notice a couple of older boys behind him until one shoved into his back, sending him stumbling a few steps down the hall away from the cabinet.

"Don't think you're going gold anytime soon, new kid!"

Nicholas rolled his eyes as the Kings Row guys passed him, talking in pretend whispers that were intended for Nicholas to hear.

"Can't believe he's on the team, even as a crappy second reserve."

The other guy sniggered. "I heard his last coach was basically a hobo."

Nicholas threw the guy against the wall.

He'd had to trail Coach Joe all around his tumbledown old gym back in the city, bugging the coach to teach him how to fence. Coach Joe hadn't wanted to train Nicholas, but he had, and he'd done it the best way he knew how. Now that he had Coach Williams, he understood Coach Joe hadn't been exactly all a coach should be, but it wasn't as if Nicholas were the ideal student. Coach Joe had texted *Happy birthday, kid, hope you had a blast* a couple of days after Nicholas's last birthday. He was the only person who'd remembered it at all. Coach Joe was great.

Nicholas whirled his fist around, already imagining the satisfaction when it connected with this smug idiot's jaw.

Then Nicholas remembered if he got caught fighting, he'd be thrown out of Kings Row. It had never mattered before. One school was pretty much the same as another. Nicholas had nothing to lose.

Thinking of all Nicholas had to lose now—*real fencing, Seiji, Coach Williams, Bobby and Eugene and Harvard, being at his dad's old school*—it would matter a lot.

Nicholas took a deep breath and stepped back. Stepping back didn't come naturally to him, and he didn't like it.

"Watch your mouth," Nicholas muttered. He didn't care what they said about him. They were mostly right about him, but they could leave Coach Joe alone.

After a moment, he remembered to unclench his fists. Both the boys wore slightly startled expressions, but after a moment they shrugged off whatever was holding them back and resumed their swagger down the hall.

"Sorry, didn't realize the hobo was like a *father* to you!" the older boy scoffed over his shoulder.

Nicholas waited until they were gone, then made his way toward the *salle*. Coach Joe wasn't anything like Robert Coste.

Nicholas's father being one of the greatest fencers of all time hadn't mattered to Mom. She'd been mad that he'd hit it, quit it, and skipped town with his fancy friends. That was all she ever said on the subject. Robert Coste was just one more in the list of men who'd let Mom down, a passing mention in a string of drunken bitterness.

The only one his father mattered to was Nicholas.

Sometimes Nicholas imagined that the truth might matter to Robert Coste, too. Some day. Not right now, obviously. But one day, possibly, when Nicholas was so great at fencing that he was officially acknowledged rivals with Seiji, and he had lots of trophies. Maybe after they won the state championship, the way Coach wanted. Nicholas might then casually hint at the facts, and Robert Coste would immediately be like, *Wow, my son— makes total sense. I'm so impressed... if only I'd known before; would you call me Dad?*, and Nicholas would be like, *No need to make a big deal of it or anything; I'm doing fine, Dad.*

Those half-formed dreams hadn't ever coalesced into a real plan of action. They'd seemed even more far-fetched once Nicholas had laid eyes on Jesse Coste. The son Robert knew about, the son he'd had with his wife and who'd grown up in his, no doubt, fancy house. The son Robert Coste had trained to follow in his fancy Olympic footsteps. Jesse, the guy Seiji wanted to fence with, because Jesse got everything.

One look at Jesse, and the rainbow-bright bubble of Nicholas's dream had burst.

You have this shiny pedigree dog you're super proud of, but hey! Guess what. Here's some unimpressive mutt on the doorstep. Exciting, right?

No.

Nicholas shook his head as he walked into the *salle*, feeling slightly sick at the thought. He met Harvard and Aiden on their way out and brightened. Their captain was the coolest.

"Hey," said Harvard, continuing to be the coolest, and hit Nicholas in the shoulder in a bro way. "Getting some training in? You're better every day, Cox."

"Blah, blah, blah, *freshman*, blah," Nicholas heard Aiden remark. "Blah, blah, blah, *hair*, blah."

Nicholas knew Aiden thought he was ignoring him on purpose, but Nicholas actually found it really hard to concentrate on what the guy was saying. He got this particular sneering lilt in his voice, and Nicholas knew he was gonna say something to indicate that Aiden was so great and Nicholas was such garbage. Nicholas couldn't help it, his attention slid away like—what was the phrase Coach Joe used?—water off a duck's back. Nicholas had heard that kind of stuff plenty of times before.

Nicholas gave Aiden a blank look. Aiden was shaking back his fancy hair, wearing an angry expression. Nicholas wondered what Aiden had to be mad about. Aiden didn't usually seem ruffled by anything. And he'd just been training with the captain, which must have been really fun. Aiden always had someone to train with.

Harvard and Aiden were best friends, people said, who'd known each other since they were little. Imagine having someone you got along with that well, who stuck around that long. Especially someone as great as Harvard. Aiden had no idea how lucky he was.

It must be awesome to have a best friend. Nicholas had never had one, but maybe Seiji would be his best friend someday? Yeah, Seiji probably would.

He carefully put Seiji's broken watch to the side as he grabbed his mask and épée.

He chose his *piste* and moved into an *étude*, going over the footwork Coach had insisted he practice. Nicholas was left-handed, and Coach said that could be a huge advantage, but he had to know how right-handed fencers moved, too. He tried out right-handed advances and retreats; advanced, retreated, advanced six times and remembered to retreat once, reached the end of the *piste* and spun, advanced, retreated, and went into an advance lunge.

Nicholas allowed himself the luxury of moving fast and forward, the way he wanted. He fenced with imaginary partners to work off his restlessness, trying to make himself tired enough to settle into training.

Coach Joe had always said it was important to keep in shape, so Nicholas used to run laps around the block until it was dark, even though the neighborhood was lousy. If you moved quickly, that wasn't a problem. Safe within the unblemished walls of Kings Row, Nicholas fenced with shadows and heard the thunder of his own heart echoing through his body, just like his feet falling hard as he raced down the cracked sidewalks of his city.

Keep moving, Nicholas. If you're fast enough, none of it can catch you.

5 AIDEN

The team was bonding. Or at least attempting to do so in the most ridiculous way possible.

Aiden, personally, was leaning against the farthest wall in order to further disassociate himself from these people.

The whole tableau was awful and unsightly.

The freshmen were being atrocious, as usual. Seiji had his arms primly crossed over his meticulously ironed shirtfront and was refusing to participate in trust falls. It was obvious Seiji would have to be clobbered into unconsciousness before he would permit himself to fall into anyone's arms. Nicholas had his arms crossed (not primly) over a hoodie that looked like he'd been using it to mop up dirt. He also seemed twitchy about trust falls. Aiden was prepared to bet the end result would be Nicholas crashing down in the wrong direction and breaking his nose. That would be at least mildly entertaining.

Eugene was running in circles saying, "Fall at me, bro! I'm open!" It was possible Eugene was Aiden's least favorite teammate.

Harvard had taken off his uniform jacket and was rolling up his shirtsleeves, ready to catch any of his teammates in his strong arms.

Well. Maybe the *whole* tableau wasn't unsightly.

Aiden looked away, across the floorboards on which the high window was casting a triangle of light, toward the wicked woman who had perpetrated this horror upon them.

Coach Williams wore a dispirited expression—who could blame her?—but she didn't call a halt to these lunatic proceedings. Whatever happened, it was on her.

"Are you ready to do trust falls, team?"

"Absolutely not," drawled Aiden. "As per our agreement, I am Trust Fall Switzerland."

"Wasn't talking to you, Aiden, but looking forward to your essay!" said Coach.

Aiden winced.

"Coach Williams," Seiji appealed, "I also wish to be Trust Fall Switzerland. If one of us got injured doing this, it would impede our ability to fence, and that would be a disaster."

"You will not get hurt falling onto practice mats. If by some freak chance you did get injured doing this, Eugene or Nicholas would substitute for you on the fencing team," said Coach. "Hence, why we have reserves."

"As I said," Seiji told her, "that would be a disaster."

Nicholas made a rude noise. Seiji shot him an annoyed look. Aiden judged that Nicholas's chances of being caught during trust falls had just taken a nosedive.

Coach, perhaps perceiving the same thing, sighed and rubbed the place between her brows where frown lines were forming. "Eugene and Harvard, you're up."

Harvard threw his unworthy mentor a brilliant smile. "Sure."

"I'm ready, Captain!" yodeled Eugene.

This was the guy who Coach Williams thought should be Harvard's roommate? Aiden gave Eugene a look of pure disdain. Eugene stopped mid-yodel, his mouth hanging open in dismay.

"Coach won't let you do trust falls because you suck at team-work," Nicholas muttered to Seiji.

"One, two, three—" said Coach.

"I don't want to do trust falls, and I'm excellent at teamwork," Seiji muttered back.

Nicholas shoved Seiji, which wouldn't have mattered if Seiji hadn't been thrumming with tension and standing at the edge of the mat. Seiji staggered off-balance, and the mat spun with him. Nicholas and Eugene, on high alert for falling, both reached for Seiji.

This left trusting Harvard obediently tumbling backward on

Coach's word onto the exposed wooden floor with nobody to catch him.

The world became a blur as Aiden leaped into action. Open-mouthed faces, light, walls, and practice mats all were streaks of color as though someone had hurled random paints at a canvas. Aiden might have done a shoulder roll. He wasn't sure of anything that happened in that handful of confused seconds, except for the result: Aiden on his knees, Harvard in his arms.

"Hey," said Harvard, and smiled.

In the distance, Aiden was aware Seiji had righted himself and was fussily brushing off his uniform as though *he'd* fallen, while loudly criticizing Nicholas and Eugene for getting in his way. Probably Coach was also still there. Weather was probably happening, of some kind, somewhere. Beyond the window.

Aiden expended a great deal of effort in not being *too* physically aware of Harvard. On a certain level. Aiden was very physically comfortable with Harvard on another level. They'd grown up together. They used to take naps, sharing the same mat or the same bed, holding hands with Harvard Paw cozily tucked between them. Even at Kings Row, their beds were pushed close together and they watched movies with Aiden kicking Harvard in the calf or Harvard's shoulder pressed up against his. It wasn't so different from the naps. It was all about context and keeping Aiden's life arranged in the correct categories: what was important, namely Harvard, and then—strictly separated—everything else.

Now everything was a mess.

There was a distinct lack of strict separation in the warm fact of Harvard in his arms. Harvard, open shirt collar blazing white against his glowing dark skin. Aiden was as close as the shadow of Harvard's collar against his skin. Harvard was looking up at Aiden, gaze calm and steady. Harvard, broad-shouldered and built for football as well as fencing, was actually too heavy for Aiden, but Aiden wasn't letting him go.

There was only one way to express the outrage Aiden was currently feeling about the universe.

Softly, because he hated even saying it, Aiden said, "You could've been *hurt*."

"Nah," replied Harvard. "This went great. All according to plan."

Aiden wasn't used to Harvard being spectacularly wrong. "This went—how did this go—"

"I fell because I knew one of my teammates would catch me," Harvard explained. He was still *smiling*. "One of my teammates did."

They heard the sound of Coach's authoritative step moving from mat to floor, coming toward them. Aiden's arms tightened around Harvard.

Harvard patted Aiden's arm. "Thanks, buddy. Now let me go. Gotta captain."

With no choice in the matter, Aiden did. Harvard climbed to his feet without a backward glance and went into a huddle with the coach from which the words *"could've gone better…"* were heard. Aiden, head reeling and utterly bewildered, found refuge in rage.

"You *miscreant idiot freshmen*," he began in scathing tones.

"I'm not a freshman—" said Eugene.

Aiden pointed at him accusingly. "Which is why you're the worst of all! You should know better!"

A throat was cleared behind him.

"Aiden," said Coach Williams, "is right."

A thunderstruck silence followed. Coach had never said anything like that before. Even Aiden found it tough to handle.

Coach Williams prowled forward as she continued: "It pains me to say this, but you guys put on the worst display of team bonding I've ever seen in my life. Maybe the worst display of team bonding since the Stone Age, when the weakest person on the team would have their skull harvested to play the next game with."

Aiden laughed.

Nicholas asked, "Did that actually happen, Coach?"

Coach pointed to a sign on the wall that read *Did that actually happen, Coach?* She made an encouraging gesture and Nicholas glumly began to run suicides.

"You all seem determined to prove yourselves extraordinarily bad at teamwork," Coach continued relentlessly.

"Is Seiji the worst?" Nicholas called as he ran by.

"I can do better!" exclaimed Seiji.

Eugene had draped himself on Harvard and was practically

weeping. Only the word *bropology* could be distinguished. Harvard patted Eugene on the back.

"You have to try harder. Take meals together. Sit beside one another. Learn to care if your teammates are in trouble. It is quite rare for there to be a situation in which not only is someone not caught during trust falls, but chaos ensues in which he could be physically harmed! Harvard came close to falling on the wooden floor and could easily have sustained a concussion. *Aiden* is the only one who was there for his teammate. He showed you all up. *Aiden*."

The way Coach said his name suggested she'd observed a great white shark saving a drowning swimmer. Aiden was beginning to feel personally offended. He felt even more offended when Seiji hung his head in shame.

Nicholas tried to argue, panting as he ran by: "Yeah, but Aiden wouldn't have tried to save anybody else, so it's not like he really cares about the team—"

"Are you suggesting that I'm biased? I'm totally impartial. It's not my fault Harvard is awesome and the rest of you suck!" Aiden snapped.

Scholarship Nicholas gave Aiden a vacant stare, then continued running. Aiden considered tripping him.

"You've forced my hand," announced Coach. "I can't make empty threats or I'll lose your respect as a coach, and more important, your fear. Tomorrow night I'm sending you out to run suicides through the woods. With raw steak around your necks."

Amazingly, the freshmen and Eugene seemed to be taking her seriously.

Eugene whimpered. "What if we get eaten by bears?"

"I may have mentioned that our team is in the uniquely fortunate position of having two reserves!" Coach said brightly. "I can spare at least one of you."

Maybe this day wasn't turning out so badly, after all. Aiden snickered. He could still feel a ghost of warmth in his arms, but—whatever. He was a world-class champion at compartmentalizing. He had a date tomorrow night, he was pretty sure. With someone hot, no doubt. He could have a date tonight, if he wanted. Everything was fine.

Aiden could've mentioned to the idiot freshmen that the manicured woods around Kings Row were conspicuous for cottontail rabbits and columbine, not bears. But why would he do a silly thing like that? This was hilarious. They deserved everything they got, especially Eugene.

"Fortunately for you guys," Coach announced, "I have, my sister tells me, no life…and that means I have no plans Friday evening! I'll be supervising your run through the woods. I plan to stand at a safe distance and note your cries of distress with interest. You accompanying me, Captain?"

"Can't make it, Coach," Harvard told her cheerfully. "Got a date."

The sky outside the windows went dark. There was a sudden sour taste in Aiden's mouth.

Coach whistled. "Good for you, Harvard!"

It was Aiden's firm opinion that the teaching staff should not be involved in or even aware of their students' love lives. This was inappropriate. Coach should be ashamed.

"Oh cool," said Worst Freshman Nicholas, though he looked startled, as though a date was a foreign concept to him. "Hope you have a great time, Captain."

Freshmen should not interfere with unsolicited opinions about the private lives of upperclassmen. Aiden didn't know why he was the only person left at Kings Row who knew the basic rules of social interaction.

"Thanks." Harvard smiled as if he thought Bad Haircut Nicholas was adorable. "I hope so, too."

Aiden hoped an unexpected hurricane would hit. A hurricane would keep everyone indoors, and Harvard safe at home.

Failing a hurricane, he hoped those freshmen would be eaten by bears.

Aiden turned away and arranged himself a date with lucky Mr. Right There When Aiden Stumbled Out of the Gym.

———————◆———————

On his date that night, he had a totally fine time. He'd have a good time tomorrow night, too, he told himself. And every night after that.

Aiden returned to their room late, and threw himself down on the bed, still in his clothes. His mouth ached as though the guy had bitten it a little too hard. He glanced over at the pillow beside his to see Harvard curved toward him as usual, crisp white bedsheet slipping down one strong shoulder. Aiden propped his arm behind his head, glaring up at the darkened ceiling, feeling taut all over as though he might snap.

Harvard blinked, not even half-awake. Maybe a tenth. "You back?"

"Yes," Aiden answered, his voice clear in the shadowed room. "I'm back."

"Tha's good," mumbled Harvard into his pillow. He reached out blindly, eyes shut again, and patted Aiden's arm. Aiden saw the moment where Harvard, sweet even in his sleep, noticed the tension in Aiden's arm and frowned. "Dun' worry," Harvard murmured, even as he fell back into slumber. "It okay."

Harvard rolled away under his blanket, burrowing his head into the pillow. Aiden looked at the line of his back, the gray material of Harvard's sleeveless T-shirt stretched tight across it.

Now let me go, Harvard's remembered voice said in his mind.

He'd always known he would have to, one day. He'd always told himself, maybe tomorrow.

Aiden reached out and carefully secured a hold on the back of Harvard's shirt. Just a pinch of gray fabric, held tight between Aiden's finger and thumb.

Maybe tomorrow Aiden would let go.

6 NICHOLAS

O n Friday, Seiji caused a sensation at breakfast.

Before he did, it was a morning like any other, though Eugene seemed uncharacteristically glum.

"'M not looking forward to being eaten by bears tonight, bro," he said as Nicholas patted him on the back and stole some of his bacon. Eugene didn't seem in the mood to appreciate it.

Eugene often ate with his weight-lifting bros, but this morning he'd slumped down beside Nicholas to seek comfort in these hard times. Nicholas always sat with Bobby, his first friend at Kings Row, and Bobby's roommate, Dante. Bobby and Dante were an odd pair, Bobby teeny and bubbly and fond of sparkly barrettes, while Dante was huge and quiet and not fond of sparkly anything except Bobby. Right now

Bobby was nodding sympathetically about Eugene's problems, and Dante was staring at Eugene as if he thought Eugene was deranged.

"What if you just say you won't put a steak around your neck and run around the forest?" Bobby suggested. "Coach can't really want to endanger the fencing team. You guys are doing so well. Just tell her you won't do it."

"I'm not going to say no to the coach!" said Eugene. "Not after I already almost gave the captain a concussion! I don't wanna let anybody down! I'm happy to do whatever the coach wants!" Eugene paused and softened his outburst by adding: "Bro."

Dante shook his head slowly and copied Nicholas by stealing a piece of Eugene's bacon.

Eugene, who was still fretting, didn't notice. "Also, I'm pretty sure Aiden hates me now."

"Don't even worry about him. Aiden doesn't like anybody except Harvard," said Nicholas. "Aiden's kind of mean."

This point of view seemed to shock Eugene to his core. "Oh no. You have Aiden all wrong. He's an amazing fencer—"

"Nah." Nicholas shrugged. "I beat him easy."

Actually, Aiden was better than he had any right to be, given how little he practiced. Harvard must be dragging Aiden to the *salle* all the time and giving him tips. Their captain was the best that way. Still, Nicholas couldn't figure out how Aiden had managed to win against *Seiji*.

"—really smart, always knows what to—"

The captain said that Aiden was always able to predict people's moves, but he sure hadn't been able to predict Nicholas's in their match. From what Nicholas had observed, Aiden was able to say stuff that made people falter during matches, but Nicholas couldn't imagine Seiji caring about anything Aiden had to say. The whole thing was a total mystery, though one that Nicholas felt great about—Aiden had beat Seiji, and Nicholas had beat Aiden, so in a way, Nicholas had already won a match against Seiji! It would be better to actually win a match against Seiji, but that'd happen soon.

"—the best-looking guy in school, everyone agrees—"

Nicholas, who found his attention wandering when people discussed the supremely uninteresting subject of Aiden, focused. "Wait, why are we suddenly talking about Seiji?"

Eugene and Dante blinked at him. While Nicholas wasn't paying attention, they seemed to have learned how to synchronize blinking.

"I agree with Nicholas!" said Bobby.

It was Nicholas's turn to blink. "About what?"

Then he realized why they were suddenly talking about Seiji. It was because Seiji was here. Nicholas had never seen Seiji at breakfast before. He didn't seem at ease in the dining hall. At first Nicholas hadn't been at ease here, either, since the room looked more like a museum hall than a cafeteria. There was art on the walls and multiple chandeliers, though at least the cafeteria chandeliers were the type that resembled fake candelabras and hung on chains. They weren't the glittery real ones to be found in other rooms at Kings Row. Nicholas knew with awful cold certainty the glittery chandeliers were actual crystal.

Seiji probably wasn't freaked out by chandeliers or smooth walls, but nonetheless he didn't seem at ease. He stood tall among the benches and tables, shirt and hair neat even though they didn't have class for more than twenty minutes, staring vaguely around as if he might be lost.

Nicholas stuck a hand in the air and waved it energetically around.

"Hey, Seiji!"

When Seiji spotted him, Nicholas thought he glimpsed a faint hint of relief on his face. Seiji came over right away, too. Nicholas grinned, feeling a warm spot in the center of his chest.

Eugene perked up as well. "Abroha! What brings you here?"

"Hello," said Seiji, sitting down. "I came here to bond with my teammates. You know . . . share a meal and a conversation."

They nodded, because they did know. Seiji nodded, too, a moment after the rest of them.

"Wow," said Bobby happily. "This is so cool! I can't believe you cut your training short to have breakfast with us."

Seiji looked shocked. "I didn't cut my training short. I just got up at three thirty in the morning instead of four so I could do this as well."

"Three thirty…in the morning…," Eugene murmured. "Always grinding. You're an inspiration, bro."

Nicholas made a horrible face around his mouthful of bacon. He didn't feel inspired by three thirty in the morning at all.

"What are we conversing about?" Seiji inquired.

Eugene put his head down on the table. "I'm not having a chill time lately. Could use a lift from my bros."

"Totally. We are here for you!" said Nicholas, and nodded encouragement at Seiji.

Seiji stared at him blankly.

Nicholas mouthed: *Team bonding*. Then he gestured from himself to Seiji, and back again.

Seiji cleared his throat. "Of course, Eugene. I will…provide you with emotional support, as requested."

This was a great morning, Nicholas decided. Seiji was having breakfast with them. Bobby was staring at Seiji, delighted and starstruck. Fencing was the first thing Bobby and Nicholas had bonded over, so Nicholas was sure Bobby and Seiji would get along well, too. Other people were murmuring and pointing at their table, no doubt jealous Seiji was sitting with them.

"Aiden hates me!" Eugene said sadly. His voice was muffled since he was speaking into the cradle of his arms.

Seiji nodded. "He does seem to dislike you. I've noticed that myself."

This wasn't what Eugene needed to hear. Nicholas kicked Seiji in the ankle.

"Nicholas just kicked me," Seiji reported, eyes narrowing. "I'm fairly certain it was on purpose!"

Bobby, who had a beautiful soul, hastily intervened. "Eugene, I'm sure Aiden doesn't hate you. He's probably feeling a bit sensitive right now, because Coach threatened to kick him off the team and make you roommates with Harvard instead of him."

Seiji and Nicholas gave a mutual shudder at the hideous words *off the team*. No wonder Aiden was in a foul mood these days.

"Is that what's going on?" asked Nicholas. "Sweet."

Bobby tilted his head, pigtails tipping to one side. "What do you mean?"

"I meant for the captain," said Nicholas. "Eugene would be a way better roommate than Aiden. Harvard could finally have some peace and quiet."

He realized Harvard and Aiden were best friends, but surely Harvard was exhausted by the constant talking at this point. Anybody would be. Nicholas viewed the dining hall, faces crowded around the long rectangular oak tables, benches crammed with boys in navy and gray. The sight of so many students assembled, all of them belonging so much more than Nicholas ever could, was as intimidating as being thrown into a really fancy sea. But Harvard would fit right in at any table. He was sure any of those older boys would be thrilled to hang out with the captain.

"Well," said Eugene, "I guess it's possible Harvard *is* tired of having Aiden's guys over at all hours. If you know what I'm saying."

"Wow," murmured Nicholas, as realization dawned. "Are you saying...?"

Eugene nodded. Bobby and Dante were nodding as well, in a resigned fashion. Apparently, this was common knowledge.

"Aiden has his friends over, like, at night? And in the mornings?" Nicholas demanded.

"Well...yeah, bro," said Eugene. "From night until morning. Sometimes."

Nicholas was scandalized.

"Does he throw *parties*? That's gotta be distracting for Harvard! The captain's fencing shouldn't suffer because his roommate is a party animal."

A silence settled over the table. Nicholas assumed everyone was as horrified as he was, but their expressions had gone strangely fixed. He looked to Seiji, whose eyebrows had drawn sharply and disapprovingly together.

"I agree completely, Nicholas," said Seiji. "Aiden shouldn't be throwing parties! Do you realize what's happening here? Because it seems obvious to me."

"Oh, thank God, someone's going to tell him," Bobby murmured.

Seiji leaned across the table toward Nicholas, as though he might whisper to him and still be heard over the buzz of chatter rising to the rafters. Nicholas leaned forward to hear what was so obvious to everyone else.

"I suspect that if Harvard wasn't being deprived of sleep by these social gatherings, the captain would be higher ranked among the fencers," Seiji informed Nicholas earnestly. "Harvard might potentially be in the top ten rather than the top fifty. No wonder Harvard can't find time to work on his low lines. I honestly can't bear to think about how this irresponsible behavior is affecting the captain's fencing."

"...Oh my God," Bobby whispered.

"Right, Bobby?" asked Nicholas. "We're all shocked."

There was another silence. Nicholas was pleased to see even Dante seemed stunned.

Seiji, making a visibly painful effort to be sociable, turned to Dante. Nicholas thought Seiji had selected Dante to address because Dante was the strong silent type, and Seiji found quiet more comfortable than conversation.

They all watched in horror as Seiji made his fatal mistake.

"What are your thoughts on low lines? When working with the épée, naturally."

"I don't care about épées," Dante told him.

"Ah," said Seiji. "More of a sabers man? Our coach feels the same. For myself, I prefer—"

Dante explained, "I don't care about any kind of fencing."

Seiji exchanged a slightly panicked glance with Nicholas. Nicholas shrugged, like *Go with it.* He found Dante's attitude puzzling as well, but Dante was a good guy. Dante and Bobby were best friends. Seemed as if everyone had one of those.

Nicholas wondered when a good time might be to bring up being best friends with Seiji. Possibly not soon, since Seiji was clearly finding a friendly breakfast to be a trial.

Bobby gave Seiji a look of rapt admiration, then, obviously torn, gave Dante a look of best-friend love. Dante's attitude about fencing must be hard for Bobby to deal with, Nicholas thought with sympathy.

"Dante's a great cook," offered Bobby. "His whole family gets together and makes these huge meals. They cook the most fantastic Italian food."

Nicholas did love pizza. The food at Kings Row was amazing, and the meals were so regular. The teachers actually got mad if you skipped any of them. Still, he really missed a delicious, greasy slice. Mom would give him the money for pizza sometimes, when she wasn't gonna be home.

"Fascinating," murmured Seiji politely. "Unusual."

"Not really," Bobby defended Dante, admirably loyal to his best friend even when addressing his fencing idol. "Cooking's a more popular hobby than fencing."

"They don't have a *Great British Fence-Off*," muttered Dante.

There was a thoughtful pause.

"Oh, that sounds like such a good show," Nicholas murmured.

"I like your idea for a television show as well," Seiji told Dante. "Why do you picture it being British specifically?"

Dante's mouth opened and closed. No sound came out.

"Could be because of the European history of dueling?" Nicholas suggested, and looked to Seiji. "Like in the book you let me borrow. Did you know that if you killed someone in a duel back in the old days, you could run away to France, because in France, dueling was still a totally cool and legal way to kill someone you had beef with?"

Seiji nodded, pointing at Nicholas for emphasis. "I did know that, but clearly not everybody does. You're right; the show would be educational for many people. Perhaps they could hold fencing displays in old manor houses and castles and châteaux? And, of course, in colleges such as Cambridge, Oxford, and Trinity, where the legacy of fencing students is so illustrious."

Breakfast conversation was so awesome now that Seiji had joined them! Nicholas bet nobody else had as much fun as they did.

Dante had clearly given up on talking and was giving Bobby a silent, pleading look. Nicholas guessed Dante was shy. Seiji was pretty famous, so maybe Dante was overwhelmed.

"Speaking of cooking!" said Bobby with speed. "Don't tell, guys, but Dante sometimes makes pasta sauce over a burner and we have a midnight feast."

"Fun!" said Nicholas enthusiastically. "We should have a midnight feast. That'd be a good team bonding exercise."

"*More* communal meals?" Seiji said. "For a team bonding exercise. Certainly."

"I can fix us a midnight feast," Eugene suggested.

He'd lifted his head from the table, intrigued by this new idea. Maybe Eugene, like Dante, cooked big meals with his family. Nicholas had seen them, all Eugene's tiny younger brothers and sisters, show up to support him at the fencing tryouts. They seemed really nice.

"Or you'd all be welcome to come by our room and eat pasta," Bobby offered. Nicholas beamed at him.

Their exciting discussion of a midnight feast was broken up by the sound of the bell ringing for class.

Seiji rose immediately. "Good breakfast, everyone. I… enjoyed it. See you here at this table, for more conversation, at the same time next week."

"Next week?" The question seemed to pop from Bobby's lips with the force of sheer surprise. Seiji bent an inquiring gaze upon him. Bobby looked mortified.

"Is this not a weekly occasion?"

Nicholas hit Seiji on the shoulder, the way Harvard had hit him, so Seiji would feel included the way Nicholas had. "We have breakfast together every morning."

"*Every morning!*" Seiji exclaimed, and then collected himself. "Oh. Good. Then I will see you all tomorrow morning, at this time sharp."

Bobby gazed at Seiji with distress. "We just turn up, you know, when we turn up."

Seiji's expression was briefly appalled. Bobby murmured feebly about how they should learn how to keep to a better schedule.

Seiji pressed his lips together and nodded. "Understood. We'll meet at this time approximately. Looking forward to that."

"We might not make it to breakfast tomorrow morning," Eugene reminded Nicholas and Seiji gloomily. "We might get eaten by bears tonight."

7 SEIJI

Seiji was finding his essay remarkably difficult to write. There simply wasn't much to say, and he was
uncertain how to put it. In Seiji's experience, he reported the basic facts, and
people became angry with him and
called him arrogant. Then they dis-
liked him for simply telling the truth.
Was he meant to lie to get them to like
him? Seiji didn't intend to do that.

*My father is CEO of a zaibatsu spe-
cializing in automotive manufacture,*
Seiji wrote. Then he remembered
that people frequently couldn't be
bothered to look up words and added
(*business conglomeration*) after the
word *zaibatsu.*

*My parents are a hardworking and
devoted couple who raised me with
every advantage. I always had the best
trainers—and the best of everything
else, too.*

What else was there to discuss

about his childhood or his parents? Seiji didn't know his parents especially well. They were always busy with work and each other. Seiji heard unpleasant gossip at his father's parties about mistresses and divorces, but Seiji never doubted for a moment *his* parents would be loyal.

He'd often seen them with their foreheads pressed together, or their eyes on each other, in their own private bubble where Seiji had never been able to reach them. At family mealtimes, they became wholly wrapped up in business discussions and seemed hardly able to hear when Seiji tried to join in. His contributions hadn't been particularly helpful, he had to admit. Then again, last time he tried, Seiji was six.

His parents were a team. Seiji didn't think he had the same capacity for devotion his parents possessed, and perhaps they knew that. Seiji suspected his parents didn't find him very likable, which was an opinion many people held.

They were always civil to him. They provided well for Seiji. They did everything they could. It wasn't their fault that once they'd had a child, they discovered they didn't want the one they'd got.

I have an excellent relationship with my family, Seiji concluded.

Surely three lines was enough chattering on about his homelife, and the rest of the essay could be about fencing.

Seiji put down his pen and sighed as he looked around. It was almost time to go into the woods. Behind the blue shower curtain, the wild disorder of Nicholas's half of the room lurked.

Outside their mahogany door, the wild disorder of the world awaited. Even if he managed to complete this essay to his satisfaction, there was the rest of the team bonding to contend with.

Kings Row was a small school compared to the towers and high walls of Exton, where Seiji had always intended to go. The fencing team at Kings Row was a stranger team than the one he'd always expected to be part of. Even their coach was strange.

Seiji respected his coach, of course, and if she felt team bonding was important, then he believed that it must be. He was still having trouble working out what the point of the exercise was, but he hoped he'd discern it with time. Until then, he was putting in his best effort.

Seiji wasn't asocial. He was perfectly good at the social situations that had proper rules. At gatherings with sponsors, whether to do with business or fencing, he knew to stay mostly quiet, murmur in a modest way, and exhibit excellent manners. Seiji's coaches and his father never had any complaints about how Seiji conducted himself on those occasions.

He *wasn't* asocial, but he wasn't sociable, either. *Keeps a distance from his peers*, a teacher had written on Seiji's report card once. Seiji did, and felt that was sensible. Why not hold yourself apart from chaos?

Kids Seiji's own age were chaotic. Nicholas was more chaotic than most. Seiji found him very difficult to reason with. It had been Nicholas's suggestion that they should be friends, not

Seiji's, and it was impossible to know what Nicholas even meant by being friends. Was Seiji supposed to watch *all* Nicholas's terrible fencing matches? None of this was Seiji's idea.

Nicholas had once saved Seiji a seat on the team bus, and Nicholas took the seat beside Seiji in their classes, but Nicholas hadn't saved Seiji the seat beside him at breakfast this morning. Of course, Seiji had to admit, Nicholas hadn't known Seiji was coming.

Would Nicholas save Seiji a seat at breakfast *tomorrow* morning? There was no telling. It would be worrying if he did, since from what Seiji had observed, Nicholas stole food from other people's plates. Seiji didn't want anyone to steal food from his plate.

It had all been so easy with Jesse. Until it hadn't.

Jesse had never said they were *friends*. He'd said they were *fencing partners*, and Seiji believed that was better. More important.

Seiji put away his papers and pens neatly, then checked his reflection in the mirror. There was a lock of hair out of place, so he produced a comb and made himself presentable.

Then he went out into the woods. He found Nicholas and Eugene already there—maybe they'd been socializing beforehand—at the edge of the forest, with Coach and a pile of raw steaks.

Seiji had been hoping the steaks were a joke, but apparently not. Nicholas was already wearing a steak around his neck, secured in place with twine. The uncooked meat was blue in parts, and dripped onto Nicholas's skin. Somehow, he was managing to remain calm. Eugene looked upset, but not as upset as Seiji felt.

"Shirt off, steak on," Coach Williams encouraged.

Seiji stared at the steak. "I cannot put this on."

"Your teammates are already wearing them," Coach pointed out. "What makes you different from them?"

Seiji fought the impulse to cling to Coach's sleeve and beg. "*I have dignity.*"

There was a pause. Seiji had never disobeyed a direct order from his coach, but he didn't think he could put some clammy, messy thing on himself. Nicholas and Eugene's appearance was absurd.

"Oh, all right," Coach said at length to Seiji's intense private relief. "But you have to stick to the others. Don't run away if the bears come. Stay and be eaten together. That's what teamwork means."

"Please stop talking about bears," Eugene moaned.

Coach gave them a wild grin.

Seiji was certain there were no bears, but when Seiji pointed out obvious facts, other people got annoyed. Sometimes he found it best to keep quiet.

Coach clapped her hands. "Off you go!"

They began jogging through the woods. The reassuring sight of Coach, in her bright-red tracksuit, was soon lost among the trees. The evening air had a bite to it, and while Seiji had to repress the urge to shiver, Eugene and Nicholas were wearing cold steaks around their necks. This wasn't responsible behavior on Coach's part. Nicholas could get sick, and Seiji, as his roommate, would have to handle the situation. Seiji could already picture snuffling and complaining from behind the curtain in addition to Nicholas's usual incessant noise. There would be tissues all over the floor.

There was a rustling in the undergrowth.

Eugene startled and threw his arms around Seiji. "Bear! I heard a bear!"

Seiji fought free with strength born of desperation. "You did not hear a bear!"

He almost tripped over a tree root getting away from Eugene. Then came another rustle, and Eugene threw his arms around Nicholas.

"Bear!"

"*Where?*" demanded Nicholas, clinging back. "I'm a city kid. I don't wanna go out in a bear attack!"

Seiji lifted his eyes to heaven and saw only evergreens and the darkening sky. He kept a careful distance from his teammates to avoid any repeat of Eugene springing at him, and tried to judge how far they'd gone and in which direction. That was tricky, since the trees looked similar to one another. When Seiji turned around to consult with Nicholas and Eugene, they were nowhere to be found. Seiji felt lost and confused in a dark-green world.

He decided to head for the road he could glimpse through the trees. Roads led to civilization. A road would lead him back to school.

As Seiji reached the road, winding through the trees like a dark snake, a gleaming black limousine turned a curve. Seiji stepped to the side to let the car go past. He had no wish to be run over.

The limousine came to a halt. A shiny black door opened, and a smooth golden head emerged, almost silver in the dusk.

"*Seiji?*" said Jesse Coste in obvious astonishment. "What are you doing out here? And where is your shirt?"

This couldn't be happening. This must be a nightmare. No, that was a panicked and irrational thought.

Seiji, perfectly able to distinguish awful reality from dreams, pulled himself together. "I'm jogging through the woods near my school. What are you doing here?"

He was grateful that his voice sounded cool and distant, as though he were doing a completely reasonable thing and asking a completely reasonable question. Jesse looked precisely as Seiji remembered him, as Jesse always did: in control without even having to try, without being aware there was any other option.

"I'm headed to the airport for a tournament," Jesse answered, then raised an eyebrow. "Your school? That's cute."

"It *is* my school," Seiji pointed out evenly.

He was getting through this ordeal with dignity, he told himself. Then he heard a rough voice calling his name. Seiji's heart sank.

Nicholas came blundering through the trees with all the grace and subtlety of a lost hippopotamus.

"Oh, there you are," said Nicholas, frowning.

Seiji was more or less accustomed to Nicholas by now, but he could vividly imagine Nicholas through Jesse's eyes at this moment, and it was hideous to contemplate. Nicholas had leaves in his hair, dirt on his chest, and a raw piece of meat hung around his neck. He was a monument to the mess Seiji's life had become.

Then Nicholas noticed Jesse and went absolutely still.

"You," Nicholas murmured in a strange, faltering voice, as though too shocked to think of any other word.

"And...you?" said Jesse. "Who are you? Did I—Never mind, doesn't matter."

Jesse made a dismissive gesture, flicking away Nicholas's existence as though it were a crumbled leaf that had fallen onto Jesse's Exton uniform. He turned his head, not a golden hair out of place, back to Seiji.

"As I was saying, before we were so *rudely* interrupted"—Jesse's tone invited Seiji to share the joke, but Seiji didn't feel like joking—"I think it's well past time you gave up this absurd notion of Kings Row. You've made your point. You don't belong at this third-rate school with these third-rate students. You need to be at Exton with me. That's where you really belong."

His voice was convincing, but then Jesse always did have conviction. Seiji knew Jesse well enough to know it wasn't false assurance. Everything about Jesse was golden: voice, laugh, skill, confidence. Everything about him said, *I'm on the winning side.* Jesse never doubted that. Nor did he have any reason to doubt. Jesse's whole life so far had proven him right.

When Seiji had first met Jesse, Robert Coste was with him, speaking proudly of Jesse's ability. Jesse's father watched every one of Jesse's matches and monitored his training. Seiji wondered what it would be like, to be able to inspire the kind of pride Jesse could. He wanted to learn how.

Always keep moving toward your target, Seiji's dad had said once at the breakfast table, talking about business. That made sense to Seiji, so he'd remembered it.

If Seiji was with Jesse, he wasn't a weird loner whose appearance in the dining hall caused widespread mockery. His intense training made sense to everybody, because he wasn't just a prodigy. He was Jesse Coste's training partner, and he had to live up to that. If Seiji was with Jesse, he was chosen and special. In Jesse's presence, Seiji wasn't lost and wandering in the dark, having taken all the wrong turns. He wasn't alone.

Seiji always tried to control his expressions, but Jesse knew him well enough to recognize the hint of surrender on his face. Jesse had seen it before.

Jesse smiled as he always did when he got his way, pleased but not surprised. He moved away from the limo and toward Seiji, smooth as when he was delivering the coup de grâce in a match, with his hand held out.

"Uh." Nicholas cleared his throat. "I'm not gonna let you kidnap my teammate in your limo."

Jesse's eyebrows almost rose through his golden hairline at the unfamiliar words *not gonna let you*. Nicholas took a step forward.

Seiji had a sudden feeling of unease. The way Nicholas was staring at Jesse was uncharacteristic. Usually, Nicholas paid more attention to Seiji than anybody else.

Jesse regarded Nicholas suspiciously in return. "Please stay back. I don't wish to contract mad cow disease."

Nicholas rolled his eyes. "You're hilarious."

"I'm serious—I don't want to," said Jesse.

Seiji was direly embarrassed by Nicholas's presence, not to mention his appearance. He hadn't wished to see Jesse again. If forced to, he would have preferred to see him while winning Olympic gold. Failing that, Seiji would've preferred to see Jesse literally anywhere other than here. In the middle of the woods, in a state of undress, with a companion who had apparently been raised by wolves and then abandoned by the pack for being too scruffy.

There was . . . another consideration, besides embarrassment.

Sometimes there were people who were obviously *not* on the winning side, and never would be. Bad at fencing or at words or at life in some crucial way Jesse could always ascertain. Occasionally, Jesse would casually amuse himself at some unfortunate soul's expense. Seiji wouldn't laugh because he never actually understood the jokes or why they were funny, but he didn't care much. It was simply Jesse's way. Now he recalled with unwelcome vividness how those people's cheeks would bear sudden swift streaks of red, as though slashed. Or they might slink off with a curious look of defeat, as if a lunch table were a fencing match. Some of them, Seiji had noticed, never came back again.

Seiji didn't want to see Jesse do that to Nicholas.

Not *Nicholas*.

The wind whipped around and around the tops of the pine trees, an almost mocking sound—like kids chasing one another around the playground, and singing taunts in thin, cruel voices.

Nicholas Cox was an absurd wreck of a person. But he'd said they would be friends. He'd once congratulated Seiji on his win, in a match that didn't even matter much—not in the gracious public way other people did, more as if they were congratulating themselves on their own good manners than anything Seiji had done—but sincerely because Nicholas thought Seiji had fenced well and was glad he'd won. Nobody else ever congratulated Seiji like that. Jesse and Seiji hadn't congratulated each other on their wins against lesser opponents. Victory was assumed.

How was Seiji supposed to stop Jesse from hurting Nicholas? He'd never been able to stop Jesse from doing anything he wanted.

Seiji edged toward Nicholas. He didn't get in front of him, but he tried to be in the position he would've taken on the *piste* in order to deflect a blow, if one came.

It was something a fencing partner would notice.

Jesse's eyes went dark.

"I have no idea what's going on here," he said, his voice bright as ice, "though it appears to be extremely sad and strange. Does it make you feel better about yourself to hang out with losers, Katayama?"

Nicholas, who apparently hadn't noticed Seiji's careful maneuvering, charged right past Seiji as if he wanted to head-butt the limousine. He hit Seiji's shoulder hard on the way past. Seiji clenched his teeth with annoyance.

"Who are you calling a loser, jerk?" Nicholas demanded.

"You," said Jesse. "I'm calling you a loser. You were born to be one. That much is obvious."

He didn't spare either of them another glance. He yawned and stretched, gold watch gleaming above the cuff of his shirt-sleeve in the dying light, then strolled back to the limousine.

"Let me know when you're tired of sulking, Seiji, and ready to fall in line." He closed the door.

Seiji watched the retreating red lights of the sleek car, like evil eyes in the shadows.

Fall in line. That was the crux of the matter.

If Seiji was with Jesse, he would be where he belonged. He wouldn't be awkward or out of place or wake up at night with a knot of misery in his chest.

And if Seiji was with Jesse, they would never be equals. Jesse had always assumed that was understood, but Seiji hadn't realized it until recently. Once he did, he shocked everyone—even himself—by finding it unbearable.

"*That guy*," Nicholas spat at the retreating car, "is—"

"Probably the best fencer of our generation," observed Seiji. "And everything he said was true."

Nicholas reared back. Seiji stared him down. For a moment, Nicholas seemed a symbol of everything that had gone wrong in Seiji's life, all order lost and only chaos remaining. For a moment, Seiji hated him.

Nicholas made a graceless snorting sound and plunged into the woods. Seiji wasn't worried about losing him. Nicholas was practically crashing into the trees and trampling the undergrowth with his stop-traffic-red sneakers. His path of destruction would be simple to follow. For now, Seiji lingered on the dark road where Jesse had been, as night fell.

Nobody could rival Jesse. Nobody could replace him, either.

Seiji was alone.

8 AIDEN

Aiden kissed a boy and saw stars. He was lying on his back in the grass, staring up at the night sky, and there were stars in it. There were also several clouds, though not as many as Aiden could wish for.

"Does it seem like hurricane weather to you?" asked Aiden.

"—you're so hot?" said Whatshisface.

"Feels like the wind's picking up a little though, right?"

"No," murmured Aiden's date. "Seems to me it's going to be a really nice night."

"Why would you say something like that?" Aiden demanded.

The boy gave him a somewhat quizzical glance. Aiden had to admit, he hadn't been bringing his A game, so he stretched out languidly on the picnic blanket, laced his fingers through the boy's long brown (red?

It was dark out here) hair, and pulled him down for another kiss. The boy gave a soft, delighted sigh.

"I used to watch you in the halls," the boy murmured in his ear, "and wonder... Did you ever think about me, too?"

Aiden wasn't thinking about this boy *now*.

Before Aiden could say "So, this is awkward," the boy kissed him again. He wasn't a bad kisser. Hooking up made Aiden think of fencing, sometimes. The sheer physicality of it, the smooth, skilled movements flowing and arching to a victorious end. Knowing your opponent's moves, weaknesses, what would get to them. Scoring all the points you could. And, in the end, turning away.

The boy began to unbutton Aiden's shirt, and Aiden turned away from stars and kisses.

"Are you finding it difficult to concentrate?" Aiden asked, and the boy stilled, looking slightly helpless. Aiden grinned and shrugged. "Just me, I guess."

When you weren't feeling it, you weren't feeling it.

Shortly after, Aiden found himself alone in his room, which hardly ever happened. On the rare occasions it did, Aiden was used to knowing where he could go to find Harvard and expect a warm welcome: at his house or hanging out with friends or in the *salle*. Tonight, Aiden couldn't go be where Harvard was. Tonight, Harvard was on his stupid date.

Aiden decided he would take advantage of the peace and quiet to write his essay. He'd done some reading about what might be expected from this sort of assignment, and one idea had been life lessons Aiden had learned from trusted authority figures.

Aiden's father had remarked once that some women were sports cars on the way to champagne brunch, and some were family vans headed to soccer practice. Aiden knew which his father preferred.

Aiden's father didn't actually talk to the women in his life, but Aiden did. Many of his dad's girlfriends got lonely. They would chatter to Aiden in order to pass the time and fill the echoing Italian-marble rooms with some semblance of life.

Sometimes what they said was useful.

Heather the professional cheerleader, who could put her hair up into a high and sleek ponytail in two seconds flat, told him once, "Other girls on the squad say couples split because of money or cheating or fights, but I don't think so. There's only one reason relationships end: Somebody loses interest. And somebody always will. Just make sure you're the one who loses interest first, Aidy."

Aiden nodded shyly. "How do you make someone interested in the first place?"

Heather's injection-paralyzed brow failed to wrinkle as she thought. "Don't be too nice. Don't care too much. Don't let them be sure of you. Always be something different and gorgeous and fascinating, so they don't know what to expect."

"Like a chameleon?"

"Sure, if you're always a beautiful chameleon. Just remember to be gone long before you lose a man's interest, I always say!" Heather added, winking and laughing merrily at her own lovely face in the mirror.

Aiden was just a prop in the room back then, a slight, unremarkable kid only useful as an audience. The only person who really noticed him was Harvard, and Harvard noticed everybody.

Heather hadn't taken her own advice. She'd lingered too long, and Aiden's dad had ditched her with particular viciousness. Aiden had heard her crying as she left, seen the proud plume of her ponytail drooping as she'd climbed into the car. Aiden never let his own head drop like that.

What did it matter how people left? What mattered was that they did.

Aiden abandoned his essay and went to sulk cross-legged on his bed, pulling his bear into his lap for comfort.

It was almost ten o'clock at night. Harvard usually went to bed early so he could get up and practice, but Aiden supposed that wouldn't be the case anymore. He'd have constant late nights now that he was dating.

"You might be in a single-parent family now, Harvard Paw," Aiden told his bear. "I'll do my best, but you know I'm not the responsible type. You'll probably run wild from lack of supervision and eat picnics belonging to hikers. Or babies belonging to hikers. I don't know, I foresee hiker-related tragedy ahead."

Harvard must be having a wonderful time on his date. He

had forsaken all his captainly duties in the pursuit of romance. Those freshmen needed him. Would nobody think of the freshmen? Aiden certainly wasn't going to.

Just as Aiden was contemplating the demise of the entire fencing team, the door opened. Harvard walked in. He'd got dressed up for his date. He was wearing a nice button-down shirt and his gray wool coat, but the coat sat differently now than it usually did. His shoulders were slumped underneath it.

Aiden cast aside Harvard Paw and leaped up from the bed. Harvard barely seemed to notice. He shut the door, and then leaned back against it. Then he slid bonelessly to the floor.

"Aw, did the date go badly, buddy?"

—*thank you, thank you, God, thank you*—

"No?" Harvard offered, as though he weren't sure.

"No?" echoed Aiden, who needed to be sure. "Did it go well?"

"I think...," Harvard said at length. "I think...too well?"

"What does that mean?"

No answers were forthcoming; Harvard seemed to be in a state of shock. He just sat there, back against the door, staring at the wall.

Earlier, Aiden had casually called Harvard's mother, acquired this awful girl's full name, and found her on all forms of social media. She updated frequently, usually about the lousy music she enjoyed. He couldn't believe he hadn't already thought to check her accounts tonight.

There was a new post—a picture of Harvard looking adorable

and attentive and holding a double scoop of chocolate ice cream. Underneath the picture was the caption *When you think he might be THE ONE!!!!!! #bestnightever.*

Oh no, oh no, oh no.

Aiden was perfectly aware, had *always* been burningly aware, that Harvard was one hundred percent boyfriend material. He'd dedicated his entire life to making sure nobody else caught on. Now all Aiden's efforts had come to nothing.

"I know what to do!" Aiden declared. "Give me your phone. Right now. Don't question me, this is an emergency."

Harvard, seemingly on autopilot, handed over his phone. Aiden stared at it, devoting intense contemplation to the task ahead. Then he swept his hair back with one hand, and with the other he began to tap out some messages.

After seven minutes, he offered Harvard his phone back.

Harvard blinked at the phone as though he wasn't entirely sure what it was. "What..."

"Congratulations!" Aiden told him. "You're now blocked on every form of social media Shirley possesses."

"Cindy," murmured Harvard. "I'm *what?*"

That was the beauty of this result. Now that the girl was out of Harvard's life, Aiden didn't have to remember her name anymore. She had nothing to do with them.

Shock was clearing from Harvard's face and being replaced with a gathering fury. There was no gratitude in this world.

"Aiden, what did you *do*? What did you say to her?"

Aiden shrugged lazily. "Nothing much. The usual stuff I say when I get impatient—the type of message that makes guys stop being infatuated and block me. I was going for speed and effectiveness, not finesse. And voilà. You're welcome."

His roommate scrolled through his own phone, making indignant faces at Aiden's messages. When he came to one message in particular, he dropped his phone on the floor.

Yeah, Aiden might have gone too far with that one.

"I didn't ask you to do this! I didn't *want* you to do this. I would have let her down kindly but firmly," said Harvard.

"I couldn't take that chance," muttered Aiden.

"Why did you do this?"

Aiden opened and closed his mouth, then opened it again and said decidedly, "You were upset. I was trying to solve your problem for you."

"That wasn't my problem."

"Then—" Aiden said. "What was your problem?"

"I walked Cindy to her doorstep," said Harvard slowly.

"For future reference," Aiden suggested, "you can leave them at the gate. Or drop them off by the side of the road and say 'See ya!' That's a real time-saver."

Harvard gave Aiden a doubtful look. "Your success with men is a mystery to me."

Aiden was aware. He forced himself to smile. "I'm sexually magnetic, so jot that down. Mystery solved." Aiden clapped his hands together. "Proceed with your story!"

Harvard did so, his face now clouded with distress. Aiden had spent the whole night praying for clouds, but not these.

"We were standing together on her porch. She told me she'd had a great time. Then she sort of—swayed in toward me, and I could tell that. Uh. That she wanted to kiss me."

Aiden had known this girl was bad news.

"You...kiss people all the time." Harvard cleared his throat, slightly awkward. "Like, you've probably kissed someone within the last five minutes."

Aiden tipped his hand back and forth. "Maybe an hour ago. Laurence."

He wasn't used to talking about kissing with Harvard. He refused to let it show this affected him.

"Wow, no, that was Byron," Harvard informed him. "You were calling him Laurence? That's worse than usual."

"Really? Byron? You'd think I would remember a guy called Byron," Aiden mused. "Anyway, enough of Byron. I won't be seeing him again. We couldn't even agree about the weather."

Harvard looked out the window. "What's to agree about? It's a nice night."

Aiden beamed approval at him. Harvard was so wise. "It *is* a nice night. And still early. Sorry your date was a lousy kisser, but what do you say we watch a movie and you can revisit dating another time?"

Such as college. Or grad school! You can't hurry love. Sometimes, Aiden had heard, you just had to wait.

Harvard stated in a distant voice, "She wasn't a lousy kisser."

"Oh," said Aiden. "She was a really great kisser?"

He regretted Cindy had already blocked Harvard. Aiden had more things to say to her.

"I don't know. I didn't kiss her," Harvard told their floorboards. "She sort of swayed in toward me, and I panicked and I, uh, kissed her on the forehead and ruffled her hair and ran off."

"Good call!" Aiden said. "There's no need to rush this stuff. When you're ready! Or never! Never is fine, too."

He wondered idly how Harvard had got the *Best Night Ever* hashtag with a forehead kiss. No, he could picture how it had been. She must have thought Harvard was the last of the true gentlemen. She wasn't wrong. Harvard had probably reached out and enfolded her in his arms, and she'd felt taken care of and cherished.

"I didn't want to kiss her," Harvard confessed very quietly.

"Why would you?" asked Aiden. "She has terrible taste in music and uses too many exclamation points!"

"I never...," said Harvard. "I never thought about it before. I always thought I'd...want to one day? That it would feel right. But I don't think I want to kiss girls at all."

"Oh," said Aiden. "*Oh.*"

They'd had this conversation before, from the opposite side. Harvard had assured Aiden of Harvard's eternal friendship and how all kinds of love were beautiful, which hadn't exactly been what Aiden was looking for.

Aiden couldn't believe this was happening. He was too surprised to be supportive.

"So...you might want to kiss guys?"

"I—maybe?" said Harvard. "I think...yes?"

As statements of ringing certainty went, this one left something to be desired. Still, it was more than Aiden had at the start of the night. Aiden remained in a place of dazed disbelief.

"Welcome to the club?" Aiden hazarded. "It's a sexy club."

Aiden shot Harvard Paw an incredulous look, to see if someone else was getting this. His stuffed bear had fallen over on his side. Aiden was fully in sympathy with the bear.

When his gaze returned to Harvard, he was smiling weakly. Harvard's wider smiles embraced everyone, but these small grins were exclusively for Aiden. "Thanks, buddy."

If Harvard felt better, Aiden felt better.

Maybe..., Aiden thought through the shock, testing the thoughts out in his mind as if he were rehearsing lines for a play to see if a role felt right. *Maybe this is great.*

Harvard wasn't going to marry Stacey with the bad taste in music and settle down in a house featuring a white picket fence and two point five golden retrievers. Aiden was saved.

"I think you know who you should talk to about this," Aiden purred encouragingly. "Lucky for you, there's an expert on hand."

"Yeah," mumbled Harvard, and scooped up his phone from the floor.

Aiden watched in disbelief as Harvard rang the second contact on his phone.

"Hey, Mom. Just called to say I love you. And, uh...Do any of your friends have a son my age? Who might be interested in going on a date? With me?"

Aiden sat down hard on their bedroom floor. He tried to have a heart attack in a cool and collected fashion.

9 NICHOLAS

eiji was mad at him. That wasn't exactly unusual, but this time it was Jesse Coste's fault.

Seiji had been silent coming back from the woods, then quiet all night without even uttering the normal bedtime stuff like *Turn off the light immediately, Nicholas*, and *Don't speak to me*. He hadn't come to breakfast this morning, even though he'd said he would, and Nicholas had saved him a seat.

He kept remembering the moment in the dark woods when Jesse had said Seiji should go with him, and the way Seiji—who never hesitated—had hesitated. Some part of Seiji wanted to go.

Seiji hadn't gone. Probably because Jesse Coste was an enormous jerk. But Seiji seemed tempted by the idea of Exton and the fencing team there.

Nicholas couldn't really imagine a school better or fancier than Kings

Row. Even when he'd got a brochure for Kings Row sent to Coach Joe's gym, the place had looked fake to him, a school out of a book or a childhood dream. Nicholas had worried he'd get grubby fingerprints on the brochures, but now that he was there, he felt—and plenty of students acted—as though Nicholas might get grubby fingerprints over the whole school. If there *was* a better school, Seiji deserved to go there.

He deserved a better fencing partner. Nicholas had figured out that when they were together, sometimes Seiji was fencing someone else, someone also fast and left-handed, but with an advanced skill that Nicholas didn't have. Yet. He'd have it soon, if Seiji would just *wait*.

Wait, and not return to Jesse.

How were they supposed to be rivals if Seiji went to a whole other school and forgot Nicholas existed? Nicholas didn't want him to leave. But he knew uneasily that he would be furious if he were Seiji, cut off from having what he wanted. If Exton was to Seiji what Kings Row was to Nicholas...then Nicholas shouldn't get in his way.

Nicholas was too dispirited to steal much of Eugene's bacon.

"Having a domestic, bro?" asked Eugene. "You fighting with Seiji again? Can't help but notice he's not here."

"Yeah, uh..."

Nicholas wasn't going to get into the whole *Robert Coste is my father and his other, legitimate son was trying to lure Seiji away from the team in a limo.* He'd never told anybody about Robert

Coste. And it seemed like a lot to spill to Eugene over scrambled eggs. Eugene would probably focus on the Robert Coste issue, and right now Nicholas was preoccupied with Seiji.

"I broke his watch?" Nicholas hazarded at last.

He'd been worrying about that off and on. It seemed like basic roommate etiquette—a word from the Kings Row brochures that Nicholas didn't know how to pronounce—not to break your roommate's stuff. Seiji must be mad about that, too. Jesse probably wouldn't have broken Seiji's watch.

"That sucks," said Eugene. "But it's Saturday. Wanna head to town with me and get it fixed? There's a fancy jewelry shop where my dad got his good watch repaired."

"Oh, great." Nicholas was relieved. He'd been at a loss about what he should do. He rewarded Eugene by saying, "Thanks, bro."

Eugene beamed. "If they can't fix it, they can totally sell you a replacement."

Nicholas frowned. "I hope they can fix it. I think this watch might be kinda expensive. Reminds me of a watch a guy from my last school had, and that watch cost a hundred dollars. Can you *believe* any watch could cost a hundred dollars?"

Outrage made Nicholas's voice louder than he'd intended. Aiden, passing their table with a cup of coffee, jerked out of his reverie at the noise. He looked a bit pale and twitchy; Nicholas figured he might've already had too much caffeine.

Aiden halted beside their table and remarked, "I *do* find that incredibly hard to believe."

Even Aiden could see it was ridiculous. Nicholas nodded, feeling fully justified in his indignation.

"Insanity, am I right?"

There was a silence. Aiden took a thoughtful sip of his coffee.

"Let me put this another way," said Aiden patiently. "How much do you think the watch, which I am wearing on my wrist right now as we speak, cost?"

"I dunno, fifty bucks?" Nicholas shrugged. "It's pretty nice."

"You keep me humble, Cox," remarked Aiden. "Of course, everyone *else* won't stop telling me how amaz—*blah, blah, blah, bloo.*"

Nicholas tuned out Aiden and reached for his toast.

His day was looking up. Eugene was taking him to get Seiji's watch fixed. Nicholas had twenty bucks. That should cover it. Seiji would be pleased. This would be simple.

It wasn't simple.

Nicholas had never been to Kingstone before, but as soon as he arrived, he knew he didn't belong there any more than he belonged at Kings Row. Nicholas and Eugene went down a broad main street flanked by white and black buildings that practically screamed *We're so fancy we pretend we live in a chess game.*

"These are bow ties." Nicholas grimaced as he gestured to the buildings. Eugene looked puzzled. "You know, stores so tiny and expensive you're not supposed to call them stores?"

"Oh! You mean boutiques, bro."

"Yeah," said Nicholas gloomily. "I think I do."

Nicholas knew at a glance, even before they went into the jewelry store, that Eugene had made a mistake.

WEIRS FINE JEWELERS was painted in discreet green and gold above the door next to a clock surrounded by fancy black iron swirls. Even the hands on the clock had little curly black iron paddles. The two Kings Row guys who'd tried to hassle Nicholas the other day were in there, talking about "Daddy's birthday present."

"Oh Lord, it's the poors," remarked the taller one as they came in.

Eugene flushed.

Nicholas did an imitation of the guy's nasal voice. "Oh Lord, it's the creeps who call their fathers *Daddy*."

Then he looked at the price tag on something shiny in a glass cabinet even fancier than the cabinets in which the Kings Row trophies were kept. He swallowed.

The jewelry store staff showed the other Kings Row students a shiny array of cuff links. The staff was dressed in white shirts and black pants that might have been a uniform but could have also just been fancy clothes. They were like weird polite penguins. One of them gave Nicholas a look up and down, then back up almost incredulously, as though he couldn't reconcile Nicholas's face with the Kings Row uniform.

"It's the *scholarship kid* who tried to have a scuffle with us the other day, isn't it?" asked the nasal-voiced student. Nicholas suspected his name might be Eustace, though that was a terrible thing to think about anybody.

Eustace's tone suggested that he'd kicked Nicholas's ass somehow due to being rich, instead of Nicholas backing off on his own. Now all three of the jewelry-selling penguin people were giving Nicholas dubious looks.

"You wanna go now?" Nicholas demanded, surging their way.

When he strode forward, a member of the staff coughed pointedly.

"Bro," whispered Eugene. "No, bro."

He tugged Nicholas aside to a shiny glass case full of watches. Nicholas stared at the price tag on one watch. Surely that was a typo. It was a watch, not a rocket.

"We could take those guys," Nicholas muttered.

Eugene seemed agitated. "There's a lot of glass in here. And I've never actually been in a fight!"

"Seriously?" Nicholas glanced at Eugene, who Coach Joe would've described as beefy. "But you're huge."

"I'm a lover, not a fighter!"

The Kings Row jerks were pointing at Nicholas and miming him slipping stuff into his pockets. The quiet, discreet staff quietly and discreetly asked Nicholas to leave.

Nicholas had been wrong. Turned out you could kick someone's ass just by having money and wearing your uniform the right way. Without throwing a single punch, those rich boys had won the fight.

Eugene's whole big, usually good-natured body was bristling as they left the store. He resembled the offspring of an angry cat and a weight-lifting porcupine. "They acted like you were going to shoplift!"

Nicholas shrugged. "Who hasn't shoplifted, right?"

Eugene said in a hollow voice, "Oh my God."

"I mean," Nicholas elaborated, more squirming than shrugging at this point, "when you're hungry? I mean, if your mom got wrapped up with work or whatever and maybe forgot you, and you could use a snack. . . ."

Eugene said, in a very different tone, "Oh my God!"

"It's not a big deal," Nicholas said with finality. "I don't care. What I *do* care about is that we haven't got Seiji's watch fixed, and I don't see how we're gonna do it. They're not going to let me back in there, and honestly, I think that place would charge more than I could afford."

"Yeah, I . . ." Eugene squinted. "I think you might be right."

He said it almost apologetically. Nicholas shrugged again. He didn't see what Eugene had to be sorry for.

"My cousin's friend works part-time at this store which mostly sells, um, maybe stolen phones," suggested Eugene. "Maybe he could help?"

He escorted Nicholas down the narrow, winding backstreets

of Kingstone until they passed a wall with some graffiti on it. Beyond some smoking kids and above what used to be a stable door, in white letters on black paint, was written NEEDFUL BLING. Nicholas felt this was definitely more his sort of place.

Eugene's cousin's friend wore an old Kings Row hoodie and was chewing gum and barely took his eyes off his phone. Eugene explained the problem.

"Bro, you gotta help us," said Eugene. "We can't go back to that store."

The guy finally lifted his eyes from his phone. Nicholas gazed at him in mute appeal.

"I was a scholarship kid myself," said Eugene's cousin's friend. "I'll see what I can do about the watch."

Nicholas grinned at him shyly. "Appreciate it."

Nicholas thought that'd been a totally successful trip into town, but for some reason, Eugene remained unusually quiet and thoughtful as they strolled out of the store and down the hill toward their school.

"My family doesn't have a lot of money compared to some of the other Kings Row kids. We can't, like, take vacays in Europe. I sometimes feel kinda lousy about it," offered Eugene as they walked back through the winding streets.

"Oh really?" asked Nicholas. "I thought you guys were totally rich. Like, you have all those brothers and sisters, and I heard them mentioning having their own rooms? Even though there are so many of them!"

Nicholas hadn't always had his own room, even though there was only one of him. Sometimes he slept on the sofa for a few months, until they had to move again. When they'd had a studio, he'd slept on the floor.

Eugene was quiet for a while longer.

"It's relative, I guess, bro." He shook himself out of whatever had him twisted up to add, "Those guys from our school? Don't let them get you down. They're jerks and bullies."

"Oh, whatever." Nicholas rolled his eyes. "They can *try*. Kind of adorable, if you ask me. *Wow, I'm so sad—I totally didn't notice I don't have any money until you pointed it out, dudes! C'mon.*"

He mimed wiping away tears running down his cheeks with his fists. Eugene was still looking a bit shell-shocked, for some reason.

Nicholas searched his mind for something to cheer up Eugene.

"Hey, you wanna know something funny? I thought *you* were trying to bully me the first time we met. When you gave me the wrong directions on my first day of school, and I got lost in the woods."

Eugene, to Nicholas's surprise, looked dismayed rather than amused.

"No!" he exclaimed. "Oh no! I thought it was a totally awesome prank! 'Cause, like...you were new, and you didn't know which way to go, and you'd get...lost in the woods. In a hilarious way. 'Cause pranks are fun, right?"

Nicholas shook his head, grinning a little.

"You know we're bros now, right?" Eugene asked anxiously.

Nicholas's grin spread. "Yeah, I know we're bros now."

They fist-bumped. Eugene went home for dinner, since it was Saturday, and Nicholas walked slowly back to Kings Row alone.

He and Eugene were bros, but Eugene didn't get it. He couldn't, not really. Other people weren't gonna make Nicholas feel lousy. It wasn't about what other people did. It was about what Nicholas did, or failed to do. Or who Nicholas failed to be.

Hey, Dad, Nicholas thought defiantly, taking a detour to stop by the framed photograph of Robert Coste beside a shining trophy. Even in his mind, it felt like a lie. Robert's blue eyes were fixed on his glittering prize. He couldn't see Nicholas.

Nicholas didn't care about limos or watches or morons. But he cared about other stuff.

Robert Coste didn't know about Nicholas, and he wouldn't want him if he *did* know. Robert knew about Jesse, though, and Jesse fit in at a school even fancier than Kings Row. Jesse was one of those rich kids who always got what they wanted.

Everything in the world that Nicholas wanted...it all belonged to Jesse. Even Seiji.

10 HARVARD

Harvard was pretty nervous about his second date of the weekend. He was afraid he'd spend another night feeling the same absolute wrongness he'd felt on Friday, wondering why he wasn't happier to be there. He never wanted to feel that vacancy in his chest again, the knowledge he was expected to do something and couldn't possibly do it. But Harvard worried if he chickened out now, he might never date again.

His mom had been understanding and embracing of all Harvard's doubts on the phone, just as he'd known she would be.

You and me, kid, she used to say in the hospital when Dad was sleeping, his father's wasted body quiet and still under white sheets. *We're a team.*

Harvard always tried to be a good

teammate, but his mom was the best. She was the one who encouraged him to go on a second date right away, told him that her friend Rita had a son he might like. She said she loved him and was proud of him, as she did every time he called, and she wanted him to be happy. She told him to grab every chance for happiness he got.

Harvard had a happy family, but they knew better than most how fragile happiness could be.

So he was going to try and be happy in a new way, which included figuring out who—if anyone—he wanted to kiss. He'd never thought about . . . physical stuff that much. That was Aiden's specialty, and Harvard's mind tended to veer away from the idea of Aiden and romance.

This wasn't about Aiden. It was about Harvard and some guy.

Maybe a date with a guy would go better. Maybe it would feel better. He could only hope so.

He had some time to kill, and he didn't want to get worked up worrying about his date, so Harvard tried to be productive and write his teamwork essay. Coach hadn't technically said he had to do it, but since everyone else on the team was doing it—even Aiden—Harvard had decided he should, too.

He'd written about meeting Aiden when he was five, how they'd got along right away and how Harvard had known at once that Aiden was cool and funny and special. He knew what came next. He'd been avoiding it, but Harvard knew he shouldn't avoid responsibility.

When I was seven, my dad got really sick, Harvard wrote. *He got better. It's all good now.*

He felt he should add more to the essay about that, before he got onto the subject of fencing. Maybe about how his mom had been brave, and they'd been lucky?

He looked helplessly around his room. Aiden wasn't there. He was probably on a date. Possibly two dates, since it seemed like Friday night's hadn't gone well. More and more over the last few years, Aiden was nowhere to be found.

When Aiden was out on dates and Harvard felt restless like this, he'd usually go to the *salle* and practice until he was exhausted enough to sleep and not anticipate the sound of Aiden coming in, accompanied or otherwise.

He could go to the *salle* now. Or he could drive around on his motorcycle. He'd got his license when Mom and Dad took him to Italy last year and had so much fun his parents had surprised him with a motorcycle on his birthday. Harvard didn't ride it a lot now that he was back at school, but Mom had forcibly suggested he should pick up his date on the bike. He didn't know why, but she seemed to feel strongly that it would improve his chances with Neil.

Driving the motorcycle would make Harvard think about the date later that night, which was exactly what he was trying to avoid.

He went to the *salle*, crossing a lawn that was half-shadow, half-gold in the setting sun, and ran through the arched doorway.

Fencing was simple, as so many things weren't. Fencing came with the assurance that if Harvard tried hard enough, it would make a difference. Harvard wasn't powerless, the way he had been as a kid. He could accomplish something real.

Fencing also came with teammates. The *salle* was already occupied. Nicholas Cox was in there. Usually, Harvard would've joined Nicholas on the *piste* beside his, and maybe offered a couple tips, but this evening the sight of Nicholas made him hang back. Nicholas wasn't practicing any of the moves Coach was trying hard to teach him, helping him catch up to the other students' years of learned techniques. Instead, Nicholas was rushing forward, ever forward, in a flurry of swings. He seemed to be fighting invisible and unconquerable enemies that came from every side.

From the look of him, he'd been doing it for some time. His T-shirt was drenched through with perspiration, his chest rising and falling so hard it was almost as though he were sobbing. As Harvard watched, Nicholas finally let his point drop and trailed his weary way across the room, sliding down with his back against the wall until he hit the floor.

Harvard hesitated, then crossed the *salle*, knelt down, and asked Nicholas, "You doing okay?"

Nicholas's head came up with a jerk, but he didn't look angry that Harvard was there. He wiped sweaty hair out of his eyes with the back of his hand, mouth trembling out of shape for a minute, then said, "What would you do if—if someone called you a loser?"

"Who called you that?" Harvard asked with deadly calm.

He knew how some of the kids at Kings Row were about scholarship students. It had never seemed to bother Nicholas, so Harvard hadn't wanted to embarrass him by making an issue of it, but now someone had clearly pierced Nicholas Cox's impressive armor. Harvard never approved of cruelty and stopped it whenever he could, but this was different. Nicholas was on Harvard's team. Nicholas was Harvard's responsibility. If anyone had hurt him, Harvard wanted to know.

"Nobody from this school!" Nicholas assured him instantly.

Harvard paused, unconvinced, but from his experience with Nicholas, he was an honest guy. After a moment, Harvard nodded.

"Well, let me know if anybody is a jerk to you. If they wanna call you a loser, they can call me a loser, too."

Nicholas turned to Harvard with his eyes popping out and so circular, they were basically flying saucers.

"Nobody could ever think *you* were a loser, Captain."

"I've lost matches." Harvard gave Nicholas a little smile. "I've lost more than that. Everybody loses. Sometimes you lose more than you knew you had."

Writing the essay had forced Harvard to recall things he usually didn't let himself dwell upon. It had all been a long time ago.

He remembered being so little that when he'd sat in the hospital chairs, his feet dangled far above the floor. His mom had talked to the doctors behind a half-shut door, and Harvard had heard the words *You might want to prepare yourself for the worst.* His mother had gone into the room where his father slept, held his hands, and sobbed. Harvard had known with the quiet terror of a small helpless thing that despite what Mom had said about them being a team, there was nothing he could really do.

"What if someone called you a loser and you knew it was... sort of true?" said Nicholas. "It's not gonna *stay* true. But it's kinda true, for now."

"It's not true at all."

Nicholas scoffed.

"Hey," said Harvard. "It's not losing that makes you a loser. It's how you deal with it when you lose. I believe that."

There was a silence as Nicholas pondered this, forehead scrunching up and mouth pursed, looking the same way he did when Coach or Harvard or Seiji suggested a new technique to practice.

At last, Nicholas shrugged. "I'm not used to losing anything." He cracked a smile. "Not because I'm such a winner, obviously. It's just I never had much to lose before. Now I have so much stuff. But at the same time, I feel kind of lousy about hanging on to it. Like I'm...maybe doing something wrong. Have you ever felt that way? I know it doesn't make much sense."

Harvard murmured, "It makes sense."

"I know you and Aiden have been friends forever." Nicholas's

124

rough voice was wistful. "It must be really cool, to have a some-one you know will always be there. I've never had that, but I get that it would suck to let go of. That you wouldn't want to, not ever. If anyone got in the way and messed stuff up between you and Aiden, you'd hate them, probably. Right?"

Harvard thought of the first time he'd looked around for Aiden and hadn't found him. They were going on fifteen and had been getting more and more into fencing. Aiden had got taller all of a sudden and started to move differently. Harvard registered it, but he hadn't really *noticed*: Aiden was always Aiden, always great and cool, and without question beloved.

Other people had noticed.

They'd been walking around Kings Row, deciding if they wanted to go there. As they'd crossed the quad, Aiden was talking about the Kingstone Fair. He seemed to really want to go.

"I was thinking," Aiden said hesitantly behind Harvard, "that we could go together? You and me."

"Sure," Harvard had told him. "I could win you a bear. To be friends with Harvard Paw."

"Friends," Aiden had said. "Great."

There was something funny about Aiden's voice when he'd said that. He hadn't sounded pleased like Harvard had thought he would be. Harvard had frowned, about to turn and check on him.

Then someone had whistled and called out: "Hello, gorgeous!"

There had been a moment of confusion. Harvard had glanced around for Aiden, expecting Aiden to be a step behind him the way Aiden always was. That was how they'd walked forever, since they were kids and Aiden was so much smaller than Harvard but trailed persistently after him.

Only Aiden hadn't been there. Aiden stood alone, attention distracted by the whistle that was clearly aimed at *him*.

"Hey," said the boy who'd whistled. "Yeah, you! What are you doing later?"

After a startled instant, Harvard had seen a slow smile steal across Aiden's face. He'd tossed back his hair—when had it got so long?—so he could see the guy who'd whistled better. His gaze had slid to Harvard, uncertain.

What had Harvard expected, for Aiden to stay in his shadow forever? Even if that were what he'd wanted, it wouldn't be right or fair. Nobody shone like Aiden.

Harvard had taken a step back.

That was the first time Harvard had realized they wouldn't do everything together forever. They hadn't gone to the fair together. Aiden had gone with some guy, and Harvard had stayed home alone.

"Sometimes it's right to let go of people," Harvard told Nicholas now, thinking about that day. "But you can still be there for someone, even if you have to let go."

"Sometimes I feel like I'm messing stuff up just by being here," muttered Nicholas.

"No," said Harvard. "Being there for someone is the most important thing you'll ever do. Not winning or losing. Just being there."

The night they'd thought Harvard's dad would die, Aiden's latest stepmother had tried to pick up Aiden from the hospital.

"I have no idea who this woman is!" little Aiden had claimed, always so smart even when they were tiny. He'd used the lethal combination of being articulate and having the cutthroat instinct for knowing exactly what to say, and secured the nurses as his allies.

When Aiden's latest stepmom couldn't tell them what Aiden's middle name was (Harvard had felt sorry for her and mouthed *Lionel* in her direction, but Aiden elbowed him), Aiden's stepmom had eventually slunk away in shame. Aiden got to stay almost the whole night.

His dad came out of a meeting to get Aiden, and he'd carried Aiden away, Aiden yelling his head off and kicking his feet against his dad's ten-thousand-dollar suit jacket. *Let me down, I want to stay! I want to be with Harvard, I have to be with Harvard!*

The hour Harvard had spent alone in the hospital outside his father's room was the longest of his life.

In the gray early morning, Aiden had showed up again. Harvard had been sitting on the chairs in the waiting room and Aiden crept in, wearing his pajama top with his jeans, hand in hand with one of the nurses he'd won over earlier.

Harvard had blinked his dry eyes, sleepless and burning. "How'd you get here?"

Aiden had shrugged his thin shoulders and smiled his timid little smile.

Harvard only found out later how Aiden effected his return. Seven years old, and he'd stolen his stepmom's credit card and called a taxi to take him to the hospital.

Aiden had climbed up onto the hard gray hospital chairs with Harvard and they'd slept, holding hands, curled up under the same thin blue hospital blanket.

"I have to be with you, too," Harvard had mumbled.

Dad had got through the crisis. Dad lived, and Harvard did, too. Because of Aiden.

Aiden's just heartless, boys would tell Harvard, and it was as if they were talking about a stranger. Aiden had more heart than anyone Harvard had ever met. If those guys didn't get that, none of them was the right guy.

One day, once Aiden was done having fun, there would be a right guy. Harvard had made his peace with that long ago.

But Harvard was tired of being good, yet not quite good enough for his mom and for his team and for Aiden. At last, he wanted something of his own.

He was, he admitted to himself, really hoping this date worked out.

Nicholas cleared his throat, and Harvard's attention was recalled to his teammate in need. "I want to keep things the way they are now. For a little while longer. Have you ever felt that way?"

Yes, Harvard thought, thinking of childhood, of being the most important person in Aiden's life as Aiden was the most important person in his. It couldn't last.

"Yeah, I have. I don't know if you can keep things the way they are, but I want you to know this. You're not messing anything up by being here, Nicholas. You're not messing anything up by having friends. We're friends, aren't we?"

Nicholas beamed, a huge stunned smile, as though he hadn't known before. "Yeah, Captain!"

"I'm glad you're here. I think we're lucky to have you at Kings Row."

He leaned against the wall, giving Nicholas's shoulder a little nudge.

"I like," Nicholas said shyly, "being part of the team. Having friends. I'd like to belong here, somehow. Sometimes I feel like I can. I keep thinking if I was just *good enough*, I could make everything work out. You know?"

Harvard nodded and thought about trying too hard. Supporting his mom, when he felt too overwhelmed and too young to do it right. Supporting Aiden's relationships like a best friend should, when he secretly felt like doing anything but.

What mattered was being there. What mattered was always doing your best and hoping one day you'd get it right.

Harvard told Nicholas, "I know exactly what you mean."

His answer made Nicholas turn to him, Nicholas's face changing as though he could tell how sincerely Harvard meant it. Turning on a dime the way he did sometimes, Nicholas flashed him a grin full of renewed determination.

"I'm gonna get good enough, as fast as I can."

"I believe in you."

Nicholas glowed. "You do?"

"I'm your captain. It's my job."

"Thanks, Captain," Nicholas told him.

"Anytime." Harvard checked his watch. "Except for right now. I'm gonna be late for my date. Gotta go. Please keep working on your retreats."

"Whoa, you date a lot, don't you?" Nicholas sounded impressed. "I mean—you must be really popular. That's cool; I totally get why. Have a great time."

Harvard wished he was as cool as the freshman imagined he was, but he was glad he'd come to the *salle*, even if he hadn't got any practice in.

When he got back to his room, he didn't immediately start getting ready for his date.

Instead, he produced his essay and crossed out *It's all good now* and wrote *My dad is better now, but it was really hard at the time. My mom and my best friend got me through.*

Then he checked the mirror, shared an expression of nervous agony with his reflection, slid on his new leather jacket he'd bought for practicality because leather protected you best if you wiped out on the roads, and went on his date.

Harvard didn't want to let down anybody, including himself.

He rode his motorcycle out through the gleaming gates of Kings Row, through the quaint, winding streets of Kingstone, and past the town toward the houses high up in the hills. Streetlights painted an orange trail for him up through the curving road. His mom had given him directions to this guy Neil's house, and Harvard followed them easily enough to a large white house with ivy growing up the walls, and a porch painted pale green. There was a boy already sitting on the porch steps, messing around with his phone.

His mom had promised him that he would like Neil. She'd said that he was the kind of guy who'd sit with his mom's friends and act genuinely charming and happy to be there. Harvard hadn't really understood that. Harvard's mom was awesome, so who wouldn't want to hang out with her? But he trusted her recommendation.

Now Harvard leaned forward against the handlebars of his bike, and understood what his mom had meant. The guy sitting on the porch steps had a relaxed air and brown hair that gave the impression of being untidy even though it was neat. He wore a flannel shirt, but a nice one. *He's*, Harvard thought, unused to thinking this way but trying it out, *cute?*

Harvard didn't experience a lightning strike, wasn't suddenly certain of who or what he wanted. But he got a good feeling about this. He felt a little surer.

"Wow," breathed the boy who must be Neil, which was— maybe? Harvard hoped?—a good sign.

Harvard smiled.

"Hey, I'm Harvard. It's really good to meet you."

11 SEIJI

Nicholas was angry with him. This was making the midnight feast even more awkward than it was always bound to be.

Seiji wished he were in the *salle*, but he was sitting in Dante and Bobby's room feeling uncomfortable instead. Dante, the one with the peculiar cooking hobby, was making pasta sauce over a burner. Bobby, who was very small and enthusiastic, had asked to take a selfie showing Seiji was in his room.

"Dormitory rooms are designed to be uniform and anonymous," Seiji pointed out. "The picture could be taken in any room, including my own. It would prove nothing."

This seemed to dampen Bobby's enthusiasm for a moment.

"I'll know you were here!" Bobby said eventually. "Let's just take it!"

Seiji took the picture willingly enough, since it would please Bobby, but it was a strain to figure out how to behave in unfamiliar surroundings. The least Nicholas could do was help him, but instead he was sulking in the corner. The only reasonable explanation was that Seiji had offended him. Seiji was always offending people, though Nicholas seemed to bounce back faster than most.

Seiji couldn't figure out what the problem was. He hadn't said anything worse to Nicholas than he usually did.

There was the incident on Friday night with Jesse by the side of the road, but that had obviously been more upsetting for Seiji himself than for Nicholas. What reason did Nicholas have to care about Jesse? Seiji supposed that Nicholas might be sad to have an excellent fencer looking down on him, but Nicholas must accept that would keep happening until he got better.

Nicholas had no personal reason to care about Jesse. Other people cared a lot about what Jesse thought of them, but Seiji couldn't picture Nicholas caring. Everyone liked Jesse better than Seiji, but Nicholas wouldn't. Not even if, for some reason, Nicholas got to know Jesse and Jesse actually tried to be charming. Even then, Seiji was sure, though he didn't have much basis for the certainty, that Nicholas would still like *him* better.

So it wasn't about Jesse. It was something Seiji had done. But what?

Seiji got up, though it seemed awkward to do so, and sat next to Nicholas. He usually sat beside Nicholas, but Nicholas hadn't explicitly saved him a seat. There was no seat to save, though. It was all floor.

Nicholas didn't say hey or anything welcoming, like usual. Seiji sat there in silence and resented Nicholas for being angry with him.

"Want marshmallows?" offered Bobby.

That made Nicholas smile, even though he was giving Seiji the cold shoulder. "Yeah."

Were they supposed to eat marshmallows as a side dish to pasta? That was disgusting.

"I don't want marshmallows," said Seiji. "Nicholas, reconsider eating marshmallows."

Nicholas turned his furious dark stare on Seiji. Seiji stared back stonily. He didn't even know why Nicholas was angry. People were always getting angry with him and never explained why. Nicholas was just like everyone else.

"If you want to go somewhere," Nicholas mumbled, "you can just go."

Many people had made clear to Seiji that his presence was unwelcome, but Nicholas never had before. Seiji glared at him and moved away. He didn't care that Nicholas didn't want him here. He was used to that, but he was shocked by Nicholas's rudeness. Seiji had been invited to the midnight feast, just the same as Nicholas. This wasn't Nicholas's room.

Not that Nicholas could uninvite Seiji to his room. Since it was Seiji's room, too.

Seiji nursed his justified outrage at Nicholas's bad manners while Nicholas continued to sit sullenly in the corner. Seiji was enduring rudeness and expected to eat carbohydrates at an inappropriate hour with strangers. Harvard, who had arrived dragging Aiden behind him, went over to Nicholas and started telling jokes to make him laugh.

Seiji supposed Nicholas must have decided to be friends with the captain instead. That was fine with Seiji.

Eugene sidled over to Seiji and offered him a protein shake. Eugene had brought enough protein shakes for everyone, which Seiji found thoughtful, though nobody else had greeted the shakes with the appreciation they deserved.

"I made you hydrolyzed whey protein isolate like you like," Eugene said encouragingly.

"Thank you," said Seiji.

It was good Eugene was drinking protein shakes, which would optimize his performance, and considerate of him to provide Seiji with the same. Eugene was the only person at the midnight feast with whom Seiji wasn't annoyed.

"You seem a bit quiet, bro," Eugene remarked in a low voice. "Not that you're what I'd describe as chatty, but normally you'd have accidentally insulted someone by now. Something wrong?"

He was tempted to snap, but Eugene was a teammate, too.

Seiji cleared his throat. "Nicholas is angry with me. I'm not sure why. Do you know why? I know you two socialize frequently."

Eugene paused. "I don't think Nicholas is angry with you."

"No, he is," said Seiji. "He told me to go away."

"He probably just meant that you could go practice in the *salle* if you're hating the midnight feast, dude," said Eugene. "Your face went all grumpy cat when we broke out the marshmallows."

Seiji opened his mouth to protest that Nicholas never cared when Seiji made faces, and never told him to go away, but Eugene continued.

"I think there's something else going on."

Seiji gave Eugene his full attention. "What?"

Eugene turned his protein shake in his hands for another moment. "We went to town Saturday, and some Kings Row guys there were awful to him. It's been bothering me all weekend, actually. They acted like they were so far above Nicholas. They made it seem like he was going to shoplift! Which he wasn't!" Eugene added hastily, as though Seiji might imagine Nicholas would.

The burner's blue flame hissed. Harvard was talking about how delicious the pasta sauce smelled. Their captain was very good at making conversation.

Seiji frowned. "Why would people from our school represent Nicholas as a common thief?"

"Right? It sucks!" said Eugene. "You might know them? They were the first two guys to wash out of fencing tryouts. They think they're so much better than Nicholas."

"They think they're better than Nicholas?" Seiji asked sharply. "But they can't fence *at all*!"

"Bro...," said Eugene. "I realize this concept might be difficult for you to grasp, but this is not about fencing. They were just being jerks."

Seiji raised an eyebrow. "I'm familiar with the concept of people being jerks. Certain people on the fencing circuit used to refer to me as a samurai."

Eugene's open, friendly face was taken over by a confused scowl.

"Because I'm Japanese, and I'm excellent with a sword," Seiji explained. He rolled his eyes. "Extremely droll."

"Yeah, I'm familiar with those kinds of jerks, too. You should hear the stuff they say about me," Eugene said, and buffeted Seiji with his shoulder. Seiji almost dropped his protein shake. "They think they're better than Nicholas because he doesn't have a lot of money."

"Oh, Nicholas is on scholarship, isn't he?" Seiji recalled. "Does his family have less money than most people at Kings Row?"

Another hissing burner silence ensued.

"Uh...," said Eugene. "You hadn't noticed that Nicholas is a bit different from everyone else?"

"Well, yes, obviously I have noticed that! What's that got to do with money?"

Eugene wasn't being very helpful.

Seiji considered this matter on his own. He supposed Nicholas spoke differently from other people, even though Nicholas didn't come from very far away. He'd believed it must be a personal idiosyncrasy.

"Have you realized that Nicholas doesn't have a lot of stuff?"

Seiji *had* noticed that Nicholas didn't wear pajamas, like a normal person. He basically wore underwear to bed.

Was Nicholas too poor for pajamas? That was so sad.

"So, because Nicholas doesn't have any money, these students mocked him by pretending he would steal?" Seiji clarified. On Eugene's nod, Seiji scowled. "And now he's upset. That's wrong."

To Seiji's horror, Eugene slung an arm around his shoulders. Seiji had no idea why he was doing that. Eugene couldn't possibly think bears would attack in Bobby and Dante's room.

"Bro, we are in total agreement. I wish there was something we could do to get those guys back. But I guess the world sucks sometimes. Anyway, don't worry about Nicholas. He's tough."

Why would Eugene have told Seiji all this information, unless he wanted Seiji to worry? Preventing Nicholas from being hurt seemed like basic friend behavior. Even Seiji could grasp that much.

Seiji squinted over at Nicholas. He didn't appear distraught. He was laughing while Bobby dared him to stuff more marshmallows in his mouth. There was already an alarming number of marshmallows in Nicholas's mouth.

"How would we get those guys back?" Seiji asked. "Like you were saying."

Eugene blinked rapidly. "I was thinking it would be cool to play a totally excellent prank on them. Make them look as dumb as they are."

Seiji shuddered. "I don't think I want to...pull a prank."

Pranks seemed undignified.

Eugene shrugged. "Yeah, I figured it wasn't your scene, my man."

My man was even worse than *bro*. Seiji endured.

He should've felt better now that he knew Nicholas was not angry with him, but somehow, he didn't. He remained uncomfortable. Of course, he was still at this midnight feast.

Aiden didn't appear to be enjoying the midnight feast, either. His face was stormy, when normally he was the kind of person who sailed through life on calm waters. Seiji sympathized with Aiden's antifeast attitude, but he didn't intend to bond with him. After all, in tryouts, Aiden had brought up seeing him lose against Jesse. He had known it would strike a nerve, and, humiliatingly, it had. Seiji had lost against Aiden, too.

Aiden's glittering eyes always seemed to read Seiji like a book, as though Aiden saw things Seiji didn't even know about himself.

Aiden's lip curled back from his teeth in a snarl, distorting his face further. "What are you looking at, freshman?"

"I was looking at you," said Seiji truthfully.

Those green eyes narrowed, seeing too much again. "Reliving the day you had to feel like a loser?"

Seiji's gaze fell away from Aiden's.

"Seiji isn't a loser. Being a loser isn't about whether you lose or win matches," piped up Nicholas, and Harvard turned around to give Nicholas a fist bump.

Seiji frowned. "Why not? Do words just not have meanings anymore?"

He took this as confirmation, though, that Eugene had been right and Nicholas wasn't angry with him, so he went back over to Nicholas and out of Aiden's line of sight.

"Don't eat an excessive amount of carbohydrates at this hour," Seiji advised Nicholas.

"I'm gonna," said Nicholas.

Seiji shook his head, pained. "Try some protein shake."

Nicholas accepted the shake and took a gulp. Then he immediately spat half of it back into the glass. Seiji stared at him in dismay.

Nicholas wiped his mouth with the back of his hand. "That's gross."

"*You're* gross!" Seiji exclaimed. "That is unsanitary! Eugene, may I have another protein shake?"

"Have the one Eugene brought for me," Nicholas urged. "Please."

Seiji accepted this peace offering. He sat by Nicholas and drank a new protein shake, and the midnight feast was slightly improved. He declined to eat pasta at midnight. After the pasta was eaten, they roasted the rest of the marshmallows over the burner. Nicholas put his marshmallows into the remnants of his pasta sauce. Seiji was absolutely revolted.

Harvard continued to make conversation. Seiji didn't know how he did it. People called these interactions *small talk*: To

Seiji, the talk was so small he never seemed able to find it, or sure why he should. Harvard was discussing someone called Neil who went to another school.

Seiji tried to make conversation as well. "Ah, a fencing opponent?"

"No, Neil's not that into fencing," Harvard said. "He's into art. He showed me some of his drawings. They're really good."

"Another unusual hobby," Seiji remarked, and gestured to Dante. "Like Dante's interest in cookery."

Sitting in the far corner being tall and gloomy, Dante sighed and gave them what Seiji found to be an unfriendly look. Seiji sympathized. If Nicholas had invited his many friends over to their room, Seiji would go sleep in the *salle*.

Bobby shook his head at Dante, sparkly clips in his hair catching the light. "They're welcome! Especially Seiji. It's an honor to have you here, Seiji!"

That was kind of Bobby to say, though Seiji wasn't sure why it would be. Seiji nodded uneasily.

"Neil did say he'd like to see one of my fencing matches, though," Harvard continued, brightening further. He seemed to be in a very good mood.

"Oh, I see," said Seiji. "Neil is a friend."

Friends watched each other's fencing matches. Seiji was aware.

"Well...not exactly?" Harvard ducked his head. Seiji stared in bewilderment.

Nicholas nudged him. "Harvard is dating Neil. The captain goes on many dates!"

"Oh yes," said Seiji, enlightened. "I remember."

He was grateful to Nicholas for explaining the matter so that Seiji understood. There had been a great deal of talk about Harvard dating recently. He hoped the captain wouldn't let dating interfere with his fencing too much.

"I didn't know you had a boyfriend, Captain!" Eugene exclaimed.

Eugene and Bobby leaned forward, both seeming extremely interested. Everyone must share Seiji's concern about the captain's fencing.

"He's not my boyfriend...," Harvard muttered. "...not yet."

There was a loud noise. Apparently, Aiden had accidentally pulled the curtain right off the wall. Dante leaped to his feet and Aiden muttered apologies.

Seiji didn't think Aiden was being a good guest, but he was focused on other things. He required further explanations.

"So is he going to be your boyfriend?" Seiji asked.

"I'm, uh," said Harvard. "I'm not sure."

"When will you know?"

"For now, we're just dating."

Wasn't dating what you did with boyfriends and girlfriends? Wasn't that what they were specifically for? Was there a probationary period? That seemed stressful. Stress was bound to affect the captain's game. Why was nobody sensible?

Was there a probationary period for being friends? Seiji glanced at Nicholas in alarm.

Why did nobody ever tell Seiji the rules of social behavior? He'd been taught the rules for fencing, and he excelled in that. He didn't see why everybody expected him to excel in life with no training.

"My dude, this is so exciting and romantic!" said Eugene.

"Do you like him a lot?" asked Bobby, starry-eyed.

Seiji had more questions, too. "Could you not find a boyfriend who was interested in fencing? It seems better to have a boyfriend who is interested in fencing."

"That does seem true," Nicholas muttered, but then raised his voice and said with loyalty to his captain: "I'm sure your boyfriend's super nice, though!"

"He *is* really nice," Harvard confirmed, sounding shy. "He's really cool and funny. He likes comics! He loaned me some and said I could give them back to him on Tuesday. When we have our next date. I do like him a lot. So far."

Tuesday was the day after next. How many dates was Harvard planning to have per week? They would never win the state championship at this rate.

Everyone seemed pleased—except Seiji and Aiden, whose face had darkened further. Seiji was glad to see someone else was worrying about the important things in life, but if Aiden wanted a shot at the state championship, he should practice more himself.

Seiji was about to voice this when Harvard's phone buzzed with a text. Harvard smiled as though it was an instinct, the others said *"Ooh"* in a chorus, and Aiden knocked over the burner. The fallen curtain caught on fire. Dante gave Bobby a look that combined pleading and total rage.

"I'm so sorry, everyone!" exclaimed Bobby. "Especially Seiji. Fencing team, you have to leave now."

Nicholas walked back to their dormitory, bumping shoulders with Seiji companionably in the way nobody else ever did, but he was still much quieter than usual. It was worrying. However, Seiji was able to go to sleep secure in the knowledge that at least he hadn't been the worst guest at the midnight feast.

12 AIDEN

Harvard liked a boy. His name was Neil. Aiden was sick of hearing the name.

The whole school was talking about it, because Eugene—Aiden might wring his stupid thick neck— was Kings Row's worst gossip. The Bons cornered Aiden to ask sorrowfully if it was true. Aiden snarled that it was, and the gaggle looked as though they might cry.

"Worse things happen at sea," said Aiden.

Did they, though? If they went to sea, Neil might fall overboard.

Aiden couldn't tell the Bons apart. They were all shiny-eyed and brimming over with effervescent admiration, like mini prosecco bottles on legs. Today, apparently, they'd gone flat, with not a golden bubble in sight.

"If you're happy for your best friend, we're happy for him!" declared the tallest Bon.

"Who said anything about happiness?" asked Aiden. "Who cares?"

"We always thought that possibly, when you were done being a glamorous playboy..."

The two other Bons elbowed that Bon in the ribs at the same time. The unlucky Bon folded over with a squeak.

"I'll never be done being a glamorous playboy." Aiden pronounced this sentence with a laugh and left the Bons shattered in his wake.

One day the sun would die, and Harvard liked a boy. Aiden's fan club needed to toughen up and accept life was pain.

Worse than hearing the Kings Row kids chatter about this in a low, continuous hum was listening to Harvard talk about Neil. Harvard didn't talk about him that much, but Aiden wished he would. If Harvard were excessive about it, Aiden would be perfectly justified in complaining. He could roll his eyes and tell Harvard to lay off, and everybody would sympathize with Aiden about his annoying roommate.

As one date turned into two dates and then metamorphosed hideously into plans for a third, Harvard let the name *Neil* drop more often into conversations. His phone went off all the time, and when it did, he would smile to himself, private and delighted. He mentioned a plan to see a movie, and Aiden knew he wasn't invited rather than just assuming he was. Neil was going with Harvard instead. From now on, Neil would be Harvard's first choice.

How was any of this just or right, Aiden wanted to know? This guy Neil didn't seem like anything special. Why did Neil get Harvard? He'd known Harvard for precisely six days, as opposed to twelve years. He'd been set up on a date with Harvard because their mothers were friends, and that was all. He didn't know anything *about* Harvard. He was some random idiot who drew pictures and played a lot of games on his phone, and he'd been chosen by fate?

Only that wasn't right. Neil hadn't been chosen by fate, he'd been chosen by *Harvard*. If Harvard liked this guy, there was nothing Aiden could do about it.

Aiden missed Cindy. The days when he imagined Harvard might get a girlfriend shone in his memory like a beacon of lost light compared to now, when Harvard seemed like he really was getting a boyfriend. Aiden supposed they'd make it official when Neil asked. Or if Harvard asked, and Neil jumped at the chance.

That Friday night, Harvard went on his third date with Neil, and only then did Aiden realize he'd forgotten to line up one for himself.

His dad called to tell him about another business triumph, and mentioned casually that he was getting married again.

"You've gotta be a killer and go for blood, otherwise what's the point?" Dad asked after delivering that news, without stopping for breath. "You've got to be the baddest shark in the ocean."

Aiden assumed he was talking about work again and not the

latest model in wives. Otherwise, Aiden had questions about his father's love life, and he didn't want the answers.

"Congratulations to you and Samantha," Aiden said.

"Aiden, her name is"—his dad paused—"Claudine?"

"In that case...*felicitations*," murmured Aiden, and hung up.

He updated the "eight" in his essay. Perhaps he could just say he had infinite stepmothers?

He couldn't write his essay for Coach. He couldn't even focus enough to hook up. His only comfort at times when he felt this desolate was Harvard, and Harvard was out on a date.

There was no choice. Desperate measures were called for. Aiden was going to fence.

He plunged out of the dormitory and down the stairs, almost blundering into the wood paneling and almost knocking a portrait of a school benefactor from a hundred years ago off the wall. The benefactor eyed him coldly from within a gilt frame. Aiden was clumsy lately, all his accustomed grace deserting him, but he could still fence. He wanted to slash at the air, to feel something simple and physical so he didn't have to feel anything else.

It was already full night, the moon turning the quad into a silver square. Aiden determinedly did not think of the first time he'd ever walked under these trees, with Harvard talking about whether they would like Kings Row. Aiden had thought he would like any school, as long as Harvard was there, and had concentrated on bringing up the fair in a casual way. It was the last time he'd tried to ask out Harvard.

When he entered the *salle*, Aiden registered a figure in white fencing gear moving silently down the gleaming wood floor, and his eyes narrowed with glee. Seiji Katayama, spine straight as a sword and black hair arranged in rigid defiance of gravity, was performing his training exercises. Exactly the exercises Coach had assigned him, performed with mechanical precision. Coach's exemplary little soldier, whose presence had inspired Coach's current ambitions for teamwork and winning the state championship.

Be a killer, his dad's voice said in his mind.

Aiden never did like to be alone. Other people were amusing. He could always use them to feel better. Sometimes he could only feel better by making them feel worse than he did. Whatever worked.

"Hey there, Katayama," Aiden called out. "Fancy a friendly sparring session?"

When Seiji glanced around, Aiden winked. In return, he received Seiji's usual look, mystified and slightly offended by the world around him.

"All right," Seiji answered slowly.

Aiden gave a showy bow. Seiji inclined his tidy dark head a bare fraction.

Go for blood, his dad whispered. *Otherwise what's the point?*

"Hope this doesn't bring back memories of the last time I beat you," Aiden remarked in a silky voice. "Or the first and worst defeat I saw, when Jesse Coste beat you. That's the one that really stings, isn't it?"

To Aiden's own astonishment, when he feinted, he was slightly off-balance. His point wavered as he pulled back, and he had to collect himself and dance backward a step farther than he'd planned. Seiji's cool black gaze tracked the motion. Seiji missed a lot in life, but on the *piste* he missed almost nothing.

Maybe Jesse Coste had driven away Seiji because he couldn't bear the continuous pressure of those stone-cold judgmental eyes. Who would be able to put up with that?

"You're upset about something," Seiji observed. "I can tell. I upset people all the time. I know what it looks like."

Aiden felt his own narrowed eyes open wide in shock. Seiji's steady dark gaze didn't falter.

Aiden attacked, slashing cat-quick, using his height as an advantage. Seiji's blade slid smoothly sideways, parried, then checked Aiden's next attack when it had scarcely begun. Neither his unflinching gaze nor the pace of his breathing altered at all.

"I didn't upset you, and I don't much care who did. But I'm not going to take advantage of you being upset. I don't upset people for fun," Seiji informed him coolly. "I don't employ cheap tricks. I'll just beat you because I'm better than you."

He delivered this devastating speech with no sign he realized it was devastating. Perhaps Seiji knew no other way to be.

Aiden couldn't help letting out a slightly impressed laugh. Seiji Katayama was relentless. It was probably what caused most of Seiji's problems, that he'd been born basically carrying a dueling sword when everyone else had safety foils.

Seiji came at him, remorseless, contemptuous, and Aiden fell back as Seiji scored point after point. No matter how much Aiden twisted and lunged, in the end, it didn't matter. The taste of defeat, bitter as ashes, had been lingering at the back of Aiden's mouth long before he'd entered this room.

"Fair enough," Aiden conceded and swallowed.

"I try to be," said Seiji.

Other people might consider that their first match hadn't been fair, and now Seiji's victory was. Aiden operated on the principle of *all's fair in everything*, so he didn't feel that way. But perhaps now he understood slightly better how Seiji had felt at tryouts. He found it less amusing than he had at the time.

"Catch you later, Katayama," said Aiden, abandoning the battlefield to the victor.

It was only after he got outside that Aiden realized he was still wearing his fencing gear and holding his épée. He refused to turn around and go back. Losing to a freshman was one thing. Looking ridiculous in front of a freshman was quite another.

The redbrick of the Kings Row buildings had turned the same color as the lake in the distance. At this time of night, everything was either silver or shadow.

Aiden stood in a wavering, sword-thin line of light between the silver grass and shadow of the parking lot. That was when Harvard's motorcycle came purring through the golden gates of Kings Row and up the curving driveway, parking close by Aiden.

Harvard took off his helmet and looked up into Aiden's face, gray Henley stretched tight over his shoulders and turned into pewter in this light, dark eyes warm with affection. No wonder half the school was buzzing about Harvard and his motorcycle.

"Fencing with the moonlight?" Harvard inquired, sounding fond and amused.

"Something like that. How was your date?" Aiden asked in a distant voice.

He could turn distance into words that came up close and cut, he thought. He wanted to. If other people were hurt, he didn't have to be.

Harvard glowed, transparent as a window with the sun coming through. "It was fun. Actually…" Harvard paused, shy but wanting to confide. Every second of his embarrassed pause felt like a year of horror. "I think it's going super well. I was worried, you know? That I would…get it wrong somehow. We can't all be you."

"No," murmured Aiden.

This was his best friend. That meant Aiden should be his best self. Sometimes being with Harvard was the only way Aiden knew he had a best self at all.

He let his point drop, electrified steel gleaming among the bright threads of moonlit grass. He fought the urge to say *arrêt*, and signal surrender.

"That's great things are going well with your guy," Aiden told Harvard. "I'm really glad for you."

13 SEIJI

Seiji frowned at Nicholas's sneakers, propped up on the common room desk. As was typical, Nicholas appeared to have given up on his essay and life in general, and was reading aloud to Seiji from *The Twenty-Six Commandments of Irish Dueling* and other purloined books.

"Spiral staircases in old castles were built so the defending swordsman could wield his blade freely, but the attacker's blows would be blocked!"

"For the last time, Nicholas, these rules are not applicable to modern fencing. Nobody is going to hold a fencing match on a staircase."

"I wish we could," mourned Nicholas. "I'm left-handed. My attack wouldn't be blocked at all. I would kick ass."

Seiji squinted at his essay. He'd

typed a list of his most notable victories in fencing and hoped this would suffice for Coach. When he hit SEND, he was reminded that Nicholas's sneakers were up on the desk.

"Why do you wear red shoes?" Red was so garish.

Nicholas shrugged comfortably. "Red means go."

"No, it doesn't," said Seiji.

Nicholas grinned. "Does to me!"

Seiji sighed. "In the name of teamwork…," he said, "…do you want to train together?" Nicholas abandoned his essay with alacrity. Seiji suspected it was barely begun.

In the *salle*, Nicholas was more tolerable than anywhere else, because here, he listened to Seiji. Seiji placed his hands, one on Nicholas's arm and one on Nicholas's waist, and guided him through the correct motions for a thrust with opposition, where your opponent's blade was pushing against your own. Nicholas went quiet for once. Seiji nodded to indicate they should proceed.

Nicholas, trying to be showy, as usual, went for a head-cut that Seiji parried with a look of disapproval. Next, Nicholas parried Seiji's attack, and then Nicholas attacked and was parried in turn. Nicholas went for Seiji with his épée like a silver storm, and Seiji resorted to feints, which wasn't his usual style. A feint in quarte, a feint in sixte, and a lunge, but Nicholas's own lunge veered off into an attack. Nicholas beamed foolishly, scoring one point, and became so instantly distracted that Seiji then scored two on him with ease.

From the door, Coach applauded. She was a bright splash of color in the room, zip-up hoodie fire-engine red and blazing white.

"You two fight together far better than you ever fight with anyone else. I like it."

Nicholas beamed. Seiji scowled.

"I fence excellently at all times."

"You're too used to being excellent," Coach told him. "Nicholas's speed pushes you to the next level. Technique is learned but it's also invented, and Nicholas makes you get creative."

Speed was the first thing Seiji had ever noticed about Nicholas: the way he moved, and how there was a certain faint promise to his tactics. It wasn't like seeing Seiji's own skill brightly reflected, the way it was with Jesse, but more like glimpsing light catching faraway water. Seiji respected Coach, so he considered this idea of hers in the context of what he'd learned from Eugene.

Technique is learned.

Good training, like pajamas, cost money. Nicholas didn't have any. Nicholas hadn't been trained properly, and it wasn't his fault. Jesse always said that being inadequately trained meant the fencer, not the fencing, was inadequate, but Jesse was wrong. Nicholas fenced like a Jesse who hadn't been trained. His flaws weren't from being lazy or arrogant, though Nicholas was occasionally both those things. It was as though Nicholas was fencing with a stick while the rest of them used épées.

"I'd love to see your flunge, Nicholas," Coach Williams mused, pining for sabers, as always. Seiji didn't feel the need to introduce sabers to Nicholas yet. Nicholas had enough problems with the épée.

Attacking with opposition meant pushing against an opponent's blade. Nicholas had been living his whole life moving in opposition.

It wasn't fair, Seiji thought with sudden decision. Something must be done. Nothing should get in the way of people being as excellent at fencing as they could be.

Nicholas didn't look downcast by the injustice of the world. In fact, he was preening. "Did you come to tell us how skilled we are, Coach?"

"Nope. The story of how you achieved your current ranking isn't an intimate personal insight, Seiji," said Coach, thwapping Seiji playfully over the head.

Seiji self-consciously readjusted his hair. "It was personal to me."

"If it was, think about why," Coach told him. "In fact, tell me—or anyone else—something that *is* personal to you. And, Nicholas, at least Seiji wrote something. Where's your essay?"

"Seiji ate it," Nicholas told her earnestly.

Seiji and Coach reached out and shoved him sideways, one hand on each shoulder, so Nicholas actually stayed right where he was. He grinned at them both, as though he was enjoying being reproached for delinquency.

"Go write your essays," ordered Coach. "Correctly this time!"

Seiji and Nicholas hastily departed the *salle*.

"You need to be trained," Seiji mused as they walked out under the oak trees. "It needs to be one-on-one, and it needs to be intense."

Nicholas cleared his throat. "Does it?"

"Yes, of course it does!" Seiji said severely. "You are years behind where you should be. There is no choice. I am taking charge of you."

"Uh," said Nicholas. "But is that fair?"

"I think it's fair," said Seiji. "Coach Williams can't do everything."

"Coach Williams is the coolest!"

"Her methods are peculiar but surprisingly effective."

Seiji'd had many coaches through the years, and received the indirect coaching of Jesse's father. Seiji had never had a coach like Coach Williams before, any more than he'd had a fencing partner like Nicholas. He wasn't sure how to feel about her not seeming to take pride in him for being advanced, nor wanting to hold on to his shoulder like a trophy. All he could think to do was to listen to her carefully so he might understand her better, and follow her unorthodox suggestions.

"She's the greatest, but that's not what I meant," Nicholas

continued. "If you're going to be training with me . . . I know I'm not exactly what you're used to."

Oh. Nicholas was worried about this being fair *to Seiji.* That was odd. Seiji didn't think anyone had ever done that before.

"It's sometimes . . . somewhat helpful for me to train with you."

It was a massive concession, but for some reason, it didn't satisfy Nicholas. He was still frowning. Seiji didn't know what Nicholas wanted from him. Did he want Seiji to ask him for something?

"What if," Seiji suggested slowly, "you helped me with team bonding? The social aspect, I mean. Since you're extremely popular."

Nicholas blinked several times. "Sorry, what?"

"You have breakfast with multiple people every morning," Seiji pointed out. "So you can indicate to me if I'm accidentally offending people."

There was a thoughtful pause. Above their heads, bright leaves sighed as the wind changed.

"Is it chill if you're offending people totally on purpose?" asked Nicholas.

"If you don't want to do it, you don't have to!"

Seiji stalked off with cold dignity, but Nicholas just jogged faster and caught up with him on the stairs to the dormitory.

"No, I do want to!" Nicholas said. "Deal. Deal?"

He gave Seiji an expectant look. Seiji watched him warily.

"If you spit in your hand and expect me to shake it," he warned, "I'm making you sleep outside. Deal."

He nodded to seal the deal. Seiji felt good about nodding.

"Hey, Coach thought we were good," Nicholas said smugly as they returned to their dormitory. "Because we're awesome rivals. We rock!"

Nicholas had probably never had a proper coach before, Seiji reflected. He didn't even know Coach Williams was unusual.

"You're not my rival," Seiji snapped.

He expected Nicholas to snap back "Not *yet*," as he always did. When Nicholas didn't, Seiji glanced up sharply to see what was wrong. Nicholas was still in Seiji's half of the room. He'd pulled the curtain back to step into his side, but now he stood in the shadow of the curtain with his head bowed.

Nicholas said, "I know you'd rather be fencing with someone else. I get that must suck. I'm starting to see that you and Jesse Coste were, like . . . best friends?"

He seemed about to say something else, but Seiji interrupted.

"Best friends," he scoffed. "We weren't *best friends*."

That was a childish concept. But they'd been children when they first met, he and Jesse. Seiji's coach had warned that Seiji was too advanced to fence against kids his own age, but Jesse's confidence hadn't wavered. He'd smiled and said he hoped they'd have a good match, and they had. Seiji had been so relieved to find someone who could really fence, and someone who wasn't put off by him. Jesse made life easier, on and off the *piste*. Jesse had enough social grace for them both.

If Jesse had suggested being *best friends* when they were young, Seiji would have agreed. But they hadn't been about that. They had been about skill.

Tell me—or anyone else—something that is *personal to you,* Coach had said.

Seiji couldn't talk to just anyone, but Nicholas had said they were friends.

"I was...Jesse's mirror," said Seiji slowly. "I reflected his— glow, his glories and his victories. I used to think it was an honor. We were similar, I told myself, in all the ways that really mattered."

Jesse was left-handed like Nicholas, so facing him sometimes felt like looking into a mirror. Like seeing yourself through the glass, a better, golden self in a different world. A self who fenced just as well but didn't have to work as hard for it. A Seiji who did everything in life with the same skill as he fenced.

"You're not a mirror," said Nicholas. "You're real."

"It's a metaphor, Nicholas."

Nicholas shrugged. "You're still not a mirror. Mirrors break. You never do."

Seiji thought of his moment of defeat against Jesse. The moment that Aiden had seen, and taunted Seiji with, making Seiji lose *again*. Seiji had trained his whole life to be strong, but somehow, he was still weak. Jesse had taken his sword, and Seiji hadn't been able to stop him. The bitterness of that defeat sent Seiji to Kings Row.

Always keep moving toward your target, his dad's voice said, but somehow Seiji had ended up getting his target wrong. He'd moved toward loss and pain he still didn't entirely understand.

"I *lost*," confessed Seiji. "Badly."

"Doesn't make you a loser," said Nicholas, having another lapse where he didn't understand what words—let alone metaphors—meant. "You didn't burst into tears and give up fencing. And you didn't follow Jesse to Exton like a little lamb, the way he was expecting. You came to Kings Row, and you came to fence. You came to fight."

This view of the matter was so shocking that Seiji said something he'd thought he would never say to Nicholas Cox.

"I suppose...," said Seiji, "...you're right."

Nicholas's gaze remained fixed on the floor.

"Being rivals shouldn't be about being someone's mirror. Both of you get to be real. Neither of you has to break."

"Sometimes you're insightful, Nicholas," said Seiji. Nicholas looked pleased before Seiji added: "I think it's mainly by accident."

At that point, Nicholas rolled his eyes and stepped into his side of the room, yanking the curtain closed between them.

Seiji lay back on his pillow, arm behind his head. He supposed he could see what Coach had meant about their fencing bout. Seiji couldn't be on autopilot with Nicholas, making all the right moves he'd been taught.

Thinking of the way he fought Nicholas, and the way he used to mirror Jesse, something brand-new occurred to Seiji. He *couldn't* mirror Nicholas's moves. Seiji had to make different ones, to adapt to such a wildly different style. He didn't have the speed to mirror Nicholas. He *was* fast enough to mirror Jesse's moves. Which meant...Nicholas was faster than Jesse.

In all other ways, Jesse was infinitely superior. Nicholas could never match up. Nobody could.

But if Nicholas had been trained, maybe he could use his superior speed against Jesse to score a point.

In another world, could Nicholas *win* against Jesse?

If that was possible, even in another world, could Seiji win against Jesse in this one?

Seiji rolled in bed and stared at a moonbeam cast against the curtain, putting one of the cheerful yellow ducks in the spotlight.

Over the past few months, stewing in the humiliation of feeling defeated and exposed and unworthy, Seiji had grown used to imagining Jesse as unbeatable and unrivaled.

Seiji couldn't help thinking...if Nicholas could be faster than Jesse, perhaps anybody could be anything at all. What else could Nicholas be?

What else could Seiji be?

Seiji didn't want them to be stopped from finding out.

14 HARVARD

$\mathbf{A}$iden was no good at mornings. When they had been younger, Harvard used to call him and act as an alarm clock, urging "Beep, beep, beep" while Aiden made cranky sounds on the other end of the line. Now that Harvard slept in the bed next to Aiden's, waking him was easier.

It still wasn't easy, though.

Their beds were pushed close together so they could watch movies in comfort and so Harvard could talk Aiden to sleep on the nights when he had insomnia. Now when he wanted to wake Aiden, Harvard could just reach over and gently shove Aiden's shoulder.

"Hey. Hey, sleeping beauty. C'mon. Wake up."

"Never," Aiden mumbled into his pillow.

"Are you awake?"

Aiden pulled his pillow and half his tawny hair across his face. "I'm hate wake."

"Let's return to consciousness just a little more and start putting the words into sentences that make sense," Harvard encouraged.

Aiden rolled over, emerging from the covers and blinking up at the ceiling. "People who talk sense before noon should be fired from cannons into the sun. Especially on the weekend."

Harvard, propped up on his pillow, looked indulgently down at Aiden, who was a tangle of limbs and white sheets and long hair. Harvard had always liked this time in the morning, trying to drag Aiden into wakefulness.

It was a chance to have Aiden to himself, and to have the conversation he'd been planning.

"Your behavior has been weird lately," Harvard let Aiden know. "I have noticed."

Aiden gave a tiny shrug, the sheet sliding a fraction farther down his bare shoulder. "As opposed to my usual flawless behavior, you mean?"

"Even for you, this has been weird," Harvard said gently. "I think I know what's going on with you."

"Do you?" Aiden said in a distant voice.

Harvard nodded. He'd read all about it in his mom's magazines.

"When friends get a significant other, they worry that their friend won't have time for them anymore. But you never need to worry about losing me. We'll always have bro time."

"Ugh," said Aiden, burying his face in the pillow and then pulling the blankets over him and the pillow. "You sound like *Eugene*. For shame, Harvard!"

Harvard smiled at the lump under the bedding that was Aiden.

"If you got to know Neil, I'm sure that you'd like him."

The protesting lump under the blankets went still.

"That's why I want you to meet him," Harvard proposed, hoping this was a listening silence. "I was thinking—maybe tonight. If you're not doing anything else. We could have a double date. Have a fun time and a chat. Neil's super funny. I know you guys will get along."

Aiden sat up abruptly, sheets pooling around his waist. Harvard blinked at him in astonishment. It usually took a good thirty minutes of coaxing to get Aiden out of bed.

"I would," said Aiden in a voice shiny and brittle as Venetian glass. "Of course I would love to do that, but I'm busy tonight. Very, very busy. I have business."

"I assumed you were busy," said Harvard. "You usually are. That's why I suggested a double date. Is there another time that works for you?"

There was a pause, long enough for the sunlight to creep another inch along the rumpled sheets. Aiden looked troubled for some reason. Maybe he had dates lined up every day for a year and couldn't see how to accommodate Harvard.

"What do you mean, I'm usually busy? I'm never too busy for you."

"I appreciate that," said Harvard. "And it's true. You're always there when I need you. But—I mean, you're out almost every night. Hey, and good for you. It's great that you're having fun. I want you to enjoy yourself. I know it can't be like when we were little and we lived in each other's pockets."

"It can!"

Aiden spoke very fast and was being ridiculous.

Harvard remained determinedly reasonable. "I'm just saying—it'll be better now. You have your, uh, social whirl, and I have Neil. No more nights home alone for either of us."

"If it bothered you," Aiden said in an unusually subdued tone, "you should have told me. I wouldn't have gone anywhere if I'd known you wanted me to be here."

"I couldn't ask you to do that!"

Harvard regarded Aiden with horror. What did Aiden think of him? What kind of best friend would ask their friend to give up all that? Playing video games with Harvard would be a real step down from Mediterranean cruises.

"You could have asked me," said Aiden. "I would have said yes. Whatever you ask me for, I'll say yes."

His tone was unusually serious.

Harvard smiled. "Then I'm asking you for this. You don't have to give up every night for me, but will you please give me one?"

"Yes. Yes, I will." Aiden's voice went extremely cheerful, brittle glass catching a glaring light. "A double date tonight! What fun. I wish I'd suggested this myself."

Harvard was surprised, but pleasantly so. "Really?"

"I'm definitely not lying! Let me acquire a date right now."

"Did you not have one before?" Harvard asked, but Aiden wasn't listening.

Aiden had sprung from bed and was pulling on his uniform in a haphazard fashion. Somehow, when Aiden was a dire mess, he made it look good—in a particular way that made people stare.

This was more of a mess than usual. People were staring more than they normally did as Aiden made his tempestuous way down the hall, Harvard following in his wake. Harvard had pulled on his own clothes, too, but he feared his was not a state of alluring disarray.

Aiden halted by the first cute boy he saw. "What are you doing tonight?"

The boy seemed staggered. Harvard didn't blame him. Aiden sounded rather as though he was demanding the boy's money or his life.

"Being . . . heterosexual?" the boy answered at last.

Aiden stood there being gorgeous at him. A stunned and dazzled expression grew on the boy's face, as though he'd accidentally looked directly into the sun or encountered a pinup model.

"Or maybe . . . not?" said the boy, a long pause between the words.

Too long. Aiden got impatient with people.

"Okay, I don't have time for this, see you!" said Aiden, racing past with the boy calling "Wait!" faintly to his retreating back.

Harvard gave the boy an apologetic glance, then jogged after Aiden. Over the years, he'd developed a stride that covered a lot of ground so he could keep pace when Aiden went rogue.

People were mostly charmed by Aiden. Harvard understood that; he was, too. It didn't mean he approved of everything Aiden did, and he pointed that out to Aiden often enough, but he was always more charmed than disapproving. It all reminded Harvard of being five and having Aiden tell him that he'd named his bear *Harvard Paw*. Naming the toy after the person who'd given it to him, and making a pretty advanced pun as well, was just like Aiden. He was always whip-smart, hilarious, and secretly sweet beneath everything else.

When scorned guys asked Harvard how he put up with it, Harvard understood what they meant. He'd just answer: "I like it."

He did. He'd always wanted to be good, for his mom and his team and in general. He didn't want to let anybody down. He enjoyed doing his best, but watching Aiden go his wild way gave Harvard a sense of freedom, too.

Harvard had always thought this made him and Aiden a good team. The best.

Aiden's rush was halted when a tall guy gave him a very obvious once-over.

"Hey, you," said Aiden. "Congratulations! You're going on a date with me tonight."

"Uh … great," said the guy. "Do you want to know my name?"

"Let's keep the mystery alive between us," drawled Aiden, already turning away.

Harvard mouthed *Sorry* before he followed Aiden.

The guy mouthed back his name.

"I'll tell Aiden," said Harvard. "See you later, bye! Looking forward to it."

Aiden would like Neil, Harvard was sure. Neil was so fun and nice. And of course, Neil would like Aiden. Nobody could help liking Aiden.

This date would be amazing.

15 SEIJI

That morning when Seiji came to breakfast, he discovered Dante attempting to take the seat beside Nicholas.

"Hey, dude, no, I'm saving this seat for Seiji," said Nicholas.

Dante rolled his eyes without a word and went around the table.

Seiji took the seat with a faint feeling of satisfaction. Naturally, Nicholas didn't want to sit beside Dante. Who would?

"There's no actual need to save a seat for me," Seiji informed Nicholas.

Nicholas waved him off as if he were an annoying fly. "I'm gonna, you can't stop me."

Seiji supposed he couldn't. He started eating his breakfast, though Nicholas eyeballed Seiji's protein-rich green smoothie suspiciously. Nicholas had no idea about the importance of nutrition.

Bobby and Dante were gossiping, which meant Bobby was talking and Dante was listening. Seiji listened as well, to be polite, though it was not a particularly interesting conversation.

"My hand to God, Aiden was asking people out in the hallways," Bobby said. "I heard it from Brian and Juan told him, and Eduardo was there watching it happen with his own two eyes. So weird. Aiden always waits for them to come to him!"

Nicholas snorted. "Why would anyone come to Aiden? Like, then you have to listen to him talk. *Blah, blah, blah, rich boy being rude to people.* Um, fascinating, I don't think so. Dante, are you gonna finish your eggs?"

Dante gathered the eggs toward himself, glowering. "Yes."

Nicholas drew back a questing fork. "Just asking, asking's not a crime."

Seiji mulled over what Nicholas had just said, remembering what Eugene had told him about the boys from Kings Row framing Nicholas. He'd known that Nicholas didn't like Aiden, but Seiji didn't like Aiden much himself. He hadn't realized what Nicholas's dislike was based on.

"What do you mean," Seiji asked, "rich boy?"

"Oh, you know, Seiji." Nicholas gestured with his empty fork. "Rich boys. They're the worst."

This was becoming alarming. Aiden's father was a notoriously wealthy lothario, but Seiji had to wonder what the cutoff in Nicholas's head was. Seiji was always offending people, and his father's income was far above average.

"My father is rather well-off," Seiji admitted.

Had Nicholas not realized?

"I figured. I didn't mean rich as in *rich*," said Nicholas.

"That was the precise word you used!"

It appeared Nicholas really had decided words had no meaning anymore. Life would be so confusing from now on.

"No, see," said Nicholas, and adopted a peculiar nasal intonation. "There's a particular type of rich boy, who's all 'Daddy, I want this; Daddy, I want that; Daddy, I want to treat other people like dirt because I think it's *amooosing*—'"

"Aiden doesn't sound like this—" Seiji protested.

"It's a state of mind, Seiji, c'mon," said Nicholas. "You know the type. You must, they're all over Kings Row. Bet there's worse at Exton. They're so rich but they take cheap shots, and it's so dumb, right? They don't even mean them. They're not sincere enough to mean anything. The point is to say they're great by saying you suck, and they never *do* anything great, so why do they open their mouths?" Nicholas shook his head. "I don't get it."

Seiji put down his spoon and stared at Nicholas. At this late hour of the morning, the room was social chaos. The very chains from which the lights hung suspended were swaying with the volume of people and conversation, but it wasn't as unpleasant as usual, because Seiji had something remarkable to focus on.

"How can you tell when people don't say what they mean?"

"I just can," answered Nicholas. "And I just don't have time for it. You know?"

"What if someone who was that type *did* do something great?" asked Seiji, thinking of Jesse.

Surely Jesse was allowed to say anything he liked. And Jesse didn't hurt people who mattered.

Except he'd hurt Seiji.

And those Kings Row boys who'd framed Nicholas didn't matter, but they'd decided *Nicholas* didn't matter and hurt him. Maybe deciding other people didn't matter always ended with someone hurt.

Nicholas considered the question, and then shrugged. "Saying you're great still shows you're worried nobody will notice unless you say it. If you have to say it, how great can you be?"

"Where's Eugene?" Seiji asked abruptly.

Nicholas blinked. "Uh, think he's eating with his weight-lifting friends this morning."

Apparently, Eugene enjoyed darting like a hummingbird all over the room. Why could nobody else dedicate themselves to a proper routine? Seiji sighed and scanned the room until he found Eugene at a more crowded table than any other in the room. Not only were there a lot of students at the table, but they all seemed bulky.

Seiji sighed again and surrendered himself to his fate. He finished his breakfast, and then rose.

"You go on to class without me. I want a word with Eugene."

Seiji hesitated. "You can save me a seat. If you insist."

Nicholas paused, then smiled. His face was a lot more tolerable when he did that. "I will."

Seiji wandered gloomily over to the weight lifters' table, then cleared his throat so Eugene would notice him. Eugene glanced up and went still, his eyes going wide.

"Seiji!" Eugene said. "What are you doing here—I mean, what a surprise. A nice surprise! Hey, guys, this is my fencing bro. And these are my weight-lifting bros, Brad, Chad, and Julian. Brad, Chad, Julian, this is Seiji Katayama."

Several massive students regarded Seiji with interest. It was like being noticed by mountains in uniform.

"What up, bro?" said Julian, who was the hugest of them all.

Seiji gave him a coolly polite nod.

"Katayama," murmured Brad. "Right, the one with the stick up his—"

Eugene elbowed Brad with extreme force. Extreme force seemed like the only type of force that would work on Brad.

"Any bro of Eugene's," Chad told him benevolently.

Seiji gave him a chilling look, hoping to discourage further awkward conversation. "Indeed."

He turned to Eugene.

"I was thinking about what you were saying at the midnight feast, about those guys who implied Nicholas would steal. You said we should get them back by, ah . . . 'playing a totally excellent prank.'" Seiji had to force out the distasteful quote, and then breathed deeply in relief once he'd accomplished it. "I want to do the prank. What should we do?"

"Oh," said Eugene. "Oh wow! I totally didn't think you'd be up for it."

Seiji leaned forward. "I am. But I've never played a prank on anybody before. Explain to me how pranks work."

A stunning blow landed on Seiji's back. He supposed this was some of the teen bullying one read about in the newspapers and braced himself for more violence.

Strangely, Chad was grinning at him. The blow was apparently well-intentioned.

"My dude!" said Chad. "Brad was wrong about you. Anyone who's up for an excellent prank is all right in my book. And you have midnight feasts, too?"

"We drank protein shakes," said Seiji.

"Righteous." Chad nodded. "Always keep grinding, but don't miss out on life. You know how to have fun, Katayama."

"I really don't," Seiji murmured.

The behavior of weight lifters was mysterious, but he had an objective to achieve. Seiji was a goal-oriented person.

"The prank, Eugene," he prompted.

Eugene blinked rapidly several times. "I hadn't thought it out. Just that it'd be good to do one."

"A strategic plan of attack is vital, Eugene."

Chad was nodding along with Seiji. This was only common sense. Chad understood.

"Uh...okay!" said Eugene. "Here's a good prank: So you coat a bar of soap with clear nail polish, which I think Bobby has, so we could borrow it from him, and then the soap won't lather. They'll be so annoyed in the shower!"

"These people strike me as unwashed miscreants," said Seiji. "That prank is inadequate. Next suggestion, please."

Eugene coughed. "Right, so...you creep sneakily into their room and hide an egg in there. Then their room gets really stinky and they don't know why! Hilarious."

Eugene nodded with increasing conviction. Chad began nodding, too. Seiji was disappointed in them both.

"No," said Seiji. "The point of the prank is to teach these people a lesson. What sort of lesson does a smelly room teach?"

"It would be very funny...."

"Step up your game, Eugene," Seiji advised severely.

"So...," said Eugene. "If we hid chickens in their room, and the chickens laid many eggs, but there were also...chickens..."

Seiji only shook his head.

"I see what Katayama's saying," Chad observed wisely. "He's like, where's the justice, bro?"

"That's exactly right, Chad," Seiji confirmed. "It's about justice. They need to recognize why what they did was wrong."

Eugene rubbed the place between his eyebrows. He appeared to feel beleaguered by Seiji and Chad's united logic.

"The best prank would be if we did, like, a jewel heist of the store. Then we'd hide the cache of stolen loot in those jerks' room, and when it was discovered they'd protest their innocence, but nobody would believe them, and they'd be dragged off screaming to jail. Then they'd see what it was like to be wrongly suspected!" Eugene had brightened during his dramatic recital, but now he dimmed. "Only we're not master criminals."

Seiji considered Eugene and his new scheme for a prank. He felt it had real promise.

"That is a much better idea, Eugene."

"Yeah, except we're *not master criminals*," protested Eugene.

Seiji tapped his finger thoughtfully against his chin. "Leave it to me."

"Seiji, I'm finding your current lack of expression even more unsettling than your usual lack of expression!" Eugene said. "Bro, I'm feeling a distinct sense of disquiet here!"

Seiji shrugged. He couldn't be responsible for everyone's emotions. It was difficult enough being responsible for Nicholas.

"I love this little guy," Chad announced.

Seiji assumed he was talking about someone else, someone of below-average height, when Chad rose like a volcano from the sea and slammed a meaty arm around Seiji's shoulders. Seiji gave a faint gasp, partly from horror and partly because he felt as if his bones were being crushed.

"Whoa, be gentle with him," Eugene advised Chad. "It's his first brodeo."

16 AIDEN

The diner in Kingstone was set up to look like an old-fashioned soda fountain and ice cream shop, with crimson booths and a stained-glass sign behind the cash register reading SWEETS FOR SWEETHEARTS.

Of course Neil would pick a place like this, Aiden thought with scorn. *Classic Neil.*

"I picked the place," said Harvard quietly. "I think it's cute. Do you think Neil will like it?"

Now that Aiden looked at it again, the place was totally cute. Not that *Neil* would appreciate it, Aiden was sure.

He had to stop thinking this way. The diner was nice. They would have a nice time. Harvard would be happy.

"Of course Neil will like it." Aiden's voice rang with sincerity. Neil

181

got to be on a date with Harvard here, after all. "Who wouldn't like it?"

"Perfect place to have a milkshake," chimed in Aiden's date.

"Nobody asked you," Aiden said with a charming smile. He'd learned that if he employed the smile, he could say absolutely anything he wanted and his dates would interpret it as flirting.

The date supported this thesis by winking at Aiden. Then he reached for Aiden's hand. Aiden pulled away sharply. He was about to meet Neil, and he needed his hands free. He had to be ready for anything.

Neil was already sitting in a booth. God, Aiden hated the punctual.

"Hey, Neil," called out Harvard, and gave Neil a little wave.

Aiden was tempted to step in front of Harvard so Neil wouldn't get to see it, but that would be pointless. The wave would still be meant for Neil. Aiden couldn't keep it for himself.

Harvard had said, *I'm asking for this.* Not for Aiden to be with him, but for Aiden to help him be with Neil. This was what Harvard wanted. Instead of blocking the wave, Aiden followed up Harvard's wave with his most charming smile, aimed in the same direction.

"Hey," said Aiden. "Neil, is it?"

Neil smiled back. God, Aiden hated teeth.

"Uh, wow," he said. "You must be Aiden."

There was a lilt to the *wow*, which made Aiden think Neil was surprised that Aiden was hot. Why would Neil be surprised that Aiden was hot? It was an internationally recognized fact.

Had Harvard described Aiden as hideous? Surely Harvard wouldn't do that.

Was Neil surprised to find himself attracted to Aiden? Better men than Neil found themselves in this situation all the time.

Aiden tried to regard Neil dispassionately. He supposed Neil was okay-looking. Tall, hair that was untidy in a way some might find vaguely charming. Vacant eyes, Aiden decided, giving up on dispassion and turning to viciousness. Aiden might while away a Tuesday night with a guy like Neil, but he'd save Fridays and Saturdays for someone more compelling. Why was Harvard wasting his time with a Tuesday-night guy?

Aiden slid into the booth opposite Neil. Harvard and Aiden always sat on the same side of the table, but today it would be different. Harvard wanted it to be different.

Harvard also wanted his best friend and his boyfriend to get along. Aiden smiled with the concentrated intensity of a star, leaving Neil no choice but to be dazzled or go blind.

"Sorry we're late," said Aiden. "My fault. Always is."

Neil sounded slightly dazed, as well he might. "That's okay."

Aiden's face was beginning to hurt, but he had to keep the smile pinned in place. Harvard would now be sitting next to Neil. Aiden would be forced to watch it.

Then Harvard slid in next to Aiden.

Aiden was just turning to Harvard and beginning to smile for real, when Neil said, "Uh, Harvard?"

"Oh God, sorry!" exclaimed Harvard. "Force of habit."

He slid out of Aiden's side of the booth, abandoning Aiden with a stranger. The random date sat down, and Neil made an interrogative sound. "This is . . . ?"

"This is, ah, my date," said Aiden.

"Whose name is . . . ," prompted Neil.

"Blair," Aiden answered.

Harvard coughed. Aiden glanced over at his date and Harvard, who were both shaking their heads.

"Huh," said Aiden. "Brandon? Still no? Tip of my tongue."

"This is your date whose name you don't know?" asked Neil, blinking.

Aiden had been right to dislike Neil on sight. Neil was a judgmental and unkind person, but for Harvard's sake, Aiden offered a sheepish shrug.

Harvard said quietly, "His name is Bruce."

Aiden tried to be a carefree rogue, winking at Neil and then his random date. Usually, carefree roguery came to Aiden more easily. "Clark and I are more about the raw animal passion than the in-depth conversation."

Random date seemed pleased to hear this. He moved in slightly closer to Aiden. Aiden felt crowded.

"In-depth conversation . . . about names," said Neil. "Also, his name is Bruce."

"And your name is Neil," said Aiden in a conciliatory fashion. "We're all introduced. Fabulous to meet you, Neil."

That was a shocking lie but told in a good cause. Neil leaned his shoulder into Harvard's, smiling back at Aiden. Of course Neil was pleased with how his life was going.

"Likewise," Neil told Aiden. "I've heard a lot about you. You and Harvard grew up in each other's pockets, Harvard says."

Harvard smiled.

"You're like brothers, I guess," Neil proceeded.

Harvard stopped smiling. Aiden bit his tongue. The taste of blood made him feel nauseous.

"Not really," said Aiden's random date. "My brother and I used to try to make each other eat dirt. Mom had to put us in time-out on opposite sides of the house. Aiden and Harvard are, like, inseparable. Everyone at Kings Row thought they were dating for, wow, the first five months of school."

Harvard seemed surprised by this information. Neil seemed deeply displeased to hear it.

"When we want your input, we'll ask for it, Peter!" snapped Aiden.

His random date stopped trying to slide his arm along the back of the booth behind Aiden's shoulders, whistled under his breath, and took out his phone.

The server came to take their order. Harvard frowned at the menu.

Aiden relaxed, feeling on familiar ground. "Why do you always do this? You know you always look through every item on the menu and then pick the sweetest thing. French toast for him. Oh, and then let's split the brownie sundae."

Harvard smiled over the menu at Aiden. "Yeah, you're right."

"Oh cool," said Aiden's random date, still looking at his phone. "Bring three spoons."

Aiden raised an eyebrow, slightly shocked by his date's bad manners. "You can't just share our dessert, Tony."

"His name is Bruce!" Neil exclaimed in the tone of one sorely tested.

Aiden didn't even know why Neil was annoyed this time. He was glaring from Harvard to Aiden, and back again. Aiden might well have done something wrong without noticing, but he was confident Harvard had done nothing wrong. Neil was being deeply unreasonable.

"Of course you can share the sundae, Bruce," Harvard said. "Would you like a spoon, too, Neil?"

"I absolutely wouldn't!"

Aiden was completely at a loss. Who hated brownie sundaes? What kind of person had Harvard brought into their lives?

Neil visibly made the decision to shake off his gloom, and gave Harvard a smile that made Aiden feel unwell. "Why don't you share a dessert with *me*?"

"I already said I'd share a dessert with Aiden," said Harvard, and then brightened. "I guess I could go for two halves of different desserts. . . ."

Neil looked dissatisfied with this genius solution. Harvard bit his lip. Aiden's date was raising his eyebrows at his phone.

The server's brow crumpled in confusion. "Sorry, how many spoons do you guys need?"

"Many spoons! We need so many spoons! Could you just bring us a lot of spoons and we'll sort it out later?" Harvard sounded rather frayed.

Harvard never usually sounded frayed. Harvard's patience was normally infinite.

Aiden had to salvage this double date somehow. He tried his charm offensive, though Neil seemed significantly less affected than he had been five minutes ago.

"Lots of desserts is always the answer, don't you think, Neil? The great thing about mine and Charles Xavier's relationship—"

"*BRUCE!*" snapped Neil.

"Leave me out of this," muttered Aiden's random date, texting away.

"The great thing about mine and Quill's relationship is that he's always so sweet."

"Uh-huh," said Aiden's date.

"That's what I think about Neil." Harvard's voice was lovely and soothing. "I guess I don't know how he feels about me."

Oh God, was this Harvard flirting? He was good at it. Aiden wanted to throw up. He kept smiling.

Neil relaxed, tipped his head, and regarded Harvard with a delighted proprietary air, as though he thought Harvard was really cute and belonged to him. "Oh, you're all right."

Neil leaned toward Harvard, and Harvard inclined his body slightly toward Neil's.

Wow, get a room, thought Aiden. Then: *Wait, please don't.*

Neil's hand was clenched in a fist on the tabletop. Harvard reached out hesitantly and turned Neil's hand palm up, lacing their fingers together. Neil nudged Harvard in a forgiving manner.

Aiden didn't see why some couples had to revolt the populace with frenzied displays of public affection.

No, Harvard had a right to hold his boyfriend's hand in public. Aiden supported him. Actually, Aiden liked displays of public affection himself. Aiden leaned sensuously into his date's side and nibbled his date's ear.

His date almost dropped his phone.

"You just bit my ear *much too hard!*" exclaimed Aiden's random date.

Aiden rolled his eyes. "Excuse me for being spontaneous and romantic, Thor!"

"Bruce," murmured Harvard.

"I could actually get into being called Thor," said Aiden's random date. "However, I don't want a pierced ear. Let's be clear on that."

The server brought their food and a dozen spoons. Neil glared at his club sandwich.

"Do you often have to remind Aiden of his dates' names?" Neil asked.

"Um, yeah," Harvard admitted.

"Doesn't that bother you?"

"Not really," said Harvard. "He always remembers mine."

Aiden winked at him. "Do I, Harley?"

Harvard threw back his head and laughed. Suddenly, Aiden felt less sick. Harvard was regarding Aiden in his usual warm way, knowing Aiden was incorrigible and embracing that in an ocean of endless affection. With Harvard, and only with Harvard, sometimes being who Aiden was seemed like it could be enough. Aiden's smile began, for the first time since they'd walked into the diner, to be real.

Until Aiden noticed Neil was looking at them both with that sour expression. Again.

"You know...I'm not feeling that well," said Neil. "Maybe tonight's a wash. We still on for bowling on Saturday?"

"Sure! Totally!" Harvard rushed to assure him. "Aiden, do you and Bruce want to come bowling on Saturday?"

Aiden's random date gave a long, loud whistle.

The whistle was followed by a longer, somehow even louder silence.

"I'm leaving," announced Neil.

He shoved Harvard, and when Harvard scrambled out of the booth, Neil darted for the door.

"Wait, no," said Harvard. "Or at least...let me take you home. Neil!"

Harvard ran after him. Aiden wondered if he should go after

Harvard, but his random date was in the way. The random date seemed absorbed by his phone, and not inclined to move.

After a time, Aiden began to drum his fingers against the surface of the table.

"*Sooo*," said Aiden's random date. "In love with Harvard, huh?"

"Why would you say that, Steve?" Aiden snarled.

"Because I've been here this whole time," said the random date. "Though I feel people watching from space may also know. How long has that been going on?"

Aiden looked around for Harvard and saw only milkshakes.

"I don't know what you're talking about, Barry!"

"That long, huh?" said Aiden's random date. "So everyone else at Kings Row got 'drowning thoughts of your unattainable love in sexy debauchery,' and I got 'incredibly awkward double date'?" He sighed. "Figures."

There was a pause. Aiden glanced over at Bruce's profile. Bruce didn't look up from his phone.

Aiden didn't actively care about his dates, but he didn't want them to have a genuinely terrible time. He didn't want to hurt people like his dad did. Not really.

"Sorry," mumbled Aiden.

"Oh, don't be," said Bruce in mellow tones, waving his phone to illustrate why. "I've been commenting live on this whole date as it unfolded. Got a lot of new followers."

Aiden cracked a smile. "Good for you."

"When life gives you lemons, post a bitter tirade on social media, I always say!" Bruce put away his phone. "Anyway, I figure you'll pay for all of this when your roommate comes home after getting dumped."

"He's not getting dumped!"

"I'd give it fifty-fifty," said Bruce. "Anyway, bye. It's been real, Aiden. Real weird."

"Later, Rocket," Aiden said, and Bruce grinned. Aiden didn't grin back. Aiden had been faking a smile throughout the double date. Aiden found that at the end of this disaster, he could no longer manage to even pretend.

———————————◆———————————

Harvard had been dumped.

Aiden knew as soon as he walked in. For a tall, broad-shouldered guy, Harvard usually walked very softly, as though he didn't wish to disturb the universe. It was only when he was weighted down with misery that his tread was heavy.

He came into their room and stood in the center of the floor, hands open and helpless. Harvard normally possessed great steadiness of purpose, but right now he looked as if he had no idea what to do.

Aiden stared at him, wracked with guilt. He'd always promised himself he would never hurt Harvard. Not Harvard. He truly did not want to hear what had happened.

"What...happened?" he asked.

Harvard stared at the floor. "Uh—I walked Neil home. Well, I more or less chased Neil home. He wouldn't really look at or talk to me until we reached his porch. Once we were there, he told me...he wasn't sure we were going to work out as a couple, and he was pretty sure I knew why."

Aiden wasn't any good at apologies, which was unfortunate, because he needed to come up with an abject one fast. Aiden didn't have many rules he lived by, but this was one. He didn't ever hurt Harvard. He wouldn't do that.

Except he had.

Neil had been really into Harvard until he met Aiden. It was clear Aiden hadn't done a good enough job hiding his seething hatred, or his attachment to Harvard. Aiden's date had figured out how Aiden felt, and Neil must have done so as well. This was all Aiden's fault.

Into Aiden's fraught silence, Harvard said, "I *don't* know why, though. I told Neil I didn't. He said that if I figured it out and wanted to see him again, then I could give him a call in a week. That seems like there's hope, right? I got something badly wrong, but if I knew what it was, I could fix it."

"Wait," said Aiden. "What?"

Harvard looked up at the sound of Aiden's voice, and frowned. "Do you think it was when I snapped at the server about spoons? I read that if you behave badly with the waitstaff when on a date, you're showing your date who you really are. I should go back to the diner and apologize. I should bring her flowers."

Aiden was off the hook. He didn't know why some weird masochistic impulse was telling him to wriggle back onto it.

"You don't think Neil might have made this dumbass decision because of me?"

"Because you can't remember your dates' names?" asked Harvard, a trace of warm amusement creeping into his voice. "You're a menace, but no. I don't see any reason why Neil would break up with me because of you. Neil was clear he was breaking up with me because of something to do with *me*."

Bruce had been right about everything, except for one factor: Harvard was good, really good, in a way few people could understand. He would never blame Aiden for something if he could blame himself instead.

"God, I just don't know how to date." Harvard sighed. "If I'd dated some people before now, maybe I'd understand what to do. Is that why you date around a lot? So if you find someone you like, you won't mess up?"

Aiden shook his head wordlessly. He hadn't realized Harvard liked Neil so much.

"*Is* it all just practice? Like fencing? I don't know why this is so difficult for me when it comes so easily to you," said Harvard. "I don't know what I'm doing, and I'm getting everything wrong."

Aiden was lounging on the bed, fiddling with Harvard Paw

as he sometimes did when he had the urge to go to Harvard or touch him. He patted Harvard Paw on the head. Seeing Harvard this upset made him miserable, too.

"It's all right," he told Harvard soothingly. "It *is* like fencing. Remember when we were little, how you used to have to go over everything the coach taught us with me all over again? You'd move slowly so I could copy you, and tell me what to do every step of the way, and I learned how to mimic every move until I could do it on my own. Dating will start coming naturally to you."

"Well, it's not like you can carefully guide me through all the motions of dating," Harvard said ruefully. Then his tone changed, becoming the captain's voice, the one he used when he started to see a plan forming. "I mean . . . could you?"

Their familiar room seemed to tilt right into an alternate dimension. Aiden thought for a dazed moment that perhaps he hadn't heard Harvard right. Or possibly Aiden was having a hallucination. It had been a difficult day.

"What?"

"Could you teach me to date?"

Harvard was looking at him expectantly, as if he'd really asked Aiden that question. As if Aiden really had to answer.

Aiden said, "No!"

"Do you think I'm hopeless?" asked Harvard.

His shoulders slumped again, the light that had woken in him at the thought of a strategy extinguished. Aiden wanted to bring it back.

Aiden cleared his throat and said, "I don't think you're hopeless."

A light flickered in Harvard's face. "Then—couldn't you help me?"

"I . . . ," said Aiden.

His heart was beating too hard, the continuous flutter of a trapped thing that couldn't resign itself to captivity. *It wouldn't work,* he told himself. But what if it could? No matter what Aiden sometimes imagined, he wouldn't ever really try to date Harvard. Deep down, Aiden had always known that was a dream. He knew where romance always led: the sound of a slammed door and a sports car in a driveway. Trying to have everything meant losing it all.

They had to stay friends. If they were friends, they could be friends forever. Only . . . this might buy Aiden a little time, to get used to the idea of Harvard with someone else. To have something for himself. He couldn't keep Harvard, but he could keep a memory.

This wouldn't hurt Harvard. Aiden would be *helping* him. Harvard had asked him to. Anytime the practice dating started to feel too real, Aiden could remind himself that this was all for someone else. Harvard was only doing this to get Neil back. If that was what Harvard wanted, Aiden would get it for him.

Hardly letting himself think about what he was doing, Aiden nodded.

Harvard's whisper was almost wondering. "Would you really?"

Aiden's throat was dry, but he got the words out anyway. "I told you already: Whatever you ask me for, the answer is yes."

17 HARVARD

Aiden was sitting on Harvard's bed, fiddling with his teddy bear, a lock of hair escaped from his gracefully messy bun and curving into his face. His eyes were fixed on the wall behind Harvard's head.

Harvard kept reliving the moment on Neil's porch, when Neil had looked at Harvard with what seemed almost like pity, though there was anger there, too. As if Harvard had got things so wrong it was frustrating, when Harvard had thought with Neil there was a chance of getting things right. He wanted that chance back.

"Thanks so much," Harvard told Aiden. "This is going to be great."

"Yes," Aiden said at last in a slow, thoughtful tone. "This *is* a good idea. You know how dating works in theory. You read your mom's magazines, no matter how much I implore you

not to. But theoretical experience is no substitute for practical experience."

Harvard nodded, already trying to think of exactly how they should do this. "You can show me how dating works. Practically."

Aiden's voice was somewhat distant. He was sitting still. Perhaps he was planning, too. He was very good at seeing the weak points in a plan or an opponent. He was the smartest person Harvard knew, and Harvard had never been so glad to have Aiden on his team.

"Sure. This is my area of expertise. You can practice dating with me." Aiden's pause lasted a fraction of a second. "For Neil."

Something about that made unease drum a warning beat in Harvard's chest, but Aiden was right. Harvard needed to get better at dating so he could win back Neil. Second-guessing a plan was fatal. A captain had to be confident.

"Here's the most important thing to remember when we're planning," Harvard said, falling back on what he was certain of. "The thing that can't change. I don't want to—mess anything up or blur the lines between us. We're best friends."

"Always," said Aiden. "That's the most important thing. You're the most important thing. Trust me, I know how dating works. It doesn't matter, and this wouldn't even be real dating. It doesn't mean anything. It won't change anything. I promise you."

Harvard nodded slowly. Right. Of course dating didn't mean anything to Aiden. It was the fact that Harvard was so clumsy at this, so new, that was making him hesitate.

Actually, the more Harvard thought about the idea, the more he thought it was his best plan ever.

Learning how to date was so uncomfortable and stressful. Harvard worried at every turn that he was doing it wrong, that he wasn't living up to other people's hopes of what he could be. Aiden wouldn't have any false expectations of Harvard. Aiden *knew* Harvard, everything about him, dreams to doubts, in-jokes to night terrors.

"Well...," said Harvard. "I would like to try. If you're sure you don't mind."

"I'm sure," Aiden said.

As easy as that.

"How..." Harvard swallowed. "What would we do? If we were dating. Let's plan it out. I wanna come up with a dating strategy."

Aiden's mouth formed a thoughtful shape.

"We take it step by step. I'll pick you up, we'll go on a date or two. And I'll teach you some moves. If you want me to."

Harvard had made no mention of moves, but they were part of dating. He was aware of that.

Harvard suddenly didn't feel equipped to deal with this situation. This had always been Aiden's territory, and Harvard had always stayed away, as though it were a place on a map marked *Here Be Dragons*. He'd asked Aiden to help him, and he did really want Aiden's help. Very badly.

Harvard swallowed and said, "What else?"

"I suppose you *could* walk me to class," suggested Aiden.

Harvard raised an eyebrow. "I do walk you to class. Otherwise you don't *go* to class."

They exchanged a smile.

"Ah, but if we were dating, you would carry my books," Aiden said.

"Why aren't you carrying *my* books?" protested Harvard.

"Because you're a gentleman!" Aiden said triumphantly, and hesitated. A new thought seemed to occur to him. "If you wanted to start slow you could . . . hold my hand."

That was starting slow. The idea of it shouldn't have hit Harvard with shattering force. He really was hopeless at this dating thing. Harvard bit his lip, not able to help himself.

"If people see us holding hands in the hall," Harvard hazarded, "they might think we're really together. I wouldn't want to cramp your style."

Aiden's mouth curved. "Let people think what they want. People are used to seeing me with one guy or another. I don't care."

Another snag in the plan occurred to Harvard.

"I care if it's my mom," Harvard stipulated. "My mom can never hear of this!"

Aiden raised an eyebrow. "I thought your mom liked me. But, fine, agreed. I won't text your mom with any fake news. What else do you not want? Tell me."

Harvard's mom *did* like Aiden, whom she thought of as being eternally tiny and a total scamp. She'd immediately begin planning a June wedding. Harvard could only imagine Aiden's horror.

If this went on too long, she would find out, and Harvard *would* cramp Aiden's style. He was bound to.

"We should put a time limit on this," Harvard suggested.

Aiden nodded crisply. "Fine. Let's take the week. Friday night you can go back to Neil, wow him with your new skills, and make it official. What else?"

Aiden's tone was extremely brisk and businesslike. Harvard's head was whirling.

"Um...," said Harvard. "I don't know; this is *your* area of expertise. Like you said. We have to make this plan together. You tell me. What else could go wrong?"

Aiden considered. "Being roommates could make this messy. After a date, we should leave the practice at the door."

As opposed to taking it inside. Into the room. With the beds in it. Harvard's mind felt like it was bending and might fracture under immense weight.

"Look," Harvard said. "There's one flaw in this plan. I know we don't talk about it, but it's pretty obvious. Right?"

Aiden hesitated. When he spoke, he seemed to choose his words with care. "I'm not certain what you mean."

Oh God, was it *not* obvious?

Harvard would have to say it.

"I don't think you understand the profound depth of my inexperience. I've never even kissed anybody!"

201

This seemed to take Aiden aback. Harvard had feared it might. Probably Harvard didn't even qualify for practice dating. Obviously, you didn't plan a team strategy with someone who'd never fenced in his life before.

After a stunned pause, Aiden said carefully: "I thought you and Neil must have—"

"No," said Harvard.

A few times, Harvard had thought a kiss might happen. Both nights Neil had let Harvard take him home, Neil had lingered, talking to Harvard on the porch for some time as though he might be waiting for something. But Harvard had no idea how to make the first move.

In retrospect, Harvard regretted the motorcycle. He thought the motorcycle might've led to Neil having certain expectations of Harvard that Harvard couldn't fulfill.

"Oh," said Aiden, softer than breath.

He was probably wondering what he'd got himself into, and how to get out of it. They'd known each other since they were five.

Since they were five, Harvard thought with sudden misgiving. Surely that would make everything weird.

No matter what people said about Aiden, Harvard knew he didn't just indiscriminately kiss everybody. Usually, Harvard imagined, the people Aiden did kiss tended to know what they were doing.

This might be a solution to Harvard's problems, but Aiden

didn't have any problems in this area at all. He should give Aiden the chance to back out gracefully.

"Look," said Harvard. "We've known each other a long time. I understand it might feel…very weird to try anything."

Aiden's voice was mild. "Are you physically revolted by me?"

"I mean, of course I'm not!" said Harvard.

They'd slept tangled together on hospital seats and lying on the ground camping and in beds, too. They were very physically comfortable together. They always had been. Aiden's touch had always been welcome and natural to him as sunlight.

He was afraid of losing that.

"There you go. I'm cute. You're cute," Aiden said. "So that's not a problem, but if you don't want to, that is a problem. If you don't want to, we shouldn't try this."

Harvard had no idea how to deal with the jolting sensation caused by part of what Aiden had said, so he fastened desperately on to the last sentence.

"I do want to!" Harvard exclaimed.

He lifted his chin and stood up from the bed. Aiden's upward glance seemed like a challenge, familiar from times when Harvard got Aiden to take a match seriously and Aiden's eyes gleamed above their crossed swords. The look was wildly out of context, and seemed far more dangerous, when thrown in their room.

Aiden's voice rasped as he asked, "Are you sure?"

"Yeah," said Harvard. "Come on."

Something flickered in Aiden's gaze. Harvard nodded encouragement at him. *Come on, let's get with the plan.*

"You said nothing should happen in the dorm room, right?"

Aiden answered, "R-right?"

Harvard said recklessly, "So let's leave the room."

18 AIDEN

Harvard had never been kissed. *Was Neil actively deranged?* Aiden wondered. Would Harvard be safe with someone who might at any time progress from inexplicable inaction to delusions that he was a teapot?

He didn't want to think of Neil at this time or any other.

Harvard led the way, down the back stairs of the dormitory and out into the quad of Kings Row. Once they were outside, Aiden took deep breaths of cool night air. He couldn't possibly have agreed to this. He wasn't actually going to try to teach Harvard about dating.

Aiden was clearly in the process of losing his mind. He thought he could actually feel his mind dissolving. The tiny fragments that used to be his mind would float away up into the night sky and get lost among the stars.

The stone pillars that surrounded

them glimmered silver in the gathering dusk. Their school buildings were lost in shadows, but Aiden knew exactly where they were. They had crossed this stretch of lawn hundreds of times.

Aiden had imagined the date to Kingstone Fair in excruciating detail, lived it in a hundred vivid daydreams, but he'd never planned out any date he'd actually had. Who cared?

Only now it was Harvard, so now Aiden cared, and literally all his experience was worse than useless. He couldn't be cold to Harvard or careless or hurt him. If Harvard understood what he was asking for, he would be horrified.

None of Aiden's experience applied to Harvard. He couldn't *do* this.

"I'm not sure...," Harvard began.

"You're so right, this was a terrible idea!" exclaimed Aiden. "Obviously you're overcome with shock. You were panicking. It's fine. Neil is deranged, but that's his problem. He probably thinks he's a teapot. Don't worry. There are a lot of teapots in the sea. I mean, fish. I mean, guys."

Silence reigned under the stars.

"There are a lot of teapots in the sea?" Harvard repeated.

Aiden took a deep breath.

"You can tell me that you've changed your mind. I'm not the guy who could plan a perfect date, but I'm not...I know you haven't done anything like this before, and I wouldn't push. I'm not that guy, either."

He whirled away, intending to escape, but then Harvard

followed him. Harvard was wearing a button-down shirt—one of his uniform shirts, but with jeans. When Harvard wore shirts that buttoned, he buttoned all the way. Harvard committed like that. What Harvard wasn't wearing was the woolen sweater or the blazer that came with the uniform shirt. When he leaned his shoulder against Aiden's, the warmth of his skin spread to Aiden. His shoulder against Aiden's was strong and solid. He was right there, a warm and astonishingly comforting presence. Aiden was enveloped in that strength and comfort.

"Hey," Harvard murmured, running his hand down the line of Aiden's back. Aiden felt every muscle in his body go liquid and his head go dizzy from the release of tension. "I know that. I know you. Calm down."

Aiden leaned his head against Harvard's and breathed. "I'm cool and poised at all times."

Harvard laughed. "Oh sure."

They stayed like that in a perfect silence, in which Aiden could breathe easier than he had in days, until Harvard made a sound that wasn't a snort but was still too close to scoffing for Aiden's taste.

"I haven't changed my mind."

"You can," said Aiden. "Anytime."

"I know that, too. Would you give a guy a minute before you enact a whole dramatic scene?" Harvard grumbled. "Why are you like this? I cannot believe you chose this moment to decide I'm a wounded fawn you hit with your dad's limo."

"My dad let my last stepmother take the limo," Aiden mumbled.

He had calmed down. He should pull away. Aiden knew exactly how to extricate himself from moments like these, had learned from long habit, and he was about to do so in a smooth, practiced maneuver when he became aware Harvard's attitude had shifted.

"We should—" Aiden began, and would have finished with *go back inside*, except his mouth was dry.

"Yeah," murmured Harvard. "You said we should hold hands."

There was a certain set to Harvard's shoulders and tilt to his jaw when he came to a decision and decided nothing would sway him from his course. When this determination gathered during a match, Aiden would always grin, knowing Harvard's opponent was about to be decimated.

He wasn't certain what Harvard's familiar determination would lead to in a moment as strange as this. Aiden held still and waited.

Harvard drew in a deep breath. It seemed as though he were drawing in all the air from the sky.

"If you don't like it," Harvard murmured, "tell me."

He slid his hand from Aiden's back, palm skimming lightly down Aiden's arm, and laced his fingers with Aiden's. They had held hands before many times. When they were little, Harvard and Aiden used to grab hands before crossing the street. They would swing their joined hands as they went, happy to be together, Aiden knowing he was safe with Harvard.

It was different now. They were older. It felt different—to actually twine their fingers together rather than clasp hands. It was such a small thing, this tiny advance of intimacy. Palm to palm, linked together. This didn't feel entirely safe.

"So," Aiden said, slightly breathless.

Harvard squeezed his hand. "Yeah. Well, what next? Do we try going on a date?"

"Yes," said Aiden, trying to sound calm and judicious in his capacity as a teacher of the ways of dating. "I think that would be a good next step."

"Where would you like to go on our date?" Harvard asked.

If he'd asked *What should we do?*, Aiden wouldn't have known how to respond. They shouldn't be doing any of this. But Aiden knew where he would like to go.

It was years late. It wasn't real, but it could finally be the way Aiden had always imagined, since the very first day they saw Kings Row.

"I'd like . . . to go to the fair," Aiden confessed.

Harvard smiled at him, the tiny smile that was just for Aiden, and said, "That sounds really nice."

19 NICHOLAS

In the name of teamwork, Nicholas insisted that he and Seiji must talk when they were going from one class to the other, and that at the end of the school day they should meet and discuss the day's events.

"Nothing has changed in the eighty-seven minutes since I last saw you," Seiji reported on Monday afternoon. "I don't know how anything could have changed significantly in that amount of time. I cannot elaborate on my classes. You wouldn't understand advanced mathematics even if I tried to explain it."

Nicholas nodded happily. "It's good to catch up. Hey, who do you sit with in the classes we don't have together?"

"I sit by myself," replied Seiji. "It is pleasant and restful."

"Cool," said Nicholas. "I sit with Bobby and Dante. We pull up a third desk so we can all be together in an extra-long row. Dante says Bobby and I aren't allowed to talk about fencing for more than eighteen minutes at a stretch."

Seiji squinted. "Dante is such a strange person."

Nicholas privately agreed, but Dante was Bobby's best friend, so Nicholas owed him loyalty.

"Don't think you can call anyone else a weirdo, Seiji."

"Nor can you!" Seiji said sharply.

Nicholas nodded. "Fair."

The hallways were filled with boys hooting and jumping and running around and throwing paper airplanes. One got caught in Seiji's black hair and he halted, a look of affront descending on his face like winter. The thrower of the offending plane retreated hurriedly. Nicholas plucked it out of Seiji's hair and sent the airplane flying after its maker.

Right after the end of classes, Kings Row was always a zoo, but this was more than the normal rush to escape education. People were high-fiving in midair. Kally and Tanner, who Nicholas knew from fencing tryouts, were playing air guitar and singing to each other. Students were shoving into Seiji, who normally projected a force field and stopped strangers from touching him by will alone. Nicholas saw someone leap up and grab the top of the arched doorway leading to the stone steps outside. He was starting to think there was something unusual going on.

Eugene ambled over to them in the middle of the chaos. He was grinning broadly.

"So, are you guys going to Kingstone Fair?" he asked.

"Don't know what you're talking about," said Nicholas.

"I never go places," answered Seiji.

Eugene seemed daunted by this response to his conversational overtures.

"See, the thing is, Eugene, unless you or Bobby or Dante tell us about something, we're not going to know about it," Nicholas explained. "We have no other friends at Kings Row. Nobody talks to me because I'm a vandal with a scholarship, and nobody talks to Seiji because...well, because..."

"Because of my personality," said Seiji.

Nicholas nodded. "Right, because of that."

"Or lack thereof," Seiji added in a brisk, factual tone.

Nicholas raised his eyebrows. "Oh, you've got one," he said. "Don't know that I can describe it, but you've got one."

Eugene slapped Seiji on the back. "Totally, bro."

Seiji endured being slapped on the back, his jaw setting. Another boy whooped and swung around a marble bust of a former principal. Seiji gave him a look, and the boy backed away.

"Kingstone Fair is held in the woods on the other side of Kingstone," Eugene told them, seeming happy to share his lofty experience with the freshmen. "It's every September. Everyone's really excited to go. There's fried dough."

Seiji's interest seemed caught. "This is a popular social event?"

"Yah, bro, obviously. Fried dough!"

Eugene offered Seiji a fist bump over fried dough. Seiji made a fastidious shape with his mouth, and glanced at Nicholas in search of help. Nicholas intervened to accept the fried-dough fist bump.

"So everybody will be at this fair," mused Seiji. "And the school will be deserted. What a perfect opportunity."

"To go to the fair!" Nicholas nodded with enthusiasm. "Let's all go together! As a team."

"I do not intend to go to the fair, Nicholas," said Seiji. "It seems frivolous. I meant it was a perfect opportunity for me to catch up on some of the training I've been missing by having indulgent breakfasts. It's also a perfect opportunity for Eugene to take you away from school so that I can have some peace. As Eugene and I were talking about earlier. Remember, Eugene?"

Seiji's tone was slightly sinister. Eugene's eyes went wide.

Nicholas ignored this in favor of complaining to Seiji. "If you're in the *salle* and I'm in our room, you could still have peace."

"Not enough peace," said Seiji. "You could show up at the *salle* at any time. You often do. I wish you to be entirely off the premises, so I may attain complete peace of mind. Eugene will take you away. *As previously discussed.*"

Nicholas had no objection to going to the fair, but Eugene seemed shaken. Maybe he was afraid of heights? They didn't have to go on the Ferris wheel or anything.

"Whoa, bro," Eugene remarked in hollow tones. "Having peace of mind sounds fun. I wish I had some."

"Uh, Seiji," said Nicholas. "I think you're overlooking one important thing."

Seiji blinked interrogatively.

"If Eugene and I go to the fair together, then we will be rocking at teamwork, as usual"—Nicholas accepted another Eugene fist bump, this one actually intended for him—"and you will suck at it. As usual!"

"Is that so?" Seiji asked, his voice extraordinarily calm.

Eugene made a faint protesting sound.

It seemed as though there was something going on here that Nicholas didn't understand. Nicholas felt grievously injured. He'd become Seiji's friend *first*, but here Seiji was having secrets with Eugene.

On the other hand, Seiji didn't train with Eugene, so that was sort of like Nicholas having a secret with Seiji. And going to the fair with Eugene would be fun, though obviously it would be better if Seiji were there, too.

"Fine, Eugene and I will go to the fair without you."

"Enjoy yourselves," said Seiji. He seemed in a weirdly good mood.

"What're you doing, Seiji?" Eugene was speaking from the corner of his mouth.

"I haven't done anything," said Seiji blandly.

"What are you *going* to do?" Eugene asked in an unnecessarily loud voice. Nicholas wasn't fussy about indoor voices like Aiden, but there were limits. Seiji obviously wouldn't do anything bad. "I'm starting to get that intense feeling of disquiet again, bro! Bros don't let other bros fret. Tell me what . . . Okay, everybody shut up right now."

Seiji frowned, his particular frown of being imperiously disappointed that the world was failing him by making no sense.

"Do you wish for me to tell you something, or do you wish for me to shut up? Your requests strike me as contradictory."

"Shut up!" Eugene hissed. "Some truly momentous gossip is unfolding right before our eyes!"

Nicholas knew Eugene enjoyed gossip. He looked around with interest to see what had caught his attention but saw only boys rioting excitedly over the fair to come.

Then he noticed the captain was here. Nicholas brightened. Harvard and Aiden were walking down the hall together, as they often did, but today they were holding hands.

One of Aiden's fans stopped beside Eugene and clutched his arm. "Is it happening, do you think?" the Bon whispered. "Is it finally happening?"

"I don't know, bro, but I think so, bro!"

Eugene over-bro'ed when he was excited.

Nicholas liked to see the Bons' enthusiasm for fencing but found the specific target of their enthusiasm mysterious.

Aiden wasn't that good a fencer. Why not support Seiji or the captain instead?

Someone gave a piercing whistle as Aiden and Harvard passed by. "Hello, gorgeous! What are you doing later?"

Aiden glanced around without much interest, accepting whistles as his due. Harvard was the one who actually responded to the whistle. His face clouded and he stepped back immediately, moving as though by instinct. His hand fell away from Aiden's grasp.

Then a new idea seemed to strike their captain.

He stepped forward with a purposeful air, linked his fingers with Aiden's, and tugged Aiden to his side. Aiden went easily, leaning close.

Eugene and the Bon made sounds like steaming kettles. Nicholas exchanged a questioning look with Seiji to see if he understood what was happening. Seiji gave him a tiny shake of the head.

Aiden was ignoring the crowd in the way Aiden did, taking for granted that he was being watched. All his attention seemed focused on Harvard.

Enlightenment descended upon Nicholas. "Oh, are Aiden and Harvard *dating* now?"

Harvard glanced again at Aiden, who nodded. Then Harvard nodded, too.

While light had only just dawned for Nicholas, Eugene's eyes were glowing with unholy joy. "I must tell everyone!"

"Wait," said Nicholas. "What about that Neil guy?"

Aiden's green eyes narrowed. "Neil's out," he reported.

"Like, taken out?" Nicholas muttered.

Aiden proceeded: "Harvard made the *excellent* decision to upgrade *blah, blah, blee, bloo* ..."

Aiden's mouth kept moving, but Nicholas had not bought tickets to the Aiden Kane Is So Great Show. He refused to hear.

Harvard was nodding along indulgently. This kind of heroic patience was why Harvard was the captain, Nicholas supposed.

They wandered off toward the open doors, hand in hand, still smiling. The Bon was texting frantically. Nicholas caught a glimpse of many exclamation points and capital letters on the Bon's screen.

"That's good that Aiden and Harvard are dating," Seiji decided.

Everyone exchanged surprised glances that Seiji had an opinion on this matter.

"If the captain is determined to date, and it seems he is, then he should choose someone who has at least some interest in fencing. My parents are a very devoted couple," Seiji explained.

"Are they?" Nicholas felt unexpectedly touched. Seiji's parents were together, and they loved each other.

That must have been nice for Seiji to grow up with.

"I understand that must be a surprise for you all, since you've met me, but my parents aren't much like me," Seiji continued. "They have very dedicated hearts. They say—how did they put it in that magazine feature?—that their personal partnership leads to more effective teamwork between them."

Nicholas frowned. "Wait, and you think they're *not* like you?"

"That's what I said."

"You and your lack of dedication to anything. That makes sense."

Seiji nodded absently.

"I was being sarcastic, Seiji!"

"Were you?" Seiji made a face. "Why?" Before Nicholas could answer, Seiji gestured dismissively. "Never mind that. I can't hang around making small talk all day. I have many things to do. Eugene, please remove Nicholas to the fair, thank you, goodbye."

He walked off, a stern, remote presence among the joyful crowd. A guy hopping on one foot almost crashed into him. On reception of a chilling glance from Seiji, he decided to throw himself upon the floor instead.

Nicholas grinned watching it happen, then turned to Eugene.

"We're going to the fair, then!"

Eugene seemed to be absorbed in a private, horrific vision, but he answered, "Looks like."

"We can go into Kingstone and pick up Seiji's watch, too."

Nicholas thought it would be a fun evening. Before he went to get his blazer, he glanced back at Harvard and Aiden heading out the door.

"I honestly think the captain can do better," Nicholas remarked.

The Bon tried to kick him. Nicholas dodged out of the way and ran laughing down the hall, the doors to Kings Row wide open and the sunlight of late afternoon spilling onto the stone floor.

20 HARVARD

It wasn't a real date, so Harvard shouldn't be nervous.

Somehow, he still was.

Probably, he told himself, he was nervous because this was his last chance at getting this dating thing right. He'd messed up with a girl, then messed up with a boy. From years of mapping out team strategy, Harvard knew how to pinpoint the recurring issue when a situation kept going wrong. Clearly when it came to dating, the problem was Harvard himself. Thank God Aiden had agreed to help him out.

He'd put on a button-down shirt, and then—in a panic—added cuff links. Dad said cuff links made an outfit look sharp, but old people made strange fashion choices. Harvard got worried looking at the cuff links, so he put on his leather jacket, but maybe the shirt and the jacket didn't look right together.

Harvard made intense eye contact with the mirror, willing himself to be more reasonable. This was *Aiden*, who had seen Harvard wearing dinosaur footie pj's. There was no possible way to impress him.

Aiden had called him *cute* yesterday. Obviously, Aiden had only said that to be a supportive friend, but it wouldn't leave Harvard's brain.

The door opened. Harvard started and knocked over the cuff link case.

Aiden was wearing a desperately clinging green cashmere sweater Harvard had never seen before. Harvard felt slightly uncomfortable about Aiden wearing a gift from one of his many pursuers on their date, but it would be outrageous to complain when Aiden was already doing him a huge favor.

"New sweater?" he asked in as neutral a voice as he could.

"Yeah, I just bought it," said Aiden. "For our date?"

Harvard smiled. "You look—" began Harvard. "Um."

Aiden knew how he looked.

"Amazing?" offered Aiden.

See, Aiden knew how good he looked. There was no need for Harvard to mention it.

"That's good, paying attention to what your date wears. Next time you have a date with … Neil, comment on whatever it is he wears," Aiden instructed.

Aiden always paused when he said *Neil*. Harvard guessed that Aiden had to take a minute to remember Neil's name. He appreciated Aiden making the effort. Harvard tried to visualize what Neil generally wore.

"Shirts?"

"You could stand to be a little more specific than that."

Harvard tried to remember the color of Neil's shirts. "Flannel shirts?"

Aiden made a face. "Maybe you shouldn't encourage that behavior."

He shouldn't encourage Aiden when Aiden was being mean and hilarious, so he only raised an eyebrow and repressed a smile. Aiden grinned as though he could tell about the smile Harvard hadn't permitted himself.

"*You* look great," Aiden added.

"Oh. Thanks," said Harvard.

He knew Aiden didn't really mean it, but it felt good to hear anyway. He felt a little less nervous.

Aiden held out his hand, and Harvard grasped it gratefully, linking their fingers together. He'd thought he would get used to holding hands, but every time it felt new and a little scary. At the same time, he didn't want to let go.

Dating had gone wrong for him, but maybe fake dating could go right. He could trust Aiden. He could believe this plan would work out.

Maybe it was because of Aiden's fair outings that fair-going had always seemed to Harvard like mostly a date activity. He'd always stayed home and practiced in the *salle* instead or hung out with Coach and made plans for the team's improvement.

The fair was held on the outskirts of the town, so on one side were the fieldstone walls encircling Kingstone, and on the other the encroaching woods. In the trees, lanterns hung from the boughs, and twinkly lights peeped from behind the golden leaves, creating luminous pools and sweet little gleams of light in the dark. Even the evening sky still had a broad sweep of gold painted over the dark line of the trees, and the fair made one of the brightest nights Harvard had ever seen.

They walked through a line of vendors. At a maple stall, Aiden and Harvard bought fudge. The woman there was obviously charmed by Aiden and gave them many free syrup samples until Harvard's brain felt like it was buzzing mildly inside his skull. At another, they had cider and cider donuts, which didn't help with the skull-buzzing. And at another, they bought freshly made lavender lemonade.

Harvard downed his wild-blueberry pie with a cup of lemonade and thought the fair was really fun so far. He'd been missing out.

They strolled around hand in hand, and it was strange how *not* strange that was, the easy physicality that had always been between them translating effortlessly. It wasn't slightly awkward like with Neil. Harvard supposed that was because they knew each other so well and it wasn't real, so there was no pressure.

To celebrate Kings Row's latest victory, there was a butter sculpture of a man fencing. The butter sword was melting slightly, but Harvard still pointed it out with pride.

"You should come to our next match," he urged Aiden.

"Don't nag, honey," Aiden teased, then said: "Fine, I will. Happy?"

"Yeah," said Harvard. "Very."

A guy working at the fair whistled at Aiden, but then shrugged and said, "Can't blame a guy for trying!" when Harvard raised an eyebrow at him. Aiden truly didn't seem bothered by it, only shaking back his hair, mouth curving.

One of the best things about this arrangement was that now Harvard got to stop guys from admiring Aiden and whisking him away. He was allowed to. For a little while.

They paused by the ring-toss.

"Hey," said Harvard. "Didn't you say you wanted to win a friend for Harvard Paw?"

Aiden hesitated. "I might have."

"Let's try it out," Harvard suggested. "My aunt told me these games are set up so you think you should be throwing a couple inches to the right of where you should really throw. It's an optical illusion our own eyes create for themselves."

The guy working the ring-toss didn't look impressed by this information, but Aiden did a little. In any case, he was smiling at Harvard, and that seemed encouraging.

Harvard threw a green ring, and what his aunt said must have been true, because he won.

He turned around and gave the stuffed giraffe he'd won to a passing child with pigtails. She stared up at Harvard uncertainly. Her mother regarded him with a doubtful gaze. Harvard gave the mother a reassuring smile.

Being reassuring didn't always work—ever since Harvard was eight years old, certain people hadn't found him reassuring, as he was both Black and tall—but in this case it did. The mother might also have noticed her child was now clinging to her giraffe, and it was clear she would scream if parted from her new toy.

"Thank you," the little girl's mother said stiffly.

Harvard said, "No problem."

The mother swept on, the kid waving shyly as they went. Harvard gave her a little wave back. She gave him a big gap-toothed smile and his own grin was pure reflex.

"What?" Harvard asked Aiden, who was watching him with an expression Harvard couldn't read.

Aiden gave a little smile, not meant to charm and thus entirely charming, and shrugged the matter off. "I'm horribly offended and insulted you gave away the first stuffed animal you won on our date. You shouldn't...do anything like that with Neil. You should make it up to me. Win me a bear."

Harvard concentrated, since this time it was important, carefully measuring the difference between actual depth and the perception of depth. Harvard threw, and the yellow plastic ring flew and spun and settled onto the peg.

Harvard looked around for Aiden to ask which stuffed animal

he wanted, and was quietly pleased when he turned and Aiden was right there, taking his hand.

"Well done, baby," Aiden whispered—oh, a dating thing to call somebody. After a surprised moment, Harvard smiled, the taste of lemonade bright in the back of his mouth. That was sweet.

"Wanna pick a bear?"

Aiden's small smile was like the sparkle behind the leaves, hinting and promising at light. "First, show me how to win my own."

"I'll do my best."

He put a hand on the small of Aiden's back and positioned him in the correct stance. Aiden promptly dropped the plastic ring he was holding. Harvard picked up the ring for Aiden, shaking his head. He guided Aiden's arm for the practice throw, leaning in to ask if he could see where it should land. When Aiden glanced back, Harvard smiled at him encouragingly, closing an arm around Aiden's bicep and squeezing in a reassuring fashion.

The ring Aiden threw almost hit the guy behind the stall in the head.

"Wow, that wasn't good," Harvard said. "You're not good at this!"

Aiden gave him an outraged look. Harvard supposed he was partly to blame for not being a skilled teacher, but he still couldn't lie and say the throw had been good. Without honest feedback, how was Aiden supposed to improve?

He picked out a bear about the same size as Harvard Paw, who had an approachable air...for a bear.

"You're bad at this game, but you're still cute," he told Aiden, and gave him the bear. "There, a friend for Harvard Paw at last. What do you want to do next?"

Aiden was hesitating. Harvard was suddenly concerned he'd messed up. Maybe he shouldn't have said that.

Harvard had won the bear and so he'd thought he might be allowed to call Aiden cute; Aiden had said Harvard was cute yesterday, so he'd been thinking...that must be an acceptable thing to say. Surely Harvard hadn't messed up too badly yet. Surely everything was okay.

Aiden tucked his new bear under his arm. He paused for long enough that Harvard worried everything wasn't okay after all, but when he spoke his voice was soft. So Aiden must have only been thinking through his fairground options. "I think it would be nice to go on the Ferris wheel with you."

Harvard wasn't actually crazy about heights, but he wanted Aiden to enjoy himself, so they went and Harvard tried not to focus on the ground. He had good feelings about the ground when they were together, but he became deeply uncomfortable when he and the ground were apart.

It became far easier not to focus on the ground when Aiden said, "You should put your arm around me."

"Sure," said Harvard, thankful for the guidance. He did. "Like this?"

His arm slid easily around Aiden's shoulders, and Aiden's body fell in naturally against his. The lights of the Ferris wheel, gold and blue and crimson, caught and sparkled and spangled in Aiden's long, curling lashes. Aiden turned in toward him, and Harvard mirrored the movement without thinking, chests pressing together.

Aiden murmured, "Just like that. Then I distract you from the heights!"

He was pretty distracting, all right. The fairground beneath them became a background, blurred, like a calm sea of multicolored lights beneath them.

As they departed the Ferris wheel, they ran into someone who was a spot of darkness among the bright lights. Jay was one of Aiden's many exes, if you could describe guys who Aiden saw for one wild never-to-be-repeated night as exes. Some of those guys accepted this with the philosophical attitude that good things were not meant to last. Some of them took it hard.

Harvard had felt bad for Jay at the time. Now that he saw Jay storming toward them with narrowed eyes fixed on Aiden's and Harvard's linked hands and a clear intent to spoil their evening, Harvard felt considerably less bad for him.

"Oh, so that's how it is?" Jay snapped.

"That's how it is," Harvard responded in a level voice.

Jay didn't even glance at him. His eyes were fixed on Aiden, as they usually were, hungry and mad about it.

"I guess this was always gonna happen." Jay's smile was

humorless. "But you wanted to, what's the phrase, sow your oats? Have fun with as many people as you could before you finally put Harvard out of his misery?"

It was such a bizarre misread of the situation that Harvard didn't know what to say. What he couldn't say was that this was a fake date, and Aiden was just doing his romantically inept best friend a favor. He went quiet.

"Thanks for your input, Z!" said Aiden. "Or whatever letter of the alphabet you are. I don't know why you imagine you were so much fun, but can you get lost?"

"Or what?" snapped Jay.

He took a step forward, as though he figured it would make him feel better to fight.

Harvard took a step forward, putting himself in the middle.

"Hey," said Harvard. "Stop it. Aiden never promised you anything. I'm sorry your feelings are hurt. But that doesn't give you the right to lash out at him. You can want him to like you, and be upset that he doesn't. But you don't get to *expect* that he'll like you, and you don't make yourself look like a good guy by making a scene."

Jay's eyes fell from Harvard's, head hanging as he muttered, "You don't understand."

"Sure, I do. I'm sure you think you're a good guy, because you're nice when things are going your way, but you're being awful right now. The time you learn if someone's a loser," said Harvard, "is when you see how they lose."

That made Jay's head jerk back up.

When it did, Jay's smile had twisted in on itself. "And now get lost?"

"Do whatever you want," said Harvard. "I already saw you lose a match. And now I know why you did."

Jay slunk off without another word. A cold drop of water fell on Harvard's nose, and he glanced up. Clouds were twisting above the Ferris wheel and the treetops, tangled like his Mee-mee's dropped knitting.

"Hey, it's starting to rain."

Aiden's voice was mild. "Is it? I guess I didn't notice, what with the radiant heat from the epic burn you just delivered."

Harvard's gaze traveled from the sky to Aiden and stayed there. Aiden didn't look particularly upset, but Harvard felt he should check anyway.

"Was I too mean? I just—I hate it when your guys get demanding. I always have. Just because you're . . . you, it doesn't mean they have a right to act that way. I always wished I could step in when they behaved like that. I'm sorry if I went too far."

"Don't be sorry. You should do it all the time," Aiden urged. "They are trash. Throw them away."

"Wow, buddy, don't, like, give up on love," said Harvard. "There are good ones out there."

A look of extreme irritation crossed Aiden's face, and Harvard was puzzled before he realized he was epically failing at practice dating right now.

He was about to apologize for saying *buddy* when the heavens opened and poured down a deluge onto their heads. The gold lights of the fair blurred with continuous silver.

"Where's your raincoat?" Harvard said, and when Aiden made a face: "*Aiden*."

"Carrying around a stupid bulky raincoat detracts from my air of insouciance!" Aiden protested.

This was why Aiden got colds all the time, Harvard was sure. Harvard got out his raincoat from his backpack and covered both their heads and also Harvard Paw's new friend.

"Does it, you insouciant idiot?" Harvard muttered fondly.

There were people splashing past in the mud and quickly forming puddles, and laughter ringing behind the sound of the drumming rain. Aiden slid his hands under Harvard's leather jacket. "This is romantic," he informed Harvard. "Young couple caught in the rain with only one coat to shield them from the elements!"

"I don't know that I find this romantic. It's happened constantly since we were ten!" Harvard said in severe tones.

"You'd find it romantic if it were Neil!" Aiden paused. "Which is why I'm telling you this. Next time it rains, you can seize your opportunity."

"Next time it rains, I'll probably be worrying you've wandered out somewhere with no raincoat *or jacket*," said Harvard.

Aiden hummed, sounding pleased again, and ran his cold

nose down near Harvard's ear, since he knew Harvard wouldn't push him out into the rain, though Aiden deserved it. Harvard pushed him a little, and then caught his arm so he wouldn't stumble out of cover, and Aiden snickered.

"Yeah, yeah, *you*," said Harvard, and held the raincoat over their heads as they made a run for it to Kings Row, Aiden clutching his new bear and laughing and being absolutely no help whatsoever.

By the time they reached the hall, both were laughing and had got more than a bit wet. Aiden's sweater was clinging far more than it had been before. Harvard couldn't believe Aiden hadn't even worn a jacket today. He hauled him up the back stairs toward their room, footprints leaving a watery trail on the mahogany steps behind them as they went.

At their door, Aiden hesitated. Harvard leaned against the doorframe, looking over Aiden's shoulder at the rainy dark through a mullioned window rather than at Aiden's sweater.

"Was this okay?" Harvard asked. "Was it kind of like your first date, the one at the fair a couple years back? That's why you wanted to go, right?"

Aiden must have liked that guy more than Harvard realized.

"This was like the first date I wanted," Aiden said eventually.

"Oh," said Harvard. "I'm sorry."

First-date guy must have turned out to be a jerk.

Harvard removed his gaze from the window, skipped over

looking at Aiden, and frowned at the floor, miserable at the idea of Aiden being hurt—he'd never seemed as if he could be hurt by any of those guys—when there came a sudden warm interruption to his worries.

"Nothing to be sorry for," Aiden murmured, leaning against Harvard. "I had a really good time."

Oh, Aiden was right there. Oh.

Harvard glanced up, and then found himself unable to look away.

"Me too," he whispered. "What should come next?"

As soon as he spoke, he knew the answer. He hadn't realized what he was saying.

Or had he?

A teasing smile was playing around Aiden's mouth. "What should come next, when you're at someone's door after a date that went well? Come on, Harvard. You know what."

A kiss at the door, after a date. Harvard's first kiss.

Harvard's stomach swooped and curled.

He couldn't tear his gaze away from Aiden's smile.

"That's what that girl wanted. That's what Neil was waiting around on the porch for after every date." Aiden added, "I assume he did."

The idea of Neil was distant and uncomfortable with Aiden this close. Aiden must have caught the flash of unease as it crossed Harvard's face.

"Just so you know, for the future," Aiden told him. "Hey. I, uh, I know this is . . ."

Aiden was speaking very low. Harvard had to lean in nearer just to hear him.

"I know we're talking about your first kiss. You don't have to do anything. Consider me kissed. Or . . ." Aiden paused again. Time drew out for a long moment, as Aiden's teeth drew slowly across his own lower lip. "If you wanted to practice this . . . then I would like to. It's up to you."

Aiden was being so good about this. Harvard felt terrible taking advantage of his kindness.

But Aiden had said he would *like* to.

Consider me kissed.

"No?" asked Aiden.

Harvard whispered, "Yes."

"What was it you said?" Aiden mused. "If you don't like it. You should tell me."

Aiden curled his fingers around the loops of Harvard's jeans and pulled him in a fraction closer. Aiden kissed him. Aiden's mouth was soft. The whole kiss was soft, like a question gently asked.

Then, a little less soft. Harvard liked it.

This was new territory for him. He was in a place between terrified and thrilled, tipping one way and then another as Aiden's kiss deepened and his head spun.

A kiss at the door. That made sense, as a thing to do at the end of the date. It didn't matter that this was *their* door, because it was just for practice. Harvard only had to follow Aiden's lead.

A kiss at the door wasn't exactly *one* kiss, it turned out—any more than rain was only one raindrop. Aiden kissed him and held him pressed up against the doorframe as though Harvard wanted to get away, when Harvard wanted anything but. Harvard slid an arm around Aiden's waist, grasping a soaked handful of Aiden's sweater. Harvard was reliably able to reproduce any fencing move he was shown. He had to be shown only once, and he'd know the rules. But this wasn't fencing, this was kissing, and there were no rules. Aiden's mouth tasted of lavender lemonade, and the warmth of his body was radiating right through his wet clothes. Aiden ran his hands up the lines of Harvard's arms and shoulders. Harvard's hand went to the nape of Aiden's neck, tangling in his hair, pulling so the elastic came loose and the rain-dampened hair fell around their faces. The wet hanks of Aiden's hair got in the way of the kiss, and Aiden pushed them back with a confused murmur of complaint as though he didn't understand what his own hair was.

Harvard pulled back from the lavender-lemonade kisses to murmur, "I love your hair."

"Stop not kissing me," Aiden commanded softly. "Stop it at once."

Harvard kissed Aiden's mouth and his jaw and the cool raindrops running down Aiden's throat as heat ran under Harvard's skin. Aiden made another, different sound, hands falling away from his hair to cup Harvard's face between his wet palms, and smiled, biting at the corner of Harvard's mouth. Harvard made a helpless noise. Aiden half murmured and half moaned in return, sounding both pleased and wounded, and arched in even closer.

That is so sexy, Harvard thought, and froze in horror.

At that precise moment, there came the loud sound of many pairs of footsteps clattering up the stairs. Harvard and Aiden broke apart. Harvard realized that they'd been sliding down against the doorframe, pressed together. They'd almost tumbled onto the floor.

And then what? What had he thought he was doing? Harvard was extremely disappointed in himself.

There was always much discussion of Aiden's...wiles or whatever. Harvard usually tried not to listen, since this was his *best friend*, thank you very much, but sometimes you couldn't help overhearing.

So...good wiles, buddy! Everybody who kissed Aiden felt the same way. Harvard already knew that. He'd known that for years, seen a hundred boys cut off at the knees by Aiden. He'd set them on their feet and given them a pat on the back, and always believed he was different. He was Aiden's best friend. He wasn't going to be like Jay.

Harvard took a deep breath and reminded himself to be different. He nodded thanks, not quite able to speak just yet, then swung open the door so he had space to take a step back.

"Leave it at the door, right?" murmured Aiden.

"Yeah." Harvard's voice scraped in his throat. "Leave it at the door. Right."

They weren't standing far apart, but it seemed as if there was too much distance between them. Harvard tried to think of a way to show that he was grateful, and he wasn't presuming anything like the other guys did. This was *practice*.

"Thanks," he said awkwardly. "I'm sure...I think Neil will like that?"

Aiden nodded, still distant. "He'll like it."

21 NICHOLAS

Eugene and Nicholas stood on the sidewalk outside Needful Bling and stared at Seiji's watch for a long time. The cracked glass face had been replaced by a large, faintly pink plastic dome. The hands were moving, but they were in the shape of mouse ears.

"My God, bro," Eugene said at last.

"Wow," Nicholas murmured.

"Strongly agreed, wow!"

"Works great," said Nicholas, much pleased, and pocketed the watch. "And your cousin's friend did it for free! Now I can buy corn dogs for us at the fair. I feel totally rich."

"I'll buy corn dogs, bro," Eugene said hastily.

"Sweet," said Nicholas.

Everything was going his way today.

"You're actually happy?" Eugene asked. "You're not just being polite?"

239

When they got back from the fair, he'd give Seiji the watch. He was sure Seiji would be thrilled.

Nicholas grinned. "Yeah. Can't wait to see Seiji's face."

"I am picturing Seiji's face as well," Eugene said. "I'm very worried about him in general right now."

"Why?" asked Nicholas.

"No reason!" said Eugene. "Let's go to the fair!"

They arrived at Kingstone Fair a little late, when it was already in full swing. The yellow of the stalls matched the yellow leaves fluttering down from the trees. Nicholas wasn't used to all this nature, but, like most things surrounding Kings Row, he thought it was nice.

When Harvard and Aiden wandered by, still looking happy and hand in hand, it seemed like they were having a nice date.

Aiden's face was far more pleasant now that he was dating Harvard. Nicholas was coming around to the idea. Eugene started forward to intercept them, but Nicholas grabbed Eugene's jacket. Harvard and Aiden were clearly in their own little world right now and should not be disturbed. Nicholas really thought Eugene could employ more tact.

Eugene turned to Nicholas in distress. "If I was concerned that one of my teammates might be a master criminal, the captain would want to know, right?"

"Don't interrupt the captain on his date!" commanded Nicholas, and dragged Eugene away.

Eugene protested faintly, but Nicholas felt Eugene deserved to be dragged. The captain must be left alone to do his romance.

"Eugene, if this is about the shoplifting, I don't do that anymore!" Nicholas snapped once they were safely behind the popcorn vendor.

"That's not it, bro...," Eugene mumbled, but what else could he have meant?

Nicholas shook his head, but he tried to be understanding. Eugene didn't get how the real world worked, so he thought Nicholas shoplifting a few candy bars when he was a little kid made him a thief. Whatever. Nicholas didn't want to spoil the fair. They met up with Eugene's weight-lifting buds, and they all went on the roller coaster together. Nicholas thought it was totally fun, but afterward, Brad threw up fried dough and cotton candy in a nearby trash can.

"Aw, no, bros," murmured Chad. "Our delicate flower."

"He's gotta toughen up," grunted Julian. "You spoil him. I'm only saying it for his own good!"

Nicholas and the bros got Brad water and stood around patting him on the back and commiserating that he must've got a bad corn dog. ("Every time, bro," Eugene whispered in Nicholas's ear. "This happens every time. Brad can't accept he doesn't have the stomach for the fun rides.")

By the time Brad felt better, it'd started to rain. It started off as only a sprinkle, but the sky above the Ferris wheel looked gray and serious. Rain in Kings Row was different from rain in the city, where no matter how much rain fell, the sidewalks only got a wash. Here, the whole fairground would turn to mud, and Seiji got extremely sharp about mud being tracked into the room.

Other Kings Row students had navy raincoats that went with their uniforms, and all across the sparkling fairground, Kings Row boys were producing raincoats to go over their jeans and sweatshirts, transforming them into proper Kings Row students again. Not Nicholas, though. Raincoats were considered an accessory and seemed to Nicholas a wasteful luxury. He held his jacket over his head and ran home, happy enough that the rain had started. He'd enjoyed the festival, but he wanted to go back to Kings Row and show Seiji that he'd gotten his watch fixed.

He found Seiji not in their room or the *salle* but in the common room, sitting at one of the desks and frowning at his essay in the light of a stained-glass green lamp that cast an otherworldly glow on Seiji's face. A raincoat hung on the back of Seiji's chair, and his attitude was one of intense concentration.

"Sorry for interrupting your peace and quiet," said Nicholas.

Seiji didn't appear surprised to see him. "That's all right; I'm done now."

"You're . . . done with peace and quiet now?"

"I assume," said Seiji after a moment's pause. "Since you're here."

Nicholas dismissed Seiji behaving oddly. It happened all the time. He and Seiji found each other hard to understand,

Nicholas was used to it, and Seiji wasn't mysterious in a jerky way like Aiden or Jesse. With pride, he laid the mended watch down on the desk Seiji was working at.

"Just wanted to give you back your watch."

"My watch?" Seiji asked blankly. "What watch?"

"The one I broke?"

"Oh," said Seiji. "I'd forgotten about that."

After all the trouble Nicholas and Eugene had gone through. Nicholas rolled his eyes and pushed the watch across the desk in Seiji's direction.

Seiji considered the watch for a long moment. The lamp on the desk with its green glass shade caught the new plastic surface of the watch, making the plastic look pinker than it had outside. Nicholas felt a brief moment of misgiving. Was the watch ... too pink?

"That's good the watch is working efficiently again," Seiji told him, taking the watch and fastening the band around his wrist. "I'm glad you had the basic consideration to replace what you broke."

Nicholas glowed. "Knew you'd be pleased."

Then he frowned. Seiji's raincoat was hanging on the back of his chair, which Nicholas was leaning against. When Nicholas touched the coat, his hand came away wet.

"Seiji!" said Nicholas. "You weren't in the *salle* the whole time. Where were you? Did you ... try to join us at the fair after all?"

"Of course I didn't!"

He must have. Nicholas thought Seiji definitely looked shifty. He was totally fibbing about something.

"Aw, bro," said Nicholas, trying out Eugene-speak.

"Bro?" Seiji repeated with evident horror.

"No?"

"No," Seiji said with decision.

"Okay, no to bro. Noted," said Nicholas. "Anyway, next year you should come to the fair with us."

That was a nice idea. Being at Kings Row next year, belonging at Kings Row, maybe, more than he did now. By then, Nicholas would be so much better at fencing, and he and Seiji would officially be rivals.

"By next year I will probably have killed you," said Seiji.

Score, Nicholas thought. *That wasn't a no.*

22 AIDEN

Usually when Aiden had trouble sleeping, Harvard would bore him to sleep. That custom had started during their first sleepover as kids, when Aiden was nervous in a new house and worried that if he got something wrong, he wouldn't be invited back to Harvard's. They had put the blanket over their heads, and Harvard had told Aiden the most boring story he could think of, all about Harvard Paw's adventures in the adult world.

"And then Harvard Paw went all the way to the bank," Harvard would whisper. "And then Harvard Paw said, 'I know you don't like politics at the dinner table, dear, but I simply must say...'"

Aiden would always fall asleep quickly when lulled by the sound of that voice.

There was no story tonight, only

silence, and Aiden wakeful through many silent hours of the night.

He had a suspicion Harvard was awake, too. The steady and reassuring noise of Harvard's breathing was missing from the room.

Aiden was very aware of every sound—and every other sensation as well. The sound of sheets, rustling over Harvard as he shifted in the bed next to Aiden's. His warmth next to Aiden's, lying close in the night, when that body had been all over Aiden's at this very door.

What total idiot suggested pushing our beds together? Aiden wondered, then had a vivid and terrible memory of making this suggestion on their first day of the semester.

That night, Aiden slept incredibly badly.

The next day, Aiden woke up with the certain knowledge there were some truths that could not be denied.

He reached out and touched Harvard's shoulder. Harvard came awake almost at once, sitting up and leaning over Aiden with soft eyes and a softer voice.

"Hey, Aiden. You all right? You can't be, if you're awake."

"I don't wish to alarm or distress you," Aiden said in a low but impressive tone. "But I am dying."

"Okay, so it's a bad cold."

Harvard was a fool, but a beautiful fool with gentle hands, so Aiden allowed him to talk nonsense while he laid said hand carefully upon Aiden's brow.

He frowned. "So, I think you're running a fever."

"I may be running a fever now," Aiden said with dignity, "but I will soon be cold *in my grave*. Bury me with my best épée. Make sure my hair looks great and everyone weeps that someone so foxy was taken so young. Don't let Nicholas Cox attend my funeral; he'll only lower the tone, and removing him will leave space for more weeping suitors."

Harvard didn't seem to be paying attention to Aiden's important instructions about his funeral. Instead he was rising, dressing, and preparing to abandon Aiden to his wretched, lonely death.

"I'll tell the nurse," Harvard told him. "You'll feel better soon."

When Aiden was little, he used to get sick constantly. It was a nuisance for his dad and the stepmoms, though they mostly made Aiden go to bed and stay there so he didn't bother anybody with his whining. Except the time the sweet Brazilian singer, the one who had pretended she wanted to adopt him, sat at his bedside and sang to him. That was the only time anybody at home even faked concern.

Aiden used to beg to go to school, even when he was sick, because Harvard would be there, filled with tender concern and bearing juice boxes.

Once he grew up and started going to Kings Row, with Harvard there all the time and much less exposure to slamming doors and the screech of sports car wheels, Aiden got sick far less. He still did occasionally, around the time of important fencing matches or tests. It was always a swift thing, fever running high then vanishing in a day like steam in cold air. It only happened when Aiden was at his most stressed out. Harvard always took good care of him.

Maybe Aiden was stressed now.

Maybe Aiden was consumed by guilt. He should be. He was lying to his best friend in the entire world. He hadn't *exactly* lied, he told himself, but he was aware his behavior wasn't on the up-and-up.

If Harvard knew how Aiden felt about him, Harvard wouldn't want to lead Aiden on. He would never have suggested the practice dating if he had all the information. Getting Harvard to agree to something by withholding vital knowledge from him felt uncomfortably like a lie.

Aiden didn't want to act the way his dad did, lining up stepmother number nine while stepmother number eight waited at home. His dad always laughed and said, "What they don't know won't hurt them." He'd never wanted to be like that. What they didn't know always *did* hurt them eventually.

He'd just wanted…a memory to live on. A few days to remember, when Harvard had been his and not Neil's.

Now he was being punished by fate or his own treacherous immune system. Aiden coughed into the pillow. His mind felt fuzzy, thoughts trying to swim in pudding, all his feelings as oversensitive as the surface of his skin. He didn't want to feel small or helpless ever again. He wanted to make a huge fuss so somebody would tell him it would be all right. He wanted Harvard back at once.

He went back to sleep, having confused dreams in which he was lost and searching, and occasionally was harassed to drink medicine.

He surfaced from fuzzy dreams and hot blankets when he felt relief, and knew it must be Harvard. There was a cold facecloth being dabbed on Aiden's forehead and his flushed cheeks. Aiden made a soft welcoming sound and tilted his head so the cool droplets of water would run down his neck.

"Cease forcing vile concoctions upon me and accept the fact I am doomed."

Harvard sighed. "The nurse was the one giving you cough syrup. She said you had a nasty cold, but you'd be right as rain in no time."

Aiden cracked open one eye. "I did think you looked less attractive than usual," he admitted.

Harvard hit him on the head with a pillow, which was simple brutality to an invalid.

"I'm gonna get you something to eat."

"I can't eat, I'm dying!" Aiden yelled as Harvard shut the door.

Harvard shouted back: "Try!"

Aiden didn't know why Harvard wouldn't just have the decency to accept that Aiden was fated to perish, and hold a nice vigil at his deathbed and not let go of his hand until Aiden passed.

Harvard returned with chicken soup he'd coaxed from one of the dining hall ladies, caramel waffles in a little packet, and tea with honey in it. Then he sat beside Aiden and cajoled him to sit up, half leaning against the pillows, and half leaning against Harvard's chest. Harvard held a glass to Aiden's lips, and the water soothed the hot ache of Aiden's throat. Then Harvard bullied Aiden into eating soup.

Aiden complained, but Harvard was patient. Aiden was privately incredulous that Harvard actually believed that he needed lessons in how to be a good boyfriend.

Harvard was a dating savant: He was a natural. There was no way to teach him anything, and Harvard would soon realize that himself.

He was so good at this, it was sickening, and now Aiden was literally sick.

Harvard also brought gossip, which was deeply interesting and a welcome distraction.

"Apparently...," Harvard said once he'd taken away the dishes and come back, climbing onto the bed and sitting cross-legged in the dip just beside Aiden's bed, where they often sat knee to knee when telling each other the news of the day. "And I heard this from Roy, who heard it from a Bon, who heard it right from Eugene's mouth—a group of masked boys in Kings Row uniforms broke into the Kingstone Bank and stole all the money and the safety deposit boxes. One of the students in school currently has four dozen gold bars in a safe under their bed. Everybody's on high alert!"

This information was so compelling, Aiden almost forgot he was dying so tragically young and attractive. He eased himself up on his pillows.

"Go back outside!" commanded Aiden. "Find Eugene! He's our teammate; he should have brought this gossip directly to us! Discover who these thieves might be!"

Harvard went and returned, but sadly he did not come bearing updated information.

"I found Eugene," he reported. "But he turned a funny color and said, 'Please don't make me say it to *you*, Captain.' He seems more shaken by this than I would've thought."

Aiden moaned with outrage, then started coughing and couldn't stop. He was enraged by his own body, which didn't happen a lot. Usually, Aiden felt he and his body were in this together, making each other look good.

In less than a week, Harvard was going to call on his darling Neil and explain how sorry he was for all his imaginary offenses, and Neil would say that he'd only been put off by Harvard's awful best friend. Then Harvard would realize everything had been Aiden's fault all along, and also Neil would tell Harvard that he missed him, and they would get back together. Aiden would have to pretend he was happy for them.

This was one of a very few, very precious days, like fairy gold turning to dust and leaves as they slipped through his fingers. And Aiden was wasting it by being sick and disgusting.

"Sorry for being gross," Aiden murmured into his pillow.

"Hey, no," said Harvard. "You're still really cute."

Aiden scoffed into the pillow, which turned into more coughing. Harvard patted him on the back.

Harvard was so good at this boyfriend thing it was *ridiculous*. He was screwing up the boyfriend curve for all other boyfriends. That was why Aiden didn't want any of the others.

He felt horrible and unpleasantly hot, and he could only bear this when Harvard was with him. Most of life was generally unfair and unpleasant, but it was all right if Harvard was there.

"Stay with me until I go to sleep," Aiden murmured, willfully forgetting that lunch was over and Harvard should go to class.

For Aiden, Harvard would usually break the rules.

"If you want me to," Harvard murmured back.

Aiden was ill and miserable and unguarded enough to whisper, "I never want anything but you."

"Okay." Harvard laughed quietly, kindly. "I think the cough syrup has made you a little loopy."

Aiden wanted to be angry with Harvard for never understanding, but thank God Harvard didn't. Besides, Aiden never could entirely manage to be angry with him. The emotion wouldn't coalesce in Aiden's chest, always collapsing in on itself and changing into different feelings.

As Aiden slid into sleep, like tumbling beneath a blanket of darkness, he felt an awareness even with his eyes closed that someone was stooping over him, like an intuition of a shadow, and then the soft press of Harvard's lips against Aiden's forehead. More a blessing than a kiss.

He woke up when two teachers knocked on his door and asked if they could search the room. Aiden was interested enough to let them.

"Have you found any information about the gold bars yet?" he asked when they were done searching.

"Oh dear," murmured Mr. Gaudet, their history teacher. "The boy's delirious."

Aiden feared Harvard was bringing him inaccurate gossip since he wasn't actually very good at gossiping. All that believing the best of people got in Harvard's way when it came to getting the real dirt.

Once Aiden had risen from his bed of sickness, he would ascertain the awful, criminal truth.

The vile medicine seemed to be doing its job. His head felt marginally clearer. Aiden now believed he would live.

Before he was restored to his full power, though, he needed more beauty sleep. Aiden had a lot of beauty to maintain.

When he woke up next, it was dark outside. He'd slept and coughed and dreamed the whole day away.

Harvard was sleeping in the bed next to his. Whenever Aiden

was forced to go home, he'd wake up feeling sick with panic in the night. He'd realized years ago that what woke him up was not any noise, but silence. He missed the steady sound of Harvard's breathing. You could ask a friend to sleep over, but you couldn't ask him to sleep over every night. In order to get away from the echoing quiet of his own house, Aiden was willing to go on vacation with practically any guy who offered.

If they were hot and going somewhere cool.

Harvard was having the untroubled sleep of someone who never woke in the night with wild panic caught at the back of his throat, who was never cruel or careless. Someone who never did terrible things to satisfy longings he didn't dare to speak.

The word *tantalizing*, being endlessly tormented by the presence of something so near but always out of reach, came from the name of the king Tantalus. After the king died and went to hell, he was tortured by being forced to stand in water he could never drink, with fruit hanging above his head that he could never eat.

Enough of being tortured.

Aiden wasn't going to make it to the weekend. This had to *end*. Everything ended; everyone went away, if you tried for love. Friendship was safe. Aiden had thought this would make him feel better, to practice and pretend, but it only made him feel worse. Like having the taste of fruit lingering ghostly and sweet in your mouth, all the while knowing you could never eat.

Aiden's throat ached, as it had earlier, but he didn't want water.

He turned sharply away from Harvard, tossing under the bedsheets and trying to find a cool, soft place in bed. Somewhere he could rest.

Turning his back on Harvard didn't work. Harvard stirred because of Aiden's incautious movement and reached out. When Aiden felt Harvard's hand gentle on his arm, he went still.

"Aiden?" Harvard whispered drowsily.

Aiden turned back to face him and said, "Yes."

Harvard's eyes were still closed, but his grip on Aiden, while gentle, was firm. Aiden didn't want to get away, and never had. Moonlight made the contrast between Harvard's skin and the sheets deeper, and caught at the gleam of white teeth as he spoke.

"'S all right," Harvard murmured.

His mouth barely moved as he said the words, shaped for gentleness, for soothing and sweet long kisses that made the world seem different. Not like Aiden's own mouth, made for curling and cruelty, for wicked kisses and worse lies.

"It's not all right," Aiden told him, his voice clear as a confession in the dark. "*I'm* not all right."

He had to stop this. And, he vowed, he would. He would give himself just one more day. Just one more day, to live on for the rest of Aiden's life. Then he'd tell Harvard they should stop.

23 NICHOLAS

That morning Nicholas woke up to an undeniably startling sight. Seiji's face was hovering over him, pale and intent, like a vampire who came in the too-early morning rather than the night and made you do fencing drills rather than drink your blood. Nicholas flailed and made an incoherent sound of protest at the fencing vampire.

"Wake up, Nicholas," said Seiji, poking him.

"It's not even dawn!" Nicholas objected.

"It is ten minutes before the time you usually rise," Seiji corrected. "And you could use those ten minutes to present a more appropriate and put-together appearance to the world."

"'S inhumane," Nicholas told him, hiding under his blanket.

Seiji stripped it efficiently off him.

"Come now, Nicholas, I require your presence. I will be waiting on the other side of the curtain."

Curiosity killed the cat, *and* it even got Nicholas Cox out of bed early in the morning. Nicholas climbed out from under the covers and into his clothes, though since Seiji had made a crack about his appearance, Nicholas made sure his tie was even more haphazard than usual.

When he stepped out from behind the curtain, Seiji's face went dark with surprised disapproval. It was possible that Nicholas literally throwing his tie over his shoulder had been a step too far.

"I was thinking," Nicholas offered. "Now that we're friends, maybe we don't need the curtain at all? I could take it down."

Seiji clung to the curtain as if it was a security blanket and he was a big baby. "I need the curtain."

"You need me," said Nicholas.

Seiji blinked. "What?"

"You require my presence?" Nicholas reminded him. "You said so five minutes ago, on the other side of the curtain. What do you require my presence for? Is this about fencing?"

"Oddly," said Seiji, "no. I want you to come sit at breakfast with me."

"But we eat breakfast together every day?" Nicholas pointed out.

"It's very strange you characterize something that only started last week as a regular appointment," Seiji said. "In any case, I wish for you to accompany me to Eugene's weight-lifting acquaintances table."

Nicholas raised both eyebrows. He would've liked to raise just one eyebrow, to be cool and sardonic, but whenever he tried, he just ended up raising both. "I'd *characterize* them as his weight-lifting bros. Why do you want me to do that?"

Seiji gave him a measuring look. The curtain fluttered in the breeze from the window that Seiji insisted on opening every day, for fresh air. Yellow ducks rippled on the blue surface, as though they were escaping downriver.

"I wish to speak with Eugene on an urgent matter, but I don't find the weight-lifting bros to be congenial company. You must not let any of them fist-bump me," said Seiji. "Warn me if they make any sudden movements. Chad hits me on the back."

"Slaps you on the back?" Nicholas asked. "So do you mean, like, he likes you?"

"I don't like it!" Seiji exclaimed. "Will you come or not?"

Nicholas didn't understand why Seiji was resisting popularity. Nicholas thought it would be awesome to have lots of people admire you, but apparently it stressed out Seiji.

"I will come with you and protect you from the bros' friendship," Nicholas promised. "I will be your social bodyguard."

Social secretaries organized people's social appointments, and Nicholas figured social bodyguards prevented people from having them.

After a moment's consideration of this proposition, Seiji nodded. As they walked together down the halls and the back staircase, Nicholas studied the ceiling, which was all white with twirly bits like a wedding cake. He had a troubling thought.

"You hate fist bumps?" he asked. "But you've fist-bumped me and Eugene."

"I don't mind if it's you," said Seiji. "And I don't mind *much* if it's Eugene. But not Chad!"

"Okay, not Chad," Nicholas soothed, and grinned at the back of Seiji's head as they entered the dining hall. Seiji was wearing his mended watch again today, Nicholas couldn't help but notice.

He mouthed an apology to Bobby as they passed their table, pointing to Seiji. Dante eyed Seiji and made shooing "take him far away" gestures.

Dante didn't seem to enjoy Seiji's company. Nicholas wasn't sure why.

The weight lifters' table was easy to spot since their combined muscles almost formed a landmass.

Chad was the first to see them coming. "My man! Up top!"

He lifted a meat hook. Alarm unfurled but didn't get a chance to blossom on Seiji's face. Nicholas swept in between them to deliver the high five in Seiji's stead.

"Yo, Chad!" he said, and sat down firmly between them. Seiji slid quietly onto the bench at Nicholas's side.

"Hello, Eugene," Seiji said in a voice that was cool, distant, and relieved to be separated from Chad.

Eugene jumped convulsively, and then landed with a heavy thump, like an electrified rhinoceros.

"Oh my God, what?"

"Just wanted to say good morning," said Seiji.

"Good morning, bro," Eugene muttered into his plateful of eggs.

"Morning, dude!" said Chad.

"Morning," Nicholas chorused, since everybody was doing it.

"Let's make casual conversation at the breakfast table," continued Seiji, while Eugene squirmed as if Seiji had said *Let's make a bomb*. "I heard a rumor."

Eugene dropped his fork.

Nicholas loyally tried to participate in the conversation. "Where'd you hear the rumor?"

Seiji frowned at him, which Nicholas found unfair. Nicholas was only trying to help. "From one of my other social acquaintances!"

"Uh," said Nicholas. "Okay."

Seiji nodded with decision. "Here's the rumor. I heard a large amount of watches went missing from Weirs Fine Jewelers in Kingstone."

Eugene reached for his protein shake and missed.

His voice squeaked as he asked: "How—how many watches would you say went missing?"

"I'm glad you asked! A very large amount of watches," Seiji replied promptly. "Practically all the watches in the store. Isn't that interesting?"

"Is it?" asked Eugene, but Chad and Julian were already nodding.

"Totally wild, bro," said Chad, grinning widely.

"But there's more!" announced Seiji, unlikely fount of gossip. "I heard two boys in particular were seen in Weirs just before the watches went missing."

"Oh my God," said Nicholas. "Me and Eugene were totally in there a few days ago!"

"*Bro*," Eugene exclaimed. "There is no need to make this *worse*!"

Seiji gave Nicholas a look of disappointment. "I do not see why you feel the need to make yourself a suspect."

"Well, Eugene and I obviously didn't steal a huge pile of watches," said Nicholas. "Who does that?"

Eugene moaned. "Who *does* do that?"

"Perhaps it is merely a rumor," said Seiji, and Eugene sagged with relief. He seemed really wound up about these watches. "But perhaps it's true," Seiji continued. "I heard the two students in question were left alone in the store by clerks fetching them trinkets from the back room. They were pretending that one of them was buying their father a birthday present. I heard a rumor they might have stashed their ill-gotten goods in their very own room, right here at Kings Row, and some concerned citizen spotted them doing it."

Nicholas was shocked and thrilled by this tale of larceny. Why would anyone in Kings Row steal stuff? They were all super rich.

On the other hand, he'd seen rich people do dumb things for kicks before. Back in the city, kids would total the shiny cars their parents bought for them, or total someone else's car. Some rich kids seemed to have a hard time understanding that the whole world didn't belong to them, and they wanted to break the world as if that would prove their ownership.

"The concerned citizen should report these guys," Nicholas muttered.

"Maybe he will in time," murmured Seiji. "Or someone else will. Rumor has it, people are keeping their eyes peeled for any signs of these miscreants' hoard. Didn't you hear this rumor?"

He bent a coolly inquiring gaze on Eugene, who squirmed like a distressed salmon on a riverbank.

"I did," Eugene gasped. "I think I did."

"Oh, I get it," murmured Nicholas, as everything became clear. That was why Eugene had been babbling about master criminals at the fair.

He supposed Eugene was distressed because he was worried about the crime reflecting on the honor of their school or something. He reached over the table and gave Eugene a reassuring pat on the arm. There were bad apples in every bunch. It wasn't as if the master criminal was *actually* on their fencing team.

"You've been spreading the rumor all around school, in that way you do, right Eugene?" asked Seiji. "Or I expect you soon will."

"I guess . . . I guess I will," Eugene said weakly.

"I'm gonna tell everyone," volunteered Chad with enthusiasm.

"Good work, Chad," said Seiji. "Teamwork will catch these desperate criminals."

Chad tried to reach around Nicholas to give Seiji a pat on the back. Nicholas jostled Chad, to little effect, and Seiji almost fell off the bench trying to avoid the back pat.

"Wow, what criminals?" asked one of the Bons, stopping by Eugene's seat.

The Bon was carrying a fruit basket with a card that read *Get Well Soon, Aiden!* on it in glitter. Nicholas hadn't known Aiden was under the weather. He hoped he felt better soon. Aiden wasn't Nicholas's favorite person or anything, but he *was* one of Nicholas's teammates. That was more important than anything else.

Seiji caught Eugene's eye across the table.

"Well!" Eugene pulled himself together with effort. "Uh, yes! Rumor has it there was an awful crime committed in Kingstone. At that jewelry store, you know the one?"

The Bon was agog. "I bought Aiden a pin there once as a token of my admiration!"

"Okay, bro, you do you!" said Eugene. "Anyway, a couple of Kings Row dudes were in there asking to see trays and trays of stuff, and once they were gone it was discovered practically all the watches in the store were gone, too."

"No!" breathed the Bon, sounding delighted to be scandalized.

"And I heard from a very reliable source these guys have hidden their stash in their room. Keep your eyes peeled!"

"*Who* are these guys?" asked the Bon.

"Maybe I shouldn't name names . . . ," Eugene said uneasily.

"Maybe you should," suggested Seiji. "After lunch."

Eugene had seemed to enjoy telling his tale of mystery and secret treasure, but when the Bon had scurried off to share their dark knowledge, Eugene sagged against Julian.

Julian patted him on the back, which could have bruised his ribs, but Eugene seemed to take comfort from the gesture.

Nicholas wondered what these dastardly watch thieves might look like. Those watches in Weirs had looked really fancy. This thief could potentially have stolen watches collectively worth hundreds of dollars. He stood up from his bench, scanning the crowded room. Nobody was eating in a way that struck Nicholas as especially criminal.

"Sit down and eat your breakfast," instructed Seiji.

"It's hard to eat when there could be a master criminal eating breakfast with us!"

Eugene choked.

"I guess they can't be master criminals if they've practically already been discovered, can they?" Nicholas continued. "Master criminals are never discovered."

"That seems true," Seiji murmured.

Eugene leaned against Julian's shoulder, as though he feared he might swoon.

Nicholas ignored Eugene's delicate sensibilities in order to focus on Seiji's plate. Seiji's breakfast remained disappointing.

"Next time you should get some more bacon. I'll eat it if you don't want it."

"I don't eat more than a single slice of bacon and you shouldn't, either," Seiji told him. "Excessive bacon will make your arteries clog and slow your progress on the *piste*. Your extraordinary speed is the only thing you have going for you."

Nicholas preened. "Oh, my *extraordinary* speed, is it?"

"Shut up," said Seiji.

"Quit gushing over me, 'm getting all bashful," said Nicholas.

He tried to steal Chad's bacon, but Chad shook his head. "Bro, no. I like you, but I'm still growing."

Nicholas had to be content with his own bacon. At this rate, he might starve at the weight lifters' table.

All around them, floating up to the ears of the painted dude with whiskers and a (probably not stolen) watch chain on the wall, the whispers of Kings Row rose.

By nightfall, the whole school was buzzing with reports of a hidden cache of stolen goods. Eugene seemed on the verge of nervous collapse. Seiji had the faintly smug look of the cat who got the canary and maybe a fencing trophy.

Nicholas was starting to suspect that something weird might be going on.

24 AIDEN

The next morning, despite the fact he was still weak, Aiden permitted Harvard to drag him out of bed and even suggested that they should sit with the rest of the fencing team. This was partly to make Harvard smile, and partly because Aiden was eager to get the lowdown.

"Good news, freshmen, we're gracing you with our presence," Aiden announced, dumping his tray on the table surrounded by fencers and two unfortunates who had apparently given up on life and decided to be Nicholas Cox's friends.

"Lucky," murmured one of the Bens—or was it Bins? Bons? Ben seemed more likely—passing by the table and casting Aiden a look of yearning.

Aiden gave the Ben a little wave so he would go off happy.

A tall junior named Petrarch or Boccaccio or something like that sighed: "More fencers."

"I'm like fine art, Rossetti," Aiden told the junior. "No need to comment on me. Just admire."

A muscle-bound individual lumbered by, stopping to say "My man!" and hit Seiji hard on the back. Seiji made the face of someone who'd just bitten down on his spoon. Aiden and Harvard tried not to smile. Harvard hid his grin better, because he was the kind one.

"A surprise before breakfast," observed Aiden. "You know people not on the fencing team, Seiji? And these people are willing to acknowledge you in public?"

Seiji shrugged.

Nicholas bristled in Seiji's defense. "Seiji's extremely popular," he claimed.

"I assume you're making some sort of joke," said Aiden. "Anyway! Who would like to talk to me about the crime spree in Kings Row?"

Eugene made a sound suggesting the moans of the damned. There was a gray tone to his typically golden skin and circles under his usually twinkling eyes, as though he hadn't slept. Aiden eyed him with sudden wild suspicion. Could Eugene Labao be the master criminal, the news of whose exploits were ringing through Kings Row?

"I think Eugene would like to spread a rumor about these notorious crimes," Seiji announced.

Eugene began to explain the full story about Kings Row students dropping in on Weirs Fine Jewelers and smuggling a huge array of watches, and the report that some concerned citizen had seen the criminals hiding their stash in their own room, in a weary voice.

Aiden had never seen Eugene more dispirited about spreading gossip. Aiden was also personally disappointed there were no gold bars.

"It's definitely watches. I have no idea where people came up with gold bars." Eugene made a helpless gesture. "Rumors get so out of hand."

"So these people are hiding stolen goods in their room?" asked Aiden. "Uh, devilish cunning, I *don't* think. The reputation of these people as master criminals may be somewhat exaggerated, that's all I'm saying."

Harvard nodded. "I'd hide the stolen goods in someone else's room." Eugene started, and Harvard frowned. "If I were a master criminal, which I'm not. It's hard to believe anyone at Kings Row would do anything this awful."

Eugene gave a strange bubbling laugh. "I know, right?"

Aiden decided that Eugene couldn't be the master criminal. The guy choked during fencing matches and appeared to be having a nervous breakdown right now for no reason. Master criminals needed nerves of steel.

The entire dining hall was buzzing with whispered tales of criminal exploits. Only Seiji, sitting across the table and instructing Nicholas on nutrition, seemed wholly unconcerned.

"If someone saw the cache of stolen goods," Aiden said, leaning across the table, "then someone knows who these people are.

Everybody's room has been searched! Why has the stash not been discovered? Did they move the stolen goods?"

"Not everyone's room has been searched yet," Seiji said in disapproving tones. "I don't know why."

"Some of the guys with rich dads and lousy tempers must have made it clear they'd put up a stink about being searched," Polidori commented.

The little sparkly junior looked impressed by his friend's intelligence. The tall junior didn't talk a lot, but he wasn't stupid. Aiden appreciated this.

"That is very wrong, Dante," Seiji announced flatly.

"Wow," said Aiden at the same time. "*I* have a rich dad and a lousy temper. Why didn't I think of forbidding them to search *my* room?"

There were two types of people in the world, Aiden guessed.

"I wouldn't let you do that," Harvard told Aiden. "And you're not as nasty as you like to think."

He reached for Aiden's hand, which was swinging by the side of Aiden's chair in a convenient location for Harvard to grab in case Harvard might want to. Harvard not only laced their fingers together, but also brought Aiden's hand to his lips and kissed the back. Then he let their joined hands rest on the lapel of his uniform blazer, against the golden crown over crossed swords of his captain's pin . . . and his heart. Harvard did it all absentmindedly, as though he didn't have to think about his actions because it came so naturally.

Aiden lifted a coffee cup to his lips purely in order to make a *Can you believe this?* face behind it.

There went Harvard again, raising the ideal boyfriend bar to the sky. Could the man not be stopped?

"Aw, are you having faith in me, sweetheart?" Aiden murmured. "That's so nice. And so misplaced."

Harvard murmured, a lovely little sound, patently unconvinced. *This is the last time*, Aiden thought, and held on.

The others ignored Aiden and Harvard's romantic moment in order to focus on crime.

Seiji's eyebrows looked as though they had been drawn on with a fat black marker and a ruler. "Why should the rules not apply to some students? People shouldn't use their privileges in order to escape punishment."

Apparently, Seiji had been too preoccupied with fencing to notice all the rules of the society he lived in up until now.

"Wow," Aiden remarked. "It's almost as if this cruelly unjust world is set up in such a way to favor those who already got lucky with riches, good looks, or, not to point fingers at myself, both."

Seiji frowned. "That's exactly what it's like. Well put, Aiden. In any case, it must be stopped."

Aiden blinked. "Capitalism must be stopped?"

Seiji nodded, his face even sterner than usual. "I have an idea."

"Oh Jesus, bro!" exclaimed Eugene, and banged his own forehead against the table. When he righted himself, there was a red mark on his brow.

Aiden sympathized to a certain extent. Seiji Katayama was a lot to deal with. However, Eugene was the one who chose to hang around Seiji, which nobody could possibly enjoy, except for Nicholas Cox, who was obviously mentally deranged. Eugene could deal with the misery thereof.

"How sad life must be for anyone who's not rich and hot," Aiden murmured. "Personally, I wouldn't know. Nicholas, tell me how it feels. Not now, some time when I'm in the mood to hear a sob story."

"What?" said Nicholas.

Aiden shrugged. "The wealthy and unkind only see the poor as entertainment."

"No, like, what are you saying, dude?" asked Nicholas. "I have problems focusing when you talk."

Nicholas didn't catch Seiji's faint smirk, but Aiden did. So did Eugene, who fixed Seiji with a betrayed stare.

Eugene was acting as if he knew who the real thief was. Actually, with the way Eugene was twitching and eyeing him, Eugene was acting as though *Seiji Katayama* was the true criminal. Though that would be a hilarious twist, Aiden couldn't imagine Seiji actually doing anything illegal.

He glanced around the table to see if this behavior was exciting anyone else's suspicions. Harvard was looking sympathetically at Eugene, because of his beautiful heart. Nicholas was staring around vacantly, because he was a simpleton.

Aiden felt he *could* figure out the riddle, but this was his last day with Harvard, and he refused to waste it on the freshmen. If the mystery was still ongoing tomorrow, Aiden would unravel it. He guessed after he'd finished the process of crushing his own heart to powder, he could become a cynical, world-weary, impossibly attractive detective.

Aiden brightened. Finally, an upside to this whole horrifying business.

"Here's my idea," proposed Seiji. "I will report the names to the authorities."

Nicholas's brow knitted. "Do you *know* the names? Why haven't you told me?"

"Bro, don't tell the cops!" Eugene exclaimed.

Seiji ignored Nicholas in favor of Eugene. "I meant I would report the names to the school authorities, not the legal authorities."

"I don't think you should report to anyone!" snapped Eugene. "Oh wow, I wish this wasn't happening to me. But since it is, here's the thing about gossip: The more gossip people hear about something, the more it starts to sound like fact. Once the gossip is started, bro, all you have to do is wait. Other people will do the rest. By tomorrow, someone else is gonna report seeing those guys hiding the watches. Bet on it."

Matters were truly sad for the freshmen when they were looking to Eugene Labao for wisdom and guidance.

On the other hand, it wasn't as if Aiden were planning to provide any.

"But they won't have seen the guys hiding the watches," said Seiji.

"They'll have heard about it so much, they'll feel like they did," promised Eugene.

"So, eventually, someone who hasn't seen the stash will believe they *did* see it, because they've heard about other people seeing the stash often enough?" Seiji's nose wrinkled judgmentally. "Then they will report it? That makes no sense."

Eugene shrugged. "Don't know what to tell you, bro. That's how gossip works."

Seiji seemed to accept his words. "I will leave this matter in your expert hands, Eugene. That's what teamwork is about. I look forward to seeing results."

Horror visibly descended on Eugene, just as the bell rang for the start of classes and everybody rose from the breakfast table. Only Aiden noticed that Eugene was in the grip of a nameless dread. Eugene looked up to find Aiden's amused gaze upon him.

Eugene mouthed *Help me, bro.* Aiden gave him a little shrug, a little smile, and a little wave. Then he waltzed off and left Eugene to his fate.

Classes were tedious, as usual, but Aiden was cheered by the fact that Harvard stopped in after each one to check up on him. When in class, Aiden amused himself by contributing to the gossip about gold bars and stolen watches. He noticed there were two students in his and Harvard's grade who were starting to wilt under intense collective looks of suspicion. He'd always thought those boys were worms and felt this pair deserved whatever the inexorable wrath of Seiji Katayama—aided by master of whispers Eugene Labao—had in store for them, then decided to forget all about it. He headed to his and Harvard's room for their last night.

There wouldn't ever be another night. He wanted to make the most of this one. If Harvard wanted to, as well. After the kiss on fair night, Aiden thought Harvard might be open to taking things a little further.

He wouldn't go too far. Just as much as Harvard wanted and no more.

The sun was low in the sky, spilling across the floor and half across their beds, like a gold sheet turned down and ready for someone to climb in. Aiden stretched out across the beds and waited for the door to open.

"Hey," said Harvard when it did. "Were you okay being in class today? Are you feeling sick again?"

"I'm glad you're back," Aiden told him. "I'm feeling all better."

Harvard's brow was furrowed in concern as he put down his bag, shrugging off his jacket and loosening his tie. "That's why you're lying down at five thirty in the afternoon?"

"Mmm."

It was a noncommittal, but calculated sound. Aiden made another, a long, drawn-out sigh as he lifted his arms over his head. His uniform shirt was already mostly unbuttoned, rumpled enough so that it might be accidental. He saw that Harvard noticed.

Then Harvard looked out the window. "The rules said this stops at the door of our room."

"I was thinking," said Aiden. "It's time to break the rules."

Harvard glanced back at him, almost involuntarily, then out the window again. "Why?"

He sounded as if he wanted to be convinced.

"It's time for a lesson progression," Aiden informed him. "At first, dating is going out places together. But there comes the time when you stay in...*together*. What do you do on the first night he asks you to watch a movie at his place?"

Harvard swallowed, looking almost helpless.

"Uh, what do I do?"

"Say yes, for a start," murmured Aiden. "Come over here."

"We've watched movies together, like, a million times," Harvard pointed out. "Is it that different?"

"Come over here and find out." Aiden hesitated. "If you want to."

He watched Harvard carefully for any sign of reluctance, telling himself that if he saw even a trace, he'd stop. He'd stop right now; he'd tell Harvard it was done.

Harvard nodded, bit his lip, and smiled. Shy, but eager.

Aiden had seen this expression on boys' faces a thousand times, but never on Harvard, so it was like seeing that look for the first time. Like seeing a sunrise for the first time after learning the word *sun*, wonder given bright new meaning.

Harvard put on one of their favorite movies and came over

to the bed. Aiden felt the give of the mattress under his body as Harvard crawled over to be next to him.

Initially, it wasn't that different. They *had* watched movies together a million times before. Aiden had always possessed a buzzing, constant awareness of Harvard, where Harvard was in relation to him, where they were touching and where they weren't.

The awareness was magnified; now Aiden could hope it was—to some degree—mutual.

They laughed and joked through the opening credits and romance in the sunset, then watched with more focus as a Spaniard and a masked man in black had a duel on the edge of a cliff. Then the Spaniard revealed that he wasn't actually left-handed. He switched his sword to his right hand and swung into the fight with renewed vigor. The duel at the cliff's edge recommenced, steel swinging and slicing bright in the sun's rays.

Harvard pointed. "You know, right there is when the stuntman catches the sword out of frame."

"I know."

Aiden did know. Harvard always told him this fact at this precise moment. Aiden had watched this movie without Harvard once—on a date. Seeing the sword fly without the familiar murmur had upset Aiden enough to turn off the movie.

Tonight, Harvard was here with him. They were both lying on their stomachs with their legs kicked up and their hands cupped in their chins, as though they were six years old.

They weren't.

Aiden tangled their legs together slightly, deliberately. It felt far more dangerous than crossing swords. Aiden couldn't imagine a match with so much at stake.

"During a date when you stay in," Aiden said, teaching, "you should try to see if the other person is receptive to you getting closer."

Harvard gave Aiden a look out of the corner of his eye, and let their legs stay tangled, resting with light pressure against one another. Love was a delusion, nothing but an electrical impulse in the brain, but there were many impulses running electric under Aiden's skin right now.

The man in black smiled beneath his mask and switched his sword to his right hand. The clash of swords rang over the sound of the sea.

Aiden sneaked another look at Harvard, the shine of his dark eyes and white teeth in the silvery glow from the screen. Harvard caught him looking, but he returned Aiden's look with a look of his own, warmly affectionate and never suspicious at all. Harvard never suspected a thing.

Because Aiden was his best friend, and Harvard trusted him. And Harvard *could* trust him. Aiden would never do anything to hurt Harvard, not anything at all.

Aiden moved in still closer, his arm set against Harvard's, solid muscle under the thin material of his shirtsleeve. He could put his arm around Harvard's shoulders or slip an arm around his waist or lean in. He was allowed, just for tonight.

"Why are you smiling?" Harvard asked, teasing.

"Because I know something you don't know," Aiden teased back.

Harvard raised an eyebrow. "And what is that?"

"You're *really* cute," murmured Aiden, and leaned in.

His lean was arrested when Harvard laughed. "Ha! That's such a line. These things really work on your guys?"

Overcome by the magnitude of this insult, Aiden snapped, "Invariably!"

Harvard rolled his eyes. "I hate to tell you this, buddy, but I think they're letting you get away with substandard lines because *you're* cute."

Aiden paused, torn between being deeply offended and ridiculously flattered.

Harvard bit his lip, seeming to think this over.

"I guess if you guys both know you're just playing around, what you say doesn't really count," he offered. "That's why people call them lines, like the things you say in a play. I know this isn't real, but..."

Aiden tried to keep his voice soft, to be understanding. "But it's practice for being real." His mouth twisted on the name, but he forced it out. "For Neil."

Harvard winced. Aiden supposed it might feel a little weird, to hear the name of the boy he actually liked, while tangled up with another. For Harvard, who was so good, it might feel close to cheating.

Aiden didn't want to say the name or hear it or think it. Harvard seemed to be struggling with a thought, and Aiden waited to hear Harvard tell him what he wanted. That was all Aiden wished to know or to do. What Harvard wanted.

"Have you ever...liked anyone for real?" Harvard asked in a voice that started low and sank with every word, until it almost disappeared on the word *real*.

Aiden didn't trust himself to speak, so he only nodded.

"What did you say to him?"

"I never said anything to him," Aiden answered slowly. "But there were things I wanted to say."

"Like what?" murmured Harvard, then shut his eyes, lashes black silk fans against his cheekbones. "You don't have to say. Not if it hurts. You don't have to."

It hurt, but this would be Aiden's only chance to say all the things he wanted to say. He wouldn't get another.

Life always hurt, but Harvard was the only one who could ever make it feel better.

Aiden leaned in toward Harvard as close as he could get, so close that every breath was like a storm in the tiny space between them. The blood beneath his skin seemed like thunder, every faint electric impulse turned to dangerous lightning, and every whisper to a desperate shout.

Aiden whispered: "Listen."

25 HARVARD

Aiden was very close, and it was very distracting. His shirt was off in all the ways it could be off while still being nominally on. At least if the shirt had been entirely off, it could've been normal, part of the everyday routine of getting dressed and undressed in the dormitory. Instead of this deliberate gesture toward nakedness. Half of Aiden's hair had come loose and was floating in the narrow space between them, the silky ends brushing Harvard's cheek. Harvard was having difficulty breathing.

But Aiden had asked him to listen, and Harvard always tried to do whatever Aiden asked of him. Harvard swallowed, and made an encouraging noise.

"I don't believe in love that never ends," said Aiden, his whisper clear and distinct. "I don't believe in being true until death or finding the other half of your soul."

Harvard raised an eyebrow but didn't comment. Privately, he considered that it might be good that Aiden hadn't delivered this speech to this guy he apparently liked so much—whom Aiden had never even *mentioned* to his best friend before now. This speech was not romantic.

Once again, Harvard had to wonder if what he'd been assuming was Aiden's romantic prowess had actually been many guys letting Aiden get away with murder because he was awfully cute.

But Aiden sounded upset, and that spoke to an instinct in Harvard natural as breath. He put his arm around Aiden, and drew his best friend close against him, warm skin and soft hair and barely there shirt and all, and tried to make a sound that was more soothing than fraught.

"I don't believe in songs or promises. I don't believe in hearts or flowers or lightning strikes." Aiden snatched a breath as though it was his last before drowning. "I never believed in anything but you."

"Aiden," said Harvard, bewildered and on the verge of distress. He felt as if there was something he wasn't getting here.

Even more urgently, he felt he should cut off Aiden. It had been a mistake to ask. This wasn't meant for Harvard, but for someone else, and worse than anything, there was pain in Aiden's voice. That must be stopped now.

Aiden kissed him, startling and fierce, and said against Harvard's mouth, "Shut *up*. Let me . . . let me."

Harvard nodded involuntarily, because of the way Aiden had asked, unable to deny Aiden even things Harvard should refuse to give. Aiden's warm breath was running down into the small shivery space between the fabric of Harvard's shirt and his skin. It was panic-inducing, feeling all the impulses of Harvard's body and his heart like wires that were not only crossed but also impossibly tangled. Disentangling them felt potentially deadly. Everything inside him was in electric knots.

"I'll let you do anything you want," Harvard told him, "but don't—don't—"

Hurt yourself. Seeing Aiden sad was unbearable. Harvard didn't know what to do to fix it.

The kiss had turned the air between them into dry grass or kindling, a space where there might be smoke or fire at any moment. Aiden was focused on toying with the collar of Harvard's shirt, Aiden's brows drawn together in concentration. Aiden's fingertips glancing against his skin burned.

"You're *so* warm," Aiden said. "Nothing else ever was. I only knew goodness existed because you were the best. You're the best of everything to me."

Harvard made a wretched sound, leaning in to press his forehead against Aiden's.

He'd known Aiden was lonely, that the long line of guys wasn't just to have fun but tied up in the cold, huge manor where Aiden had spent his whole childhood, in Aiden's father with his flat shark eyes and sharp shark smile, and in the long line of stepmothers who Aiden's father chose because he had no use for people with hearts. Harvard had always known Aiden's father wanted to crush the heart out of Aiden. He'd always worried Aiden's father would succeed.

Aiden said, his voice distant even though he was so close, "I always knew all of you was too much to ask for."

Harvard didn't know what to say, so he obeyed a wild foolish impulse, turned his face the crucial fraction toward Aiden's, and kissed him. Aiden sank into the kiss with a faint sweet noise, as though he'd finally heard Harvard's wordless cry of distress and was answering it with belated reassurance: *No, I'll be all right. We're not lost.*

The idea of anyone not loving Aiden back was unimaginable, but it had clearly happened. Harvard couldn't think of how to say it, so he tried to make the kiss say it. *I'm so sorry you were in pain. I never guessed. I'm sorry I can't fix this, but I would if I could. He didn't love you, but I do.*

Maybe a kiss was the wrong impulse. Harvard drew back, only to see Aiden's face darken.

"There," Aiden hurled at him, defiant. "That's what I would say to you if this was real, and I really liked you. Happy now?"

As if Harvard could be happy when Aiden sounded miserable and Harvard didn't even know why. But Harvard didn't want to seem ungrateful when Aiden was doing him a favor. When the favor had clearly cost Aiden something.

"I . . . I don't . . . Thanks," Harvard said. "Come here."

Aiden was only an inch away, but it felt like an impossible distance. Harvard missed him, even though that made no sense. Aiden *shouldn't* be so far away. Such terrible things shouldn't be allowed.

Aiden came willingly. More than willingly. More than eagerly. His body flowed in toward, then all along Harvard's. Like water to the shoreline, his arms twining right around Harvard's neck. Aiden nuzzled his face in against Harvard's cheek. Harvard felt Aiden's eyelashes fluttering shut against his skin. He ran a hand up along the curve of Aiden's back, and felt him shudder.

"Can I *please* stop talking now?" Aiden said, his voice raw with pleading, as though someone had been making him talk. As if Harvard could, or would, make him do anything.

He didn't think he'd ever heard Aiden say *please* before.

Aiden said it again between kisses, begging naturally and easily. "Please," as his mouth slid against Harvard's. "Please, please" again, as his mouth trailed up to Harvard's ear. "Please."

"Yes," Harvard murmured. "Aiden, yes."

Yes, yes, yes, anything you want, only stop, and never stop.

Given explicit permission, Aiden pounced. They were rolling together in a wild tangle of bedsheets and limbs, kissing even more wildly, Aiden pulling Harvard's shirt open and sliding his hands inside was a welcome shock. Harvard was arched over

Aiden, his body almost touching Aiden's all over. One of Harvard's arms was held over their heads to support some of his weight, his fingers knotted in the loose tumble of Aiden's hair. Aiden surged up and kissed him again.

Nothing made any sense, except the one truth that always did: Aiden shouldn't be unhappy. He often was, and it made Harvard wild with misery, too, made him wish there was something he could do to make Aiden happy again. Aiden had seemed ferociously unhappy only moments ago, but now he was smiling, eyes open again and bright.

When Aiden threw back his head, Harvard kissed the bared line of his throat, then his jaw. Aiden slid his palm down Harvard's chest to rest against Harvard's bare hip, and then hesitated.

Somewhere in the background, the movie was still playing. The world probably still existed. It didn't seem to matter much, past the white square that was their beds, pushed so close together they might as well be one.

"If this was a real date," Harvard whispered, "what would happen next?"

He saw, very clearly, that Aiden understood what he was asking. He saw Aiden's teeth slide carefully over the swollen curve of his own lower lip. Without meaning to, Harvard bent down and kissed his mouth again.

"We should stop," murmured Aiden, who usually sounded immensely sure of himself. Right now he didn't sound certain at all.

"I don't want to stop," said Harvard.

"You're sure?"

"I'm sure," Harvard answered.

He shouldn't have been sure, but he was.

"But—Neil," said Aiden, very low.

"Who the hell is Neil?" Harvard asked, kissing Aiden again.

Aiden was the whole world stretched out beneath him. Aiden's hair spread out on the sheets, Aiden moaning in his ear. The magnitude of his certainty tipped Harvard over the edge into terrifying and unwelcome knowledge.

Terrible realization dawned, remorseless illumination shed on a whole landscape. Harvard found himself looking at his entire life in a new light.

Aiden on their first day of school, on their first day of fencing class, on their last day in the hospital, on their first day at Kings Row. Inextricably part of every important moment in Harvard's life. The bright and shining center of Harvard's life, ever since he'd turned around and seen Aiden and thought, *That boy looks sad*, and wanted nothing but to give Aiden everything.

Finding Aiden and being too young to understand what he'd found. Only knowing Aiden was necessary to him and wanting Aiden there always. Of course he loved his best friend, of course he did. That was always such an absolute truth that Harvard could never question it.

Harvard gasped against Aiden's mouth. He should have questioned it before now. He should have asked himself what he was feeling. Only he'd been afraid.

Dating someone else hadn't been Harvard's idea, and with this new clarity he realized he didn't actually want to do it. He hadn't wanted to be alone, hadn't wanted to be left behind, but it was impossible and distinctly horrible to think of being like this with anyone but Aiden.

Only very recently, as Aiden dated more and more people and the potential for distance between them started to feel far more real, had Harvard started to feel lonely. If it hadn't been for Coach suggesting dating, it might never have occurred to him.

Why would he go out and look for a partner when he had one at home? Why would he go searching for a lightning strike when there was all the brightness and all the pain he could wish for, always with him?

He'd never cared about dating, never really felt the need to find someone, because he'd been otherwise emotionally committed all along. Apparently, Harvard's subconscious was insane, bent on his own ruin. Somewhere in the back of his mind he'd just decided he was Aiden's boyfriend, without consulting Aiden. Without even consulting himself.

He'd been in love with Aiden the whole time.

This was an emotional natural disaster, the equivalent of an earthquake. This could level every carefully built structure in Harvard's life.

"We have to stop," Harvard said, abrupt and desperate.

"Wait, why?" Aiden murmured, reaching to drag Harvard back when Harvard pulled away, barely seeming to understand the words Harvard had spoken. "I don't want to. You said you didn't want to..."

He trailed off, hands still grasping Harvard's shirt, exerting pressure to bring Harvard back where he had been. Aiden's eyes were heavy-lidded, almost as if he was drowsy, but it was an electric drowsiness.

For a terrifying moment, Harvard looked at Aiden and couldn't remember why they should stop. Then he looked at Aiden and did remember.

"I don't want to, but we have to," Harvard tried to explain.

Aiden looked suddenly wide awake and affronted to be so, like a cat disturbed from his rest.

His voice as sharp this time as it had been soft before, he said, *"Why?"*

When Aiden had agreed to help Harvard with practice dating, Harvard remembered vividly the exact words he'd used. *I know how dating works. It doesn't matter, and this wouldn't even be real dating. It doesn't mean anything. It won't change anything.*

He looked at Aiden, his chest feeling cold and empty, bleak with despair. Harvard was just like all the rest of Aiden's guys, only worse. He was the one who really knew Aiden, and he should know better.

Harvard said, "Because this means nothing."

26 NICHOLAS

The next day at breakfast, some teachers came and marched away two seniors. "We need to talk to you about all the *watches* we found in your room," the whole cafeteria heard a teacher say distinctly.

The boys went ashen and started pleading and protesting innocence, one of them crying and the other talking incessantly about Daddy, so Nicholas felt kind of bad for them. Then he squinted and stared at the passing criminals in shock. Oddly, Eugene didn't seem surprised at all. Eugene seemed worried, for some reason. Seiji was eating his tragic breakfast with total calm.

Nicholas jerked his thumb toward the departing guilty parties. "Wow, what a coincidence."

"There are no broincidences," murmured Eugene in a fraught voice.

"No, but seriously," said Nicholas. "I think I know those guys?"

"What do you mean?" Seiji asked, his voice suddenly a razor. "You *think* you know them?"

Nicholas wasn't paying attention to Seiji. Usually he did, but his close brush with crime had him distracted.

"Wow, Eugene, this is amazing! We were totally in the same shop as these guys. I guess we were there right before they did the job."

This seemed to puzzle Eugene, and to enrage Seiji. Many things enraged Seiji, but Nicholas wasn't following the reasons for his current episode of fury.

"You *guess* you were there?" demanded Seiji. "When they implied you were a thief and insulted your pride, and you were visibly upset all day?"

"Huh?" said Nicholas. "They what?"

He wondered what he could've possibly been upset about that day, and then remembered Robert and Jesse Coste. He couldn't tell anyone about that. He didn't want anybody to know about his dad, not until he was better, and … Nicholas realized with a sinking feeling that he never wanted Seiji to find out he had any connection to Jesse Coste.

Seiji had been violently disturbed the time he decided Nicholas fenced like Jesse.

Seiji had told Nicholas he didn't want to be Jesse's reflection. He wouldn't want to look at Jesse's reflection, either. Especially not such a currently lousy version. It was starting to seem like Seiji had refused to go to Exton and had come to Kings Row purely in order to get away from Jesse Coste. If Seiji knew Robert Coste was Nicholas's dad, Seiji wouldn't want to be roommates anymore, let alone friends. If Seiji found out, he wouldn't see Nicholas as anything but a warped version of his true rival. He wouldn't want to see Nicholas ever again.

While Nicholas wrestled with this dilemma, Seiji and Eugene were in the middle of their own argument.

"Eugene said that these boys deeply upset you with their classist and prejudiced remarks!" Seiji fixed Eugene with an accusing stare.

"Bro, I didn't think that you were going to become a master criminal in Nicholas's defense!" Eugene protested. "Nobody could have predicted that!"

"What do you mean, become a master criminal?" Nicholas boggled. "*Seiji?* In *my* defense? None of what you're saying makes any sense!"

Eugene didn't shed any light on the situation. He had his phone out and was texting busily, tongue sticking out of his mouth. Nicholas glanced at Eugene's phone screen and saw that he was texting *Please come and get me, Mom. The other kids at Kings Row are scaring me.*

Nicholas turned an inquiring gaze on Seiji.

"I have to go!" Seiji announced.

Nicholas was still gazing around in confusion, waiting for answers that never came, when Seiji rose, stalked toward the door, and walked right into the wall of impressive muscle that was Eugene's weight-lifting friends. They'd left their table and arrayed themselves in a towering line in front of Seiji.

"You *did* it," said Eugene's massive friend Chad, who'd taken a strong liking to Seiji. Chad was eyeing Seiji with even more approval than usual. "You got those guys so good."

Seiji looked apprehensive about where this was going.

"Sick, my dude!" agreed Even More Massive Julian.

"Nasty!" contributed Brad, as though making a great concession.

"Why are you all hurling insults at me?" Seiji asked in an injured voice.

"From now on, when we speak of a prank that is truly legendary, we will call it a Seiji," vowed Chad. "Boys, grab him!"

To Seiji's evident and overwhelming horror, Eugene's weight-lifting bros seized him and lifted him bodily over their heads.

Nicholas moved very fast, using all the speed he'd been born with. He grabbed Eugene's phone out of his hands and took a picture of Seiji's expression at the moment they were lifting him. Then Nicholas texted the photo to his own number. He'd found his new phone background.

"Seiji!" Chad began to chant, and the others joined him. They clearly intended to parade Seiji all around Kings Row.

Picture secured, Nicholas felt vaguely as though he should rush to Seiji's rescue, but he was also aware by now what it meant when Seiji's face set in these particular lines. Someone should probably rush to the weight lifters' rescue.

"It's true!" said Seiji in ringing tones over the chant. "I *am* a master criminal. Now put me down, or I will visit a horrible revenge on you all."

Meekly, the weight lifters put down Seiji. Seiji gave a single cool, dismissive nod, and then fled for his life.

"Gotta jet, bro," said Eugene. "My mom is unexpectedly coming to pick me up."

He tried to stand and couldn't. Nicholas had grabbed hold of Eugene's tie. He held on and ignored Eugene's imploring gaze.

"Bro...let go, bro..."

"If you don't tell me what's happening, *I'm* gonna commit a felony," Nicholas promised. "I mean it."

Eugene closed his eyes in terror. "No more crime," he whispered. "Please."

Nicholas could be beaten in fencing matches—though only by people who were super good—but he couldn't be psyched out or intimidated. He didn't know how to back down, and he found that very useful.

Right now, Nicholas raised his eyebrows, like he did in a fencing match: *Go ahead. Try me.*

Eugene took a deep breath and launched into a long and strange tale. Apparently, Eugene had made a mysterious mistake and informed Seiji that these boys had upset Nicholas for no reason. Then Eugene had decided to tell Seiji that it would be good to prank these guys for upsetting Nicholas, and that the best thing to do would be to steal a bunch of stuff from this jewelry store and frame these guys.

Nicholas listened quietly, and sneakily ate Eugene's bacon while he was too distracted to object. "Sounds like this was mostly your fault, Eugene."

"Then I'm not telling it right, bro!" Eugene defended himself vigorously. "Because this was definitely Seiji's fault. Let me stress the part where he sneaked off under cover of darkness on the night of the fair and did who knows what! Do you think he broke into the safe with, like, a blowtorch, bro? Do you think he has one of those pizza cutter things that actually cut glass? I hope he was wearing a mask, but if he was then it means he has a whole heist outfit, and I don't feel good about that, either."

All around them, Kings Row boys were discussing the thieves discovered in their midst. Eugene was wringing his hands. Nicholas waved his own hand, like *Yeah, yeah, yeah.*

"Can we get back to the important part?" Nicholas requested.

"Bro, Seiji being a master criminal *is* the important part!" Eugene exclaimed. "He is a terrifying madman!"

"No, he's not," said Nicholas dismissively. "I mean—he's not a criminal. He might be that other thing, but it's cool."

"How is it cool?!" Eugene thundered. "How is any of this cool!"

Nicholas grinned at him. "I think all of this is really cool."

Eugene stared at Nicholas's grin for a long, stunned moment. "Thanks for sharing your unique perspective on the world, bro."

"I mean, you two did a lot of strange stuff," Nicholas admitted. "But you did it to make me feel better."

The morning light was shining on the smooth walls and the gilt frames surrounding portraits of ancient bearded men. Those old dudes wouldn't have thought Nicholas belonged in Kings Row any more than the jerks who'd been led out of the room this morning did. Nicholas *didn't* belong here, but there were people who wanted Nicholas to feel he belonged.

"But you weren't actually upset. We got it all wrong. You didn't even remember those guys!" Eugene protested violently. "We did all that—Seiji committed so much *crime*—for nothing."

"You both cared about how I felt," said Nicholas. "Nobody's ever cared how I felt before."

Eugene made a funny long squeaking sound, as though he had a balloon in his lungs and someone had stepped on it, letting the air leak out noisily.

"But, I mean," Eugene said in a feeble voice. "Like. Your mom cares."

That made Nicholas think of trying—and failing—to write his essay for Coach.

He remembered an apartment from long ago. He didn't recall which part of town it'd been in, or how they'd eventually gotten evicted. What he remembered was the light of a nearby convenience store, the flickering neon-red drenching the shattered place in the drywall. At the time, his mother had a boyfriend living with them, and the boyfriend shouted and threw stuff.

He'd thrown a plate at Nicholas's head. He was fast and ducked, though, so it didn't hit him. Later that night, Nicholas traced the fractures on the wall, and thought about what that hurled plate would have done to his head. If he'd been just a little less fast.

Before then, Nicholas had assumed his mom loved him. Moms did. She was young for a mom, and they didn't have much money, so sometimes she got stressed or forgot him or yelled, but that wasn't a big deal. She was nice to him when she was in a good mood or had enough to drink but not too much. Sometimes she'd lie on the bed and hold him and say in a nice low voice that Nicholas should be quiet because Mommy's head hurt. If he was quiet, he was allowed to snuggle up against her.

After the plate hit the wall, Nicholas remembered trying to tell her, *That man scares me, Mommy.* He vividly recalled the way she'd looked at him when he did. How her eyes had been hazy with drink, but narrowed with dislike, and profoundly cold. Nicholas had understood, in that moment, that she didn't care what he was saying. She only wanted him to stop saying it. Nicholas felt as though Mom hated him for making her life even harder than it had to be.

"Nah, she doesn't care," Nicholas said quietly. He bowed his head for an instant, then bounced back and looked up. "But you guys did. You cared that I was upset, and you tried to do something about it. *That's* what matters."

This wasn't a dream of how if Nicholas proved himself worthy, his dad might be sorry he hadn't been there. Nicholas was aware that the Robert Coste who cared about Nicholas was a figment of Nicholas's imagination. These were real people, who Nicholas really knew.

"I don't know how I can ever repay you guys, but I'll think of something. I super appreciate it, bro," said Nicholas, and offered his fist for Eugene to bump.

After a very long pause, Eugene bumped Nicholas's fist with even more vigor than usual.

"Don't sweat it, my dude. I mean, I almost had a nervous breakdown, and Seiji Katayama is genuinely out of his mind, but... anything for a true bro."

Nicholas was filled with an emotion that seemed so huge it made him feel bigger, expanding so this much feeling could fit. It seemed as if he could wrap his arms all the way around the entirety of Kings Row. As if he might embrace every one of the absurdly huge redbrick buildings with the fancy windows and the shiny cabinets full of shinier trophies, and every one of the people inside those buildings.

He had to find Seiji.

27 AIDEN

Harvard had said he would come back, but he hadn't. Aiden waited all night, staring up at the ceiling and replaying the moment when Harvard had gone still and said, *This means nothing.* Harvard had wrenched himself away from Aiden as though he might catch something.

The slam of the door had echoed throughout their room.

And now it was morning and time to go to class. Surely Harvard would come to class.

Before Aiden left the room, he picked up Harvard Paw and his new friend from where they lay tumbled together on the floor. He set Harvard Paw carefully down on his pillow.

Then Aiden tossed the new bear up and down so it hit the ceiling and back again. Aiden's careless grin was reflected in its empty glass eyes.

He threw the fair bear, with extreme force, into the trash can by the door.

Harvard Paw looked a little forlorn there on the bed by himself.

"Sorry if you miss him," Aiden told his bear. "But you'll get over it. You'll thank me one day. You were born to be a carefree bachelor."

He swung by the *salle* but didn't find Harvard there. He found Coach instead.

"Where's Harvard?" Coach demanded.

"That's what I want to know!" Aiden snapped back.

Coach tried to run her hands through her hair, visibly came to the realization her hair was up in a bun, and scowled. "He was supposed to come with me and do a fencing demonstration in the town hall this morning. My students evading their responsibilities is nothing new, but—"

"Harvard *Lee*?" said Aiden. "My Harvard? Impossible."

Except perhaps it was possible. If Aiden had upset Harvard enough, though Aiden didn't even know what he'd done wrong.

He'd done plenty wrong, obviously. But he didn't know what he'd done specifically to cause that terrible look on Harvard's face last night, or what he could possibly do to make it right.

"Have you written your essay, Aiden?" asked Coach sweetly.

After a pause, Aiden shook his head.

"Are you going to write your essay?"

Another pause, then Aiden shook his head again. He tried for a rakish grin, conveying to Coach, *Don't hate the player, hate the game*. Coach gave him a look that indicated she had no time for the player.

"Do you want another roommate, then?"

Without a pause, Aiden shook his head. Maybe Harvard would want a new roommate after all this, but until Harvard told him to go, Aiden wouldn't leave their room.

"Then I think you're volunteering yourself for a fencing demonstration, aren't you?" Coach asked brightly.

Aiden shrugged. "A display *is* more suited to my particular skill set."

Everything else in his life had gone wrong. He wasn't doing that essay.

The upkeep of the Kingstone town hall was endowed by several illustrious former Kings Row students. There was a large gold clock face set in the gray stone façade of the building, and in gold letters over the double doors was written the Latin legend QUI MALA COGITAT MALITUS EIUS. Inside was a gleaming walnut platform that could be set up as a stage for mayoral debates, civil ceremonies, and—apparently—fencing demonstrations. It could hold upward of a thousand people.

The fencing demonstration in the Kingstone town hall proved extremely popular. Aiden wasn't as skilled a fencer as Harvard or Seiji, but he had better showmanship than either.

He demonstrated a few simple fencing moves, then opened his fencing jacket to show the body cord beneath to a murmur of increasing general interest and described the parts of his blade and the process of a match. He showed the cross-section blade and bell guard of the épée, while Coach sighed besottedly about sabers.

"We call the end the point both because it's where the point would be if there was one, and it's the only part of the blade with which we can score points," Aiden explained. "Which is the point."

When he laughed, an amused ripple went through the crowd.

"It isn't a particularly *useful* sport, is it?" asked one woman with a crown of stiffly processed gold hair and a rope of pearls.

Aiden winked at her. "Is any sport more useful than another? Besides, I should hope it's obvious I'm mostly decorative."

She chuckled when he did, persuaded to be charmed, and Aiden whirled into another demonstration. He explained that the épée he held was made of maraging steel, like the blades rated for international competitions. Maraging steel was ten times slower to crack under endless tiny pressure than carbon-steel blades.

"Some fencers say that maraging steel breaks cleaner, but that's actually a myth."

Nothing broke cleanly. A break was always jagged and messy, and inevitable. The only thing to do was put off the day of break-ing for as long as possible.

A little footwork, a lot more laughing, and Aiden was ready

to be done. His plan was to execute a balestra, then end with a lunge, a bow, and a flourish.

Instead, his gaze was caught by watchful dark eyes, set in the face of a woman standing at the back of the crowd. She was making no effort to be seen, but he saw her. Aiden changed his mind and ended the demonstration with an inquartata, an evasive movement hiding the front of his jacket, partially concealing the point where he could be attacked.

Then he ended the demonstration with a showy bow. He was as he was, and he refused to show he could be hurt by anything.

Aiden's hair had come loose during the demonstration. He was tying it back up and stowing away his fencing gear when she approached. He'd been braced for her to do so.

Aiden had told Harvard about her once, on their first sleepover, and cried. "She said she wanted to be my real mother," he'd confided, curled up under the covers in Harvard's room, much smaller than Aiden's room at home, and much warmer. "It wasn't true."

Safe in Harvard's house, he'd thought of his own home, so big that cold echoes stayed longer than actual sounds, crammed full of shiny things that never stayed long.

"Most things aren't real," he'd whispered.

Harvard had held his hand. "I'm real. So are you. And you're my best friend."

Then Harvard had told him a story until Aiden could sleep. It was the first time they fell asleep holding hands.

Aiden believed in Harvard, but he didn't believe in much more. Belief seemed too great a risk. Harvard was real, but nothing else was. Love was a child's dream, and Aiden didn't set himself up to be broken any longer.

Aiden was much taller than the Brazilian now. He imagined she must be shocked, remembering that pitiful kid he'd been, by how much he'd changed.

"Hello, Aiden," she said. "Do you remember me at all? I used to know you, when you were very small. I was . . . a friend of your father's."

Aiden gave her his father's shark smile and saw her flinch. "My father has a lot of friends. Check the tabloids."

"No need," she murmured. "I know."

If she was hoping she could get back with his father, she didn't have a chance. His father didn't do repeats, and she was still beautiful, but not young in the latest-model way Dad insisted on.

"I'm sure you felt you were a match made in heaven, or at least somewhere else golden and shiny," said Aiden, "but he's a busy man. I'd say ask him, but actually, it's usually best to ask his secretary."

She laughed then, though the sound was rusty and painful, not like the laughter Aiden usually wished to inspire. He wanted to be wry and in control, wanted to force life to be easy.

Only everything seemed difficult lately.

She said, "We were a match made in hell. Believe me, I didn't come here to talk about your father. There was only one reason I stayed with him for as long as I did."

"Let me take a wild guess," Aiden drawled. "Could it be money?"

Her dark eyes were level. "It was you, Aiden. You were the sweetest kid, and I hated the thought of leaving you in that big empty house all alone. He didn't even let me say goodbye. I know you must hardly remember me, and it might sound strange to hear, but I really loved you."

She must need money now.

"That's extremely touching," Aiden drawled. "But what can I say? This is so embarrassing. I can't actually recall your name."

There was a silence, ringing like a hand slapping hard across a face. Neither of them moved. Far away over her shoulder, Aiden could see the indifferent bustle of his former audience.

With an effort, the woman smiled. Her smile wasn't even a good fake.

"Ah," she said, and nodded. "Sorry to bother you, Aiden. I wish you all the best."

She turned and walked away. Aiden listened to the sound of her retreating steps, and the door slamming. He waited for the screech of car wheels.

Coach Williams approached him instead. The coach was dressed in a gray suit rather than her usual bright sportswear, her hair trying to escape its pins. She was also wearing a different expression than normal.

"Demonstration went well, didn't it?" Aiden spoke lightly. "Don't think I will be doing another, however. Next time you must content yourself with a less alluring model. Be brave, Coach. Don't weep at the thought of unworthy substitutes."

"What did you say to her?" Coach asked.

"Who?" Aiden returned, slinging his bag carelessly over his shoulder and picking up an épée.

He swished the sword about, watching the play of light on steel, and the dancing shadow against the wall. He refused to meet Coach's eyes after that first glance.

"She came to one of the very few matches you actually attended your first year on the team, and I saw how she watched you," Coach informed him. "She came to a match you didn't attend last year, and I saw she was disappointed."

"Who wouldn't be if they came somewhere hoping to see me in all my glory and didn't get to?" Aiden shrugged. "Whatever her expectations were, it's not my problem."

Coach wielded truth like one of her beloved sabers. "She didn't have any expectations. She's married. She has kids. She just wanted to see you, because you mean something to her. When I went to talk to her last year, she said she didn't want to annoy you. I was the one who told her you'd be happy if she approached you."

That was . . . a different situation than the one he'd assumed.

Sometimes, when Aiden felt the impulse to act on all his worst instincts, he thought, *Would Harvard be disappointed in you if you did that?* And then he didn't do it, whatever it was.

It had never occurred to Aiden that anyone else cared enough to be disappointed in him.

Disappointment was in Coach's usually twinkling brown eyes now. "I always thought you were a good kid at heart. Careless, but careless isn't the same as cruel. Tell me, Aiden. Was I wrong about you?"

Oddly, it wasn't Coach's eyes or the echo of a woman's voice or even the thought of Harvard that changed his mind. It was that when Aiden turned away from Coach, his roving gaze fell on the stage where he'd stood, gleaming and empty, and he thought, *Do you want to put on a show for the rest of your life?*

Aiden threw down the bag and his épée, and ran. Out through the double doors, down the flight of stone steps, and into the parking lot crowded with shining cars that would soon speed away.

She hadn't got into her car yet. She was standing with her shoulders stiff under a thick camel coat, her hand braced against the door. He noticed the wedding ring on it now, and the way her knuckles went pale on the handle before she turned and faced him.

Aiden's lungs were burning from his sprint. His hair had come loose again, flying strands suddenly a wild snarl getting in his eyes, and he was still wearing an open fencing uniform, his plastron lost somewhere in the town hall. He must look absolutely ridiculous. The wind had its freezing-cold claws curled in around the open jacket, he was breathing raggedly, and he didn't know if he had a best friend to return to. All these years trying not to break, and he would anyway. It might as well be now.

"I'm sorry, I'm sorry," Aiden gasped. "Rosina, I'm sorry. Of course I remember you."

The golden clock hands cut time like swords. She stood unmoving, watching Aiden in the clear cold light of day. It was just the two of them in the parking lot, with no audience left to impress, and Aiden knew the way he'd acted was unforgivable, that he would always mess up when it truly mattered, that every time he'd been abandoned, he'd deserved it.

Then she lifted a hand to his face and smiled.

"Look at you, Aiden," said Rosina, in her familiar beautiful voice, speaking as if she were singing to him again. "You got so tall. And you're still so cute."

They talked for a long time, standing there in the parking lot. Rosina gave him her number and offered to give him a lift anywhere he wanted to go. Aiden said he'd walk back home.

"I mean to Kings Row," said Aiden, grinning reassuringly when a flash of alarm crossed Rosina's face. "School. That's home."

It always had been, since Harvard had said he wanted them to go there together. Home was wherever Harvard was, if Aiden could live there, too.

"I'm glad you like it at school," Rosina told him. "I'm sure you have a lot of friends. Is there a special friend?"

"Yeah," Aiden answered. "There is."

Rosina smiled. "I'd like to meet them someday. Are you sure I can't take you to the gates?"

"I'm sure," said Aiden.

Several times over the years, Harvard had reached out to one stepmother or another on Aiden's behalf, trying to form a connection between them. Harvard always did this from loving concern, but it humiliated Aiden. He didn't want to be seen as begging for love he would never get. He didn't want any of them to know that he minded when they left. What was the point? They would still leave. Everybody always left. There was no way to stop them. The only thing Aiden could do was protect himself.

Aiden never bothered to try at all, but Harvard always tried so hard, for them both.

There was no way to prevent Harvard from trying without telling him the truth: *Nobody's ever going to love me but you, and I know even you will leave me someday.*

Maybe that wasn't true. For the first time, Aiden felt ready to hope for something more.

For the first time, Aiden wanted to be honest about what he wanted. A plan was forming like a path opening up before him.

He intended to walk through the woods, clear his head, and practice what he was going to say. He would make his own way back to Kings Row, the school he'd chosen with Harvard.

He was going home, and for once in his life, he would tell Harvard the whole truth.

I love you. I always have. Today, for the first time, I hope that I might be enough.

28 SEIJI

Seiji was not having a good day.
He felt he'd been horribly
misled by Eugene. He'd trusted him
to be correct in his reading of social
dynamics, but as it emerged, him
was an imbecile, Nicholas hadn't
even been upset, and the whole
prank had been an exercise in futil-
ity. As the illicit brown sugar sprin-
kled on this oatmeal of horror, he'd
been hauled around like a deeply
shamed sack of potatoes by weight
lifters.

Seiji wasn't sure he could look anyone at Kings Row in the face right
now. Any escape from their watching
eyes and embarrassing congratulations was welcome.

The last time Seiji'd been in the
woods, he'd gotten lost in them. Seiji
headed into the trees now, hoping
he could again.

Perhaps by the time he found his way back, everybody would have forgotten about the prank.

He feared not.

Seiji stalked through the woods and brooded over the horrors of the past few days.

This whole business had been unspeakably humiliating, and worst of all, sooner or later he would have to face *Nicholas*. There was no way to avoid it unless Seiji took to wearing the shower curtain draped in the center of their room over his head. Seiji had made himself appear ridiculous. Nicholas was going to laugh at him. Seiji was *not* looking forward to that last humiliation.

He'd been through too much already. He remembered when he'd called his father on the day of the fair. He'd been slightly embarrassed making the call. He didn't like taking up too much of his father's time. His father always answered his calls, but Seiji knew he was a busy man and he didn't want to bother him.

After waiting for his father's secretary to connect them, and making their greetings, he'd explained: "I am calling because I have a certain situation regarding a friend I would appreciate your help with."

His father had sighed. "Ah, I should have known this was about Jesse. Well, if you feel that Exton is the right move for you after all, I won't stand in your way, Seiji. Your mother and I never have, I hope you'll—"

"This isn't about Jesse," Seiji had told him impatiently. "Why must everyone talk to me about Jesse? Not everything is about Jesse."

His father had said, "Oh."

There was an odd startled note in his father's voice, Seiji thought later, but at the time he was focused on achieving his goal. He explained about Nicholas and about Eugene and about the prank.

"I don't see how this is a funny prank," his father had contributed at last.

"Humor is difficult to understand, isn't it?" Seiji had commiserated. "You know I never get jokes, so I don't try to figure them out anymore. I didn't understand Jesse's jokes, either."

"That's because Jesse isn't funny," his father had muttered.

Seiji had frowned. "What?"

Perhaps he'd misheard his father. Almost all adults were charmed by Jesse, who had flawless and engaging manners, and a smile that made people smile back at him. His parents had been so relieved when Seiji introduced Jesse to them: a friend his own age at last, and a friend anybody could be proud of. Seiji always presumed his parents wished Seiji were more like Jesse. He didn't blame them for wanting that. Any parents would feel the same way.

Only it was true that his father hadn't smiled at one of the jokes Jesse had made at a party last year. Seiji had wondered about that at the time.

"Do you find humor difficult to understand as well?" Seiji asked his father tentatively.

"Not usually," said his father.

Seiji sighed, and tried to think of a different way to explain the prank. He supposed it had been too much to hope for, that he and his father might have something in common.

"Apparently, it's other boys' faces once the prank is accomplished that will be amusing? The part about being amusing is not important. The part that is important is getting justice for Nicholas. Do you understand?"

Seiji hoped he had explained it right this time.

"Tell me about Nicholas," said his father.

"About—Nicholas?" Seiji repeated uncertainly.

"Would I like him?"

"I shouldn't think so," said Seiji. "He has terrible manners. And a basically unfortunate way of speaking and interacting with the world generally. He's very untidy, too."

"Oh, but you hate it when things aren't in the correct places," murmured his father. "I still remember that time we had the ambassador's son over for a playdate, and you made him cry."

"What is the point of painstakingly building castles with blocks only to knock them down?" Seiji asked. "Or sniveling?" He dismissed his father's reminiscences. "Anyway, that was when I was very young and it no longer matters, so I don't see the point of bringing it up. The point is—"

"Justice for Nicholas," said his father. "Is Nicholas—very good at fencing?"

"No," said Seiji plainly.

There was a stunned silence.

"He has a certain raw potential, but he hasn't been properly trained because of his socioeconomic circumstances," Seiji continued. "I wish to discuss this topic with you on our winter vacation. I think there must be foundations and scholarships set up. Many valuable fencers could be lost. It is almost too late for Nicholas. I shall be forced to teach him extremely rigorously."

There was more silence. Seiji wondered if his father had dropped his phone.

"What about your coach?" asked his father at last.

"She's very good but she likes us to focus on teamwork in a way I don't enjoy," said Seiji. "And she often suggests we relax. Someone with Nicholas's current technique shouldn't be allowed to relax. The way he conducts his whole life is disgusting."

"Have you said that to him—in those words?" asked his father, sounding somewhat apprehensive.

"I tell Nicholas how bad he is constantly," Seiji said. "He does not listen."

His father coughed. Seiji hoped his father wasn't unwell. "May I ask how you made friends with this boy?"

"I didn't make friends with him," Seiji answered, bewildered by this line of questioning. "You know I don't know how to make friends! He just said we were friends, so now we are, and people hurt his feelings, so—as should be perfectly obvious—I must do something about that. As I have already explained *several times*."

There was a touch of severity in Seiji's reminder. He knew his father was intelligent, so there was no need to make Seiji repeat himself.

"Nice for you to have some different friends," his father remarked irrelevantly.

Seiji thought of the constant mess in his room and weight lifters assaulting him and having to worry about people's feelings.

"I don't find it especially nice," he said gloomily.

"You were such a...distant kid," said his father. "You always seemed so hard to reach."

Seiji responded, startled, "I didn't think you were trying."

His father hesitated, then continued with an odd note in his voice: "We should have tried harder. We thought it would be easier to talk to you when you were older, and—it never was. It got more difficult instead. Love was always easy for me and your mother, and I suppose we believed that it would be easy with our child, too."

This was an extremely embarrassing subject, and Seiji could not think what to say or why his father had chosen to bring it up now. Surely this was all understood between them.

Seiji had always known he was difficult to love. His father didn't need to tell him that.

Seiji gave a noncommittal murmur. The noncommittal murmur served Seiji well at parties, in between the thank-yous and goodbyes, and Seiji hoped it would suffice as an answer.

"The only thing that seemed to make you happy was fencing," said his father.

Apparently, noncommittal murmuring would not be enough. Seiji searched desperately for something to say that wouldn't disappoint his father and came up with nothing.

"Of course, we're very proud of you and your fencing triumphs," said his father after a pause.

It made sense that excelling would please his parents.

"My name has been mentioned regarding the Olympics," Seiji offered.

"I know, Seiji," his dad told him with a touch of weariness. "And we're proud of you for fitting in so well at this new school. It sounds like Kings Row is going well."

"I must have described everything wrong," said Seiji. "You do understand that most of my fencing team is not even ranked in the top fifty?"

His father coughed again—several times.

"I think you must be getting a cold," said Seiji, concerned. "Will you help me with my prank?"

"I will. Thanks for calling, Sei-kun," said his father. He hadn't called him that often, not since Seiji was small. "I'm glad you did."

Seiji cleared his throat. He was happy if his father was happy, naturally. "I'm glad I did, too. You should see a doctor as soon as possible for that cold."

The call had been mystifying in several ways, and Seiji was certain his father had been annoyed to have his work interrupted. Especially when he was ill. And as it turned out, neither the call nor the prank had been necessary. Seiji had made a complete fool of himself.

Seiji fervently wished there was some way to escape this appalling situation.

Even as he had that thought, he saw headlights through the trees, and when he cautiously approached, he noted, to his surprise, that a limousine was driving down the road.

He was even more surprised when the limousine halted, and Jesse emerged.

"Seiji!" he exclaimed. "There you are at last."

"Hello, Jesse," said Seiji. "What an extremely strange coincidence."

Seiji nodded, and turned away from the road. This day was just getting worse and worse.

Jesse left the limousine, and walked onto the tree line, twigs snapping under his crisp steps. He snatched Seiji's arm and whirled him around.

"Get into the limo immediately, Seiji," said Jesse, who was slightly wild-eyed. "You cannot stay here. You must see that."

Seiji blinked. Had news of his prank spread to Exton already?

Jesse continued: "This is a postapocalyptic nightmare land, populated by gibbering lunatics draped in raw flesh!"

"Oh that," said Seiji. "That was days ago. Many things have happened since then."

"Worse than that?" Jesse asked, sounding appalled. "That has been haunting my dreams. Come *away*, Seiji. Do you want to be subjected to more horrors? Isn't it humiliating for a fencer of your stature to be treated like this, forced to roll around in the mud, playing pointless games with pointless people? Let's leave while you still have some shreds of your dignity left."

Seiji stayed in the circle of leaves and dirt created when Jesse spun him around. Jesse's blue eyes were as relentless as his grip on Seiji's wrist. He was pulling Seiji forward.

"Don't you want to come?" Jesse asked.

"In a way, I do," Seiji admitted slowly.

"There you go," said Jesse, used to hearing exactly what he wanted to hear. "I knew you would. Come away at once."

He tugged, but Seiji planted his feet in the ground and refused to move. Jesse gave him a look that went almost past bewildered, as though they were both lost in the woods.

"I—" stammered Jesse. "I—I'm prepared to make concessions."

"Are you?" Seiji said quietly.

Was Jesse going to *apologize*? If he did . . .

"I'll never mention this ridiculous time you spent at Kings Row," Jesse promised. "I won't let anyone else mention it, either. It will be like it never happened."

Like Kings Row and Nicholas didn't happen.

"But it did," said Seiji.

"But it *didn't*," insisted Jesse, fully prepared to argue with reality until reality backed down. "Because it didn't matter. This lousy school doesn't matter, and none of the people in it matter. Am I wrong?"

Seiji hesitated.

Jesse's eyes gleamed. "*You're* the only one here who matters, so, Seiji, would you just—"

"Do I matter?" asked Seiji. "To you?"

"Of course!" said Jesse. "Why else am I here? I'm sick and tired of training with a third-best."

Occasionally, Seiji used to force himself to smile at jokes he didn't think were funny. It seemed like he should make the effort to smile. Except when he did so, people actually took a step back.

Seiji smiled that humorless smile now. Jesse didn't take a step back, but for an instant he looked as if he wanted to.

"How flattering," said Seiji, "to be considered always second-best."

"I wouldn't put it like that," Jesse told him. "I mean, it's understood, isn't it?"

"I didn't understand," said Seiji. "Now I do."

"Just—don't think about it that way, Seiji," Jesse urged. "Think about it this way: We're the ideal opponents. I'm even better when you're with me. Without each other, neither of us is the best we can be. Doesn't that make sense?"

It did. And Seiji did want to be the best he could be.

Seiji nodded.

"So won't you come?" asked Jesse, coaxing now, almost irresistible.

He didn't want to be a broken mirror.

Seiji thought, senselessly, *I wish Nicholas was here.*

He didn't even know why he wished that. Nicholas hadn't been much help last time. In fact, he'd gotten in the way and embarrassed Seiji severely.

But Seiji hadn't submitted and climbed into the limousine last time. He was afraid this time that he would. Part of him wanted to.

But part of him didn't. He wasn't sure what part he should listen to. This was all so complicated, and he wanted life to be simple. He preferred to be certain about how he felt and what he was doing.

Going with Jesse would be simple. Jesse was always clear about what he wanted. If he were with Jesse, Seiji would always be able to see what he should do and how his future would be.

But Nicholas would be surprised and even distressed if Seiji left, and Seiji would prefer not to upset Nicholas. And though Exton was a better school and would optimize Seiji's chances for the Olympics, Seiji had the odd, nebulous feeling his father might want him to stay at Kings Row.

Mr. Coste was so proud of Jesse. Seiji had often watched them together and thought how it would be if Mr. Coste were his father and that proud of him.

Only Mr. Coste wasn't his father, and Seiji didn't want him to be. It was the pride Seiji had wanted. He'd never been sure how to get his parents to be proud of him, and Mr. Coste seemed an easier proposition, but Seiji had never turned his back on a challenge in his life.

Always keep moving toward your target, his dad said in his mind.

Which choice would make his father proud?

And, Seiji thought, *what would make me proud of myself?* He remembered the moment when Jesse took his sword with excruciating clarity. He had never been less proud of himself. He wanted to be with Jesse at Exton, but he never wanted to relive that moment. If he returned to Jesse's side, he would be declaring that low point was where he belonged.

"I won't go," Seiji said with sudden determination.

"Why not?" asked Jesse. "Explain it to me so that I can understand."

Seiji stared helplessly. He couldn't explain his reasoning to Jesse. He could barely explain it to himself. If he tried, Jesse would laugh at him and Seiji would feel ridiculous and he would get in the car.

"See?" Jesse persisted. "You can't. Look, Seiji, I understand your pride is hurt, and you don't want to back down, but there's no shame in changing your mind when you've made a bad decision. The real shame is in sticking with the decision that will ruin your game and wreck your future. Seiji, I am thinking about you. I require your presence at Exton. Deep down, you already know it's the right thing to do. You can't even give me a single reason why you would stay. Trust me. I know what you want, better than you do. I know you want to come with me."

Jesse's voice had as strong a grip on him after all these years as Jesse's hand on his wrist. Slowly, reluctantly, Seiji let himself be pulled forward a step toward the road.

Then an entirely unexpected sound stopped him in his tracks.

Ringing through the trees, more golden than the leaves still clinging to the branches, more confident even than Jesse, came the voice of Aiden Kane.

"Excuse me, Exton freshman?" Aiden said imperiously. "Why are you harassing one of *my* freshmen? Only *I* am allowed harass my freshmen, thank you!"

Jesse made a choked sound, clearly seething with outrage that Aiden didn't know who he was.

But...in the match Aiden had won, he had taunted Seiji with Jesse's name. Aiden, Seiji thought slowly, knew Jesse's name.

Aiden gave no sign of this knowledge as he strode forward to the side of the road, in a whirl of bright leaves. He was wearing his fencing uniform, and an air that suggested nobody should question it. He swept the limousine with a withering look as though to suggest such an inferior vehicle would have no place in his home, and swept Jesse with an equally withering glance.

Perhaps Aiden had *forgotten Jesse's name*, Seiji thought, lured into belief despite himself.

Aiden's sharp green eyes focused on Jesse's hold on Seiji's wrist.

"Drop," he commanded.

Jesse's grip tightened, but Seiji lifted his chin slightly. He thought he understood what Aiden was doing.

"Why do you need a limousine to go to a fencing tournament?" Seiji asked Jesse. "Not everybody can afford to go to fencing tournaments in a limousine. Also, they are environmentally unsound. You should go on a team bus with your teammates."

Jesse seemed unsure of how to respond. Aiden patted Jesse on the back, and Jesse immediately looked infuriated, which Aiden ignored.

"We're all stunned by Seiji Katayama, world's most unexpected class warrior," Aiden murmured sympathetically, and Jesse relaxed. Then Aiden's sweet voice twisted like a snake and went fang-sharp as he asked, "Might I inquire: Where *were* you going, Exton boy?"

"Um," said Jesse. "What?"

"I mean," Aiden said silkily, "where was this fencing tournament you were headed to?"

"I...Abroad," said Jesse.

Aiden sneered. Seiji knew what it looked like when Aiden believed he'd spotted a weakness in your armor. What he didn't understand was why Aiden thought Jesse forgetting where he was going was a sign of weakness. Seiji supposed it must be slightly embarrassing, but surely the limousine driver knew where Jesse was going.

Had Jesse . . . not been going to a tournament? Where had he been going instead?

Seiji wouldn't have thought to look at limousine drivers before meeting Nicholas, but now he squinted through the windscreen to make out the driver behind the wheel. She wore the usual uniform, but her cap was rakishly tilted on her curly hair, and she was chewing gum and appeared to be snickering to herself with huge enjoyment of the proceedings.

Seiji was pleased he'd decided to pay attention to the chauffeur.

"Stop ignoring me, Seiji!" Jesse snarled.

"I wasn't ignoring you," Seiji pointed out mildly. "I was just looking at someone else."

He supposed Jesse wasn't used to that.

"Who is this?" Jesse asked Seiji, jerking his chin savagely in Aiden's direction. "Who was the boy with you last time, who you—the one with the flies buzzing around him? Why am I constantly being spoken to like this at this awful school? Do they speak to *you* like this?"

After some consideration, Seiji nodded.

Jesse seemed even more incensed. "I don't believe either of these people are even ranked in the top fifty, Seiji!"

"They're not," said Seiji.

Jesse leaned his free hand against the door of the limousine as though he felt faint.

"I could be ranked if I really wanted to be," claimed Aiden. "But while you two were studying the blade, I was busy having a *lot* of fun. There are things more important than fencing."

Jesse frowned and turned an appealing gaze upon Seiji. "What's he talking about?"

"I don't know," Seiji murmured back.

Aiden rolled his eyes. "Oh my God, there are three of them."

"There's only one of me," Jesse snapped. "I'm *Jesse Coste.*"

He tossed his head up high. Seiji had seen other people quail when faced with half the fury currently gleaming in Jesse's blue eyes or contained in the arrogant lift of his chin.

"Don't flip your hair at *me*, freshman," Aiden sneered back. "I'm *Aiden Kane.*"

Aiden shook back his own light, bright, curling hair from his face and looked down his nose at Jesse.

"Who?" Jesse asked.

"Ask some of the Exton boys," Aiden drawled. "I don't remember their names, but I guarantee you they'll know mine."

"Aiden beat me at fencing," Seiji contributed.

Perhaps Aiden had also beaten some of the fencers at Exton? That must be what he meant.

Aiden should really come to practice more often. He might have more potential than Seiji had previously believed.

"I knew it, I knew horrible things were happening at Kings

Row," Jesse muttered. He stopped tugging persuasively and pulled at Seiji's wrist hard enough to hurt, so Seiji's sleeve was disarranged and the dying light caught his watch. "And what ghastly object are you wearing on your *wrist*?!"

"That's my favorite watch," Seiji snapped, and twisted his arm free.

Jesse lunged forward, but Aiden stepped in, standing shoulder to shoulder with Seiji. Jesse paid no attention to Aiden, but Seiji knew he was there.

"What?" Jesse asked blankly. "How can that be? Seiji, I feel like I can't even recognize you right now. Who even are you?"

"Kings Row's team will be fencing against Exton's one of these days," Seiji answered. "My school against yours."

He laid claim to Kings Row the same way he'd laid claim to the watch, without thinking. He couldn't justify doing so, but he didn't want to take it back.

"What are you saying?" Jesse demanded.

"You don't know who I am? Find out on the *piste*," Seiji suggested, and turned away.

He felt slightly unsteady, probably due to the fact the ground was uneven and riddled with treacherous hidden tree roots, but Aiden threw a careless arm around his shoulders as they walked over the forest floor together. That helped with the unsteadiness.

Aiden urged, "That's right. Make him chase you."

Aiden's voice was encouraging, but his actual words were confusing.

"We're fencers," Seiji pointed out. "We're not running relay races."

"I truly cannot imagine why your painfully literal milkshake brings all the boys to the yard," said Aiden, "but work with what you've got, I guess."

"I don't drink milkshakes," Seiji told him. "You're probably thinking of protein shakes. I drink those."

Aiden appeared reduced to silence by this statement.

They made their way through the trees in silence for a while. Seiji preferred a companionable silence to a difficult conversation, but he felt he should say something. Even though he didn't know how to express how relieved he'd been when Aiden showed up.

"Aiden? Thanks," offered Seiji with a small, shy smile. He was embarrassed by the sound of his own voice, sounding almost as young as he actually was. "You were really cool back there."

"Oh," said Aiden, looking vaguely startled. "No problem."

Seiji walked back to Kings Row with a teammate by his side.

29 HARVARD

When Harvard walked into their room, Aiden was standing by the window, getting changed out of his fencing gear. Aiden paused, hands tugging his jacket closed in a swift, nervous movement, when Aiden was never anything but sublimely and blithely self-confident in any possible stage of undress.

The bear from the fair was in the trash. Harvard guessed he knew what that meant.

He had really screwed up.

"Harvard!" Aiden exclaimed, jolting as though he was trying to move forward and stay absolutely still at the same time. "I thought you weren't coming back."

"This is our room? And I told you I was coming back," Harvard reminded him. "I just wanted to go see my mom."

Aiden nodded, blinking rapidly. It

was so strange to see the most familiar and dear person in Harvard's world in a new light. To recognize the light he saw Aiden in, for what it had always been. Sunset gilded Aiden's lashes and the wings of his collarbone, while the hollow of his throat was left in shadow. The curved bow of his mouth, usually curling, laughing, mocking, was today in an uncertain shape. Harvard had been such a fool.

"Right," Aiden whispered. "That never occurred to me. It should have. I know you, and I know your mom. But it didn't. I would never go home if I didn't have to." He gave an easy, looping shrug. "Of course, my home's a nightmare."

"I know," Harvard whispered back, shocked.

He knew, but Aiden never talked about it. He wondered what was different today.

Aiden was wearing a strange, cracked-open, and almost vulnerable expression. Broken, but not entirely in a bad way. Like a mask breaking, or a shell breaking, so something new could be born.

Oh God, Aiden *knew*, didn't he? Aiden had seen what had been written all over Harvard's face last night. Harvard had been afraid of this.

"I have to tell you something," said Aiden.

"I know—I think I know what you're going to say," Harvard told him.

Harvard didn't want to hear it.

Aiden's mobile mouth worked for a moment, finding a crooked path to a smile. "Just the truth."

Harvard especially didn't want to hear that.

"Can I tell you what I have to say first?" Harvard begged. "Can you please just listen for a moment? Then you can say whatever you like. If you still want to."

Aiden nodded. He'd been hovering near the window as though he might turn and jump out, but now he folded his arms tight over his chest, intent. When Aiden gave his word to Harvard, he never broke it. He was listening.

"Time for the truth, then," said Harvard, and he took a deep breath and told himself to be brave. "I love you more than anything."

New light and shock touched Aiden's face, turning his green eyes pure gold.

"I," he said. "I love you, too."

Harvard hurried on, before Aiden could say *But not like that.* "You're my best friend in the world. I can't picture my life without you. This dating mess has to stop now."

"I admit, it wasn't exactly working as planned," Aiden drawled.

Aiden was undoubtedly at this stage extremely sorry he'd agreed to the whole idea of practice dating. Harvard understood how it must have seemed to Aiden: doing a careless favor for a good friend, acting the way he did every Friday or Saturday night, sweet words and gestures that meant nothing. It wasn't

Aiden's fault that Harvard was made to take this kind of thing seriously, that every word and gesture had meant so much more than Aiden knew. None of this was Aiden's fault.

"You don't understand how badly it could go. You don't know what could happen," Harvard told him.

A pin-scratch frown appeared between Aiden's brows, his features shadowed and barely visible with his hair outlined in fire and gold by the burning horizon. "What could happen?"

"A total disaster could happen, Aiden," said Harvard. "I could fall in love with you."

That shocked Aiden into silence. Harvard had suspected it might. They were on opposite sides of the room, staring at each other across the shadowed space, darkness making the tiny space between every floorboard a gulf. There was so much between them, more precious to Harvard than anything else, and suddenly what had been rock-solid seemed both fragile and in terrible danger. The most valuable thing in Harvard's life, and it could be lost so easily, with nothing but worthless fragments between them.

Surely Harvard hadn't fallen already. There must be some choice involved, some crucial step taken off the edge that Harvard could avoid. Harvard believed in making plans. He could plan for this, too.

At last Aiden murmured, barely audible, "If you did—"

"I *don't want to*," Harvard returned, trying not to shout. "I couldn't bear that. Anything but that. I can't think of anything worse."

Aiden said, "Ah."

Harvard believed in making sacrifices—for your team and your teammates. Aiden hadn't asked for anything like this, to feel devastated with guilt for what he'd done to his best friend or for any serious interruption to his golden, charmed, carefree dating life.

There had never been anyone else looking out for Aiden: Harvard was the one who did that. He'd always wanted to, and never wanted to let him down like this. He could imagine only one thing worse than Aiden tactfully turning him down. The worst thing would be if Aiden felt forced to try dating him out of a misplaced sense of obligation.

Heirs to Swiss banking fortunes. Stacks of offerings from hopeful suitors. A legion of pretty boys with no names. A whole glittering whirl of a life that Harvard could barely understand, but he understood Aiden had chosen to live that way. It was what Aiden wanted. Harvard had no intention of taking any of that glamorous adventure away from him, when Harvard had nothing to offer Aiden in its place. His best friend, about as exciting as his grubby old bear? He knew, as he'd known that first day at Kings Row when he took his first step back, that Aiden was born to shine.

"I can't bear the idea of being without you. I always want you in my life," Harvard said. "So you can't be—you can't be in that part of it. You're not like Neil."

"No," agreed Aiden, as though it was a bleak fact as plain to him as it was to Harvard. It must be obvious to everybody.

It had certainly been obvious to Neil. Harvard had stopped by Neil's on his way home. To apologize.

"So you finally figured it out, huh?" Neil had asked as soon as he opened the door. When Harvard nodded, Neil burst out: "Can you tell me, was the double date—was dating me at all— just an attempt to show the crazy-hot bestie what he was missing or what?"

Neil's shoulders had been braced to hear the worst. Neil was like Harvard in one way. He wanted something real, and he knew getting something fake would hurt more than having nothing.

"No," Harvard said, shocked by the idea. "I wanted the date to go well. I liked you. It wasn't some attempt to make Aiden jealous, what—"

As though Aiden would ever be jealous over him.

Neil must have seen the pain on Harvard's face, as well as the regret. His hackles went down, and he opened his front door a little wider. But not all the way.

"I truly didn't know how I felt about Aiden," Harvard told him. "You knew before I did. And I'm truly sorry."

Neil had nodded, accepting. He had said Harvard could call him if he ever needed to talk. Harvard's mother had been right about him. Neil was nice, and Harvard liked him. In another world, a world with no Aiden, a world Harvard had no interest in living in, perhaps that could have been enough.

"Bye, Harvard," Neil called from his front porch, where Harvard had first seen him little more than a week ago and wouldn't be seeing him again. Even more wistfully, he added, "Bye, Harvard's motorcycle."

And that was that.

Aiden wasn't like Neil, there for a week and then gone, someone whose absence could be borne. Harvard would never stop missing Aiden. If Aiden was gone, all the years of their past were gone with him, and all the years Harvard had ever imagined in the future.

Losing Aiden would be like carving a heart out of his chest and expecting his body to stagger on as normal.

"I understand what you don't want," Aiden told Harvard, speaking very carefully. *Being careful not to hurt Harvard's feelings*, Harvard thought with a rush of guilt and affection. Now that Aiden knew he could. "Can you explain to me what you do want?"

Not to be like those other guys, who would pine for Aiden long after he'd forgotten them. To be different. Not to be foolish enough to throw away a lifelong friendship for the sake of something that couldn't last.

Harvard couldn't have everything he wanted. He had to keep what was absolutely necessary to him.

"I want what we already have. I want to know we won't lose that. I want to know you better than anyone else, and for you to know me the same. I want to know that I'll talk to you every day. I want what I can be sure of. I want to be friends," said Harvard. "I want that always."

Friends forever. For the first time, that sounded like a death sentence instead of a promise.

Aiden sighed. Harvard could only imagine how relieved he must be.

"If that's what you want. Then that's what I want, too."

His tone was entirely cool and unaffected, but something gave Harvard pause. Maybe it was purely his own masochism.

"What you want is just as important as what I want," he said slowly. "Do you want anything else?"

Aiden was quiet for a moment, contemplative. When he spoke, his voice sounded shockingly loud after the silence.

"I want one kiss that's real. To see what it would be like." As Harvard stared in astonishment, Aiden gave the same looping shrug he'd given before, though his face was entirely different, shuttered with none of that brief new openness. "Call it curiosity."

No, absolutely not. Had Aiden not listened to a word Harvard had said? Why would he prolong this torture?

Even as Harvard thought that, he was moving toward Aiden. Helpless to resist. Just like everybody else. He hated himself for it, but he didn't hate himself enough to stop.

He never knew who kissed whom first, moving together with terrifying ease and speed, as though these new moves had become instinct already. As though they would be difficult to unlearn. Aiden seized handfuls of Harvard's shirt and pushed him up against the glass, his mouth an angry demand, and Harvard only pulled him in tighter. The kiss went through Harvard like light striking through a window or fire through brush, hot and vivid.

The setting sun burned a red line against the darkness behind Harvard's eyelids. Not a sword wielded but a spear thrown in the darkness, with no way to know whom it might hit or hurt.

Aiden's hand went behind Harvard's head so Harvard wouldn't hurt himself without breaking the kiss, starving and soothing, biting and gentling at once. They were almost clinging together and almost clawing at each other, and Harvard had to stop this, had to, but he couldn't find the words.

Sunk lower than the sun and trembling, Aiden whispered, "Arrêt."

When Harvard let go his desperate hold on Aiden's fencing jacket, Aiden whirled and ran. The door slamming behind him echoed all throughout their room. Harvard listened to Aiden's retreating footsteps echoing down the hallways of Kings Row. He turned his face to the wall and the window, leaning his forehead against the cold glass. He kept his eyes closed until the sun had set and he'd convinced his wildly beating and breaking heart of what he already knew: This was for the best.

Then Harvard crossed their room, took the bear from their date out of the trash, and hid it in his backpack. He could take the bear home with him, to keep. Aiden never had to know.

30 NICHOLAS

The sun was setting, and it was almost time for the team bonfire Coach had promised them, when Nicholas found Seiji.

"I've been looking for you everywhere," he grumbled.

He felt aggrieved to find Seiji in their room, sitting on his bed and frowning at his screen, with a heap of his belongings laid out on his neatly tucked blankets. It was possible that Seiji was the only one still trying to write that essay. Nicholas had given up. He'd just run suicides until he died or whatever Coach wanted; he couldn't say any more about his childhood.

"I don't know why you would do that, Nicholas," said Seiji. "Searching for your roommate is pointless. You literally know where they sleep, because you also sleep there."

Nicholas shrugged. "Well, I wanted to talk to you as soon as possible."

"Why?" asked Seiji. "People don't tell me I'm an endlessly charming conversationalist."

Nicholas grinned. "Yeah, and they're not gonna start. Maybe I just wanna have a chat with a master criminal. You know, for my street cred."

Seiji lifted his eyes to the ceiling. It wasn't one of the fancy wedding-cake-looking ceilings like in the halls or some of the classrooms in Kings Row, but Seiji still liked to sigh and stare at the ceiling a lot. Nicholas just seemed to inspire this urge in him.

"I'm *not* a master criminal."

"Oh man," said Nicholas. "I feel all shocked and betrayed. But maybe not as shocked and betrayed as the weight lifters will."

"I don't know how everybody in Kings Row doesn't realize this," said Seiji, "but money can be exchanged for goods?"

Realization dawned, bright as the sun setting on the heap of not-actually-stolen watches in front of Seiji. Nicholas had known Seiji wasn't a master criminal, but he hadn't been sure about exactly how Seiji's plan had gone down.

"You bought all those watches." Nicholas was certain now.

"I consulted with my father to see if I could," Seiji stipulated conscientiously.

"Yeah, I just bet you consulted with your father!" said Nicholas. "You must've spent hundreds of dollars!"

Seiji paused. "Approximately."

"So you bought a huge pile of watches, and then you lied about seeing a stolen stash hidden in one of the students' rooms, and you made sure Kings Row was buzzing with gossip so the students' rooms actually got searched.... All before anybody actually checked with the jewelers to see if they *were* robbed."

"Eugene mostly did the gossip part," claimed Seiji. "I don't gossip. It involves talking to several people."

"Must have been slightly embarrassing for the school when the jewelers said they weren't robbed. Must have been slightly embarrassing for you when they gave you back a pile of watches and you had to explain where you'd got them, and how they turned up in someone else's room."

When Seiji shook his head, Nicholas realized he'd underestimated Seiji. Probably, Seiji would be a great master criminal if he really wanted to be.

"I said I wished to donate the watches to a charity," said Seiji. "My father suggested I should do this, so it wasn't a lie. I believe the school authorities think those boys stole my charity watches as an unkind prank, and they are still in trouble. Though not expelled for stealing watches."

He seemed faintly regretful about that. Seiji and Eugene had really taken a dislike to these guys. Nicholas wished he could remember anything they'd ever said, but when he tried to think back he only recalled a generalized *Blah blah, don't mind us, we're jerk faces.*

Nicholas whistled. "Gossip, misleading the authorities, and a pretend heist. Why'd you do all that?"

"It should be perfectly obvious why I did all that," said Seiji.

"For me," said Nicholas. "Because you thought those idiots hurt my feelings."

Seiji glanced up, a look of pure horror on his face. "No! Of course not! I did it to *win* at *teamwork*."

"Oh," said Nicholas, disappointed.

Well, Nicholas was *on* the team, and he was the teammate Seiji and Eugene had been supporting, so he supposed that was the same thing. He cheered up.

"Do you want one of the watches?" asked Seiji absent-mindedly.

"No, they're yours!" Nicholas protested.

"I already have one," Seiji objected in a crabby voice, as though Nicholas was being ridiculous. "Anyway, if you won't take a watch, have this. In exchange for you getting my watch fixed. My watch is of sentimental value to me," he added in a tone that suggested he didn't know what sentimental value was.

He reached under his bed and shoved a package at Nicholas while Nicholas blinked at him in confusion. The package appeared to be pale-blue pajamas made of some stiff material, the same kind as Seiji's. Nicholas gave the package a massive side-eye.

"Uh...," Nicholas said. "Thanks?"

He didn't want these and wouldn't be wearing them. They looked as if they would be itchy and horribly uncomfortable to sleep in, but since Seiji wore them to bed and presumably liked them, he probably thought they were a good gift. Nicholas smiled down at Seiji's bowed head, oddly touched.

"It's fine," said Seiji, stiff as the pajamas. "I'm sorry the prank wasn't useful. Coach is right, I'm not particularly talented at teamwork."

"No, you were right, you're crushing it," said Nicholas.

"Maybe the definitions for success and failure are different in your lexicon, Nicholas."

"I don't know what *lexicon* means," Nicholas informed him. "Nobody knows *lexicon* means. Why would you use that word?"

It was amazing how Seiji could go from concentrating on his paper to rolling his eyes at the ceiling again without even accidentally looking at Nicholas on the way.

"What I mean is, you didn't require defense from these students. So pranking them, however generally objectionable they were, was pointless."

"No, it wasn't," said Nicholas. "It was like the trust falls we did that one time."

"The trust falls we all failed at?" asked Seiji. "Yes, it was remarkably similar."

"No," said Nicholas. "Not because of that. This time, the trust falls worked. This time, I know that if I was in trouble or whatever, my teammates would come help me out. Because you came this time."

There was a pause. Seiji put away his papers. Nicholas waited, wondering if he would get ordered to his side of the curtain for being an idiot.

"Do you know…," said Seiji. "Sometimes I have the oddest thought that there might be something to be learned from you, Nicholas."

This was news to Nicholas, but he liked the sound of it.

"Oh yeah? Do you wanna copy my legendary speed in fencing?" Nicholas asked, beaming.

Seiji rolled his eyes. So much eye-rolling happened in their room, and Nicholas didn't foresee that changing anytime soon.

"This isn't about fencing."

"Who are you?!" Nicholas exclaimed. "What did you do with the real Seiji!"

"There would be no point in trying to learn anything about fencing from you. Stop persisting in the delusion you are good at fencing. You're very bad at fencing, Nicholas. I can't stress that enough."

Nicholas admitted: "Maybe it *is* the real you, after all. C'mon, we have to go to Coach's bonfire. It's gonna be totally fun; we'll roast marshmallows."

"I've spoken to you about sugar and empty calories."

"Yeah, and I've spoken to you about how they're awesome," said Nicholas. "Hey…since we've had such a good day, with you being fantastic at teamwork and everything, now would be a great time to take down the shower curtain, am I right?"

Seiji climbed off his bed to stand protectively in front of it. "We're not taking it down!"

"Aw, but—"

"No!" said Seiji.

Nicholas made a sad face.

Seiji made a martyred sound. "All *right*," he conceded in the tone of one sorely tested, and he moved the shower curtain roughly a third of a foot away from the wall.

Then he stood there with an expression indicating he was fighting the urge to twitch the curtain back into place.

"Let's open it a bit more than that," Nicholas proposed. "What if we opened it halfway?"

"Have you heard the phrase 'give them an inch and they'll take a mile'?" Seiji inquired.

"Nope."

"How strange," said Seiji. "You'd think someone would've mentioned the saying to you since it was clearly *made up about you*."

He gave Nicholas a severe look, then gave the shower curtain a stare, so Nicholas was aware that if the shower curtain was moved even a fraction of an inch farther open, Seiji would know, and there would be consequences.

"Hey, Seiji?"

Seiji was still squinting at the shower curtain.

"Seiji!"

"I won't move the curtain, Nicholas."

"I wanted to say…thanks for being a great teammate," said Nicholas. "Sorry the weight lifters lifted you."

"That was the worst part," Seiji agreed.

He put on his raincoat. Then he located a spare raincoat he had, for some reason, and fixed Nicholas with a stern and cold glare until Nicholas gave up and wore it to stop Seiji's fussing.

Raincoat on, Nicholas glanced from the opened shower curtain to the pile of watches on the bed.

"Seiji. Hey, Seiji. Seiji, I just had a thought. No problem at all if not, obviously, but I thought it might be cool. If you agreed that it would be cool?"

"What is it now?" asked Seiji in a weary tone. "We're going to be late for our social engagement."

Nicholas asked shyly, "Do you maybe…wanna be best friends?"

"Oh my God," exclaimed Seiji. "No!"

He gave a put-upon sigh, and shepherded Nicholas out the door of their room in case they were late for their social-engagement-slash-totally-fun-bonfire.

"You act like you don't even know what words mean," Seiji continued reproachfully. "*Best* implies that someone excels at an activity. It should be perfectly obvious that I am not practiced at being friends and cannot be expected to excel."

"But I think you're good at it already," argued Nicholas, prepared to be stubborn about this.

Everyone said Seiji was a fencing prodigy. It made sense he would be a prodigy at other stuff also.

"Your standards are *appallingly low*," said Seiji. "Probably due to your deprived childhood."

"Yeah, maybe so, but I still think you're great at it," Nicholas persisted. "So even if you're bad, I don't mind! Let's do it."

Chad of the weight-lifting bros had been walking past them, humming a tune, but his head seemed to spin around 180 degrees without his rather thick neck moving at all. The tune ended.

Seiji cast Chad a wary glance, but when he made no sudden movements, Seiji relaxed and returned to scolding Nicholas.

"No!" said Seiji. "Stop bothering me about this. I'm not ready."

As they made their way down the back stairs, Chad lunged. Seiji sped up to get out of the way, but Chad was actually reaching for his teammate.

Nicholas, who hadn't been expecting to be grabbed, was halted by Chad's inexorable grip. It was instantly clear that if he tried to struggle free, both his shirt and his new raincoat would rip at the seams.

Chad's face was unusually serious. "Couldn't help but overhear what you were talking about with my man Katayama back there."

"Uh," said Nicholas. "Okay?"

"You should wait until you're *both* emotionally ready, bro," Chad told him in a stern voice.

Nicholas nodded uncertainly. Chad gave him an encouraging

thump on the back that almost knocked Nicholas to the ground. Then he ran after Seiji, down the stairs, out the double doors, and into the woods. Nicholas glanced over his shoulder before plunging in among the trees and saw Kings Row waiting behind him, fancy windows blazing in the dark, as if someone had finally left a light on to guide him home.

Chad was right, Nicholas decided. He probably shouldn't bring up being best friends again for a while, not until Seiji'd had a chance to think it over.

Maybe Seiji would be ready next week?

Maybe Nicholas should wait until they'd won the state championship. Seiji was bound to be in a good mood then.

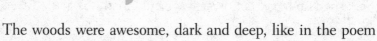

The woods were awesome, dark and deep, like in the poem his English teacher had gotten Nicholas to read. Nicholas was pretty sure that's how it went.

Coach had found a grove and taught them how to build a bonfire as a team, which largely meant that Harvard and Eugene did fine and the rest of them had various issues. Nicholas felt it wasn't fair to blame him for not being good at making fires. The teachers at all his old schools had been extremely clear that Nicholas *shouldn't* set fires.

"But if we're allowed to play with lighter fluid at Kings Row, that's cool, Coach," Nicholas said, and Coach sent him to sit on a log with Aiden, who was mysteriously in his fencing gear and wrapped in one of the stripy woolen picnic blankets.

Since the jerk had so much confidence, Aiden was able to make the picnic blanket look like something he'd chosen to wear on purpose. He was staring into the carefully constructed pyre of branches as the flames began to catch, but he nodded to Nicholas as he sat down, in a more companionable way than he usually did.

"Before you arrived, we heard Eugene's tearful confession of his crimes," said Aiden. "Actually, Coach had to pretend vigorously that she couldn't hear. You were having some trouble with various Kings Row idiots?"

That almost sounded like concern. But ha ha, who was Nicholas kidding? This was Aiden.

"Whatever," said Nicholas. "Who cares what idiots say? And they didn't say anything *you* haven't said."

Aiden nodded, pulling his picnic blanket close under his chin. His green eyes caught firelight, and Nicholas saw the moment his mouth twisted, about to say something nasty Nicholas planned to tune out.

Then Aiden didn't say it after all.

"It's possible . . . ," Aiden conceded, ". . . that I tend to go somewhat too viciously after other people's vulnerabilities so that nobody ever has the chance to go after mine."

"Oh, is that why you talk so much?" Nicholas asked. "Huh."

"Even cool, rich, devastatingly handsome people have feelings, Nicholas," drawled Aiden.

"Sorry, who are we talking about again?"

Aiden laughed. Nicholas smirked, kind of pleased with himself for amusing Aiden. After all, Aiden was older and a teammate and everybody else thought Aiden was seriously awesome.

"I know I have made fun of you frequently, for many good reasons, especially your hair," continued Aiden. "I may have also mentioned your socioeconomic status, which you can't help but could hide better, by having—just for example—some knowledge of how to dress or even basic—"

"What?" said Nicholas. "Speak up. Enunciate, as Seiji would say. Can't make out what you're babbling about."

"Anyway . . . sorry," Aiden told him.

Nicholas caught Aiden's eye. "That's okay, Aiden."

Aiden raised a single brow, because he was annoying and able to do that. It made him look cool and ironic. "Oh, *that* you heard?"

"Yeah," said Nicholas. "That, I heard."

He smiled at Aiden. After a moment, Aiden smiled back.

"Just don't fall in love with me," warned Aiden. "I'll only break your heart."

"Oh no," said Nicholas. "It's gone again . . . what was that . . . ?"

Aiden snorted and shook his head, sparks dancing in the smoke reflecting gold and red shimmers in the loose strands of his hair. Nicholas could almost see what all the fuss was about.

Not really, though.

Because Nicholas was watching Aiden, he noticed when Aiden cast a single glance through the spark and smoke at Harvard, now sitting with Coach and Eugene across the way.

Then he saw Aiden swallow and look away. A look flitted across Aiden's face, swiftly gone as the shadow of a night bird on the forest floor. Nevertheless, the sight of it made Nicholas bite his lip.

Had Aiden and Harvard had some kind of fight? Was Aiden acting like a halfway okay person purely because he'd alienated the only one who'd put up with Aiden for so long? Weren't friends meant to be forever?

Coach's gaze swept around the entire team assembled around the bonfire. Panic and guilt instantly filled Nicholas's heart and stopped him from worrying about Aiden. Seiji edged toward Nicholas so they could be in trouble together.

"Hands up, who has completed their essays?" said Coach.

Nicholas made a face at the bonfire. Nobody lifted their hand, so at least they were all failing as a team. That was a bright side!

Nicholas opened his mouth to point this out. Seiji elbowed him heavily in the ribs. There was something about the nudge that made Nicholas believe if he tried to speak, Seiji would shove him right into the bonfire.

Nicholas decided to be tactfully silent.

"I'm about to suggest an amazing bargain to you all," Coach announced. "If you succeed at this small task, you don't have to write your essays."

Aiden stirred as if he were going to protest but decided not to.

Nobody had shoved him, so Aiden must be figuring out tact on his own.

"I wish each one of you to nominate the person you believe to be the best teammate. I want you to be strictly honest," Coach stipulated.

"Harvard," said Aiden at once, to exactly nobody's surprise.

Harvard looked up from his intent contemplation of the fire. "Aiden," he said quietly, and he and Aiden exchanged a smile. It was only a small smile, but somehow it had more warmth than the bonfire.

Nicholas felt comforted by that smile. He was suddenly certain that whatever had gone wrong between them, it could be fixed. That best friends, as Nicholas had hoped, were forever.

After Harvard and Aiden spoke, there was a long silence, in which there was only the crackle of flames and the rustle of leaves in the night wind.

"Seiji. And Eugene," Nicholas said at last, since it didn't seem like anyone was going to talk unless he did. "They're really cool and great teammates. Always, but especially today."

Eugene darted around the bonfire to give Nicholas a fist bump. Nicholas was getting to like fist bumps, since it meant they were true bros.

"Nicholas," Seiji decided. "I appreciate his advice on certain subjects. Eugene is also helpful occasionally, though he shouldn't give me bad information about social situations, which are not my forte."

"Heavens," drawled Aiden. "I had not noticed that about you, Seiji. At all."

He winked at Seiji, so it didn't seem to be a malicious joke. A muscle twitched near Seiji's mouth, which might have been a gesture toward a smile.

Eugene reached out with hope for a fist bump. Seiji waved him away irritably.

"You saw what happened with the weight lifters earlier. Do you think I am in the mood for more physical contact today?"

"Understood, bro," said Eugene, lowering his fist. "Catch you tomorrow, on another righteous teammate day! I think you're all the best, bros!"

Instantly his fist shot back up in position. Seiji gave Eugene a betrayed look.

"It's a reflex, bro," Eugene assured Seiji. "I didn't mean anything by it."

Seiji made a grouchy sound and moved closer to Nicholas for protection from fist bumps. Aiden seemed judgmental of them all, as if he thought he was so much cooler than they were. Oddly, Coach was smiling, and Harvard looked as though he knew why Coach was smiling. That kind of specialized knowledge was probably why Harvard was captain.

"Did we get the right answer?" Nicholas hoped.

"You did," said Coach.

"But we nominated different people," Seiji pointed out.

"You talked about your teammates, and not yourselves. Boys,

you are ridiculous, impossible, and in the eyes of all sane people, practically past hope," said Coach. "But I'm proud of you."

They hadn't even done much fencing lately, but that still felt good to hear. Nicholas wasn't sure any grown-up had ever been proud of him before. Coach raised her can of root beer in a toast. She dimpled in Nicholas's direction.

"Here's to the wondrous bond of unity, kid."

Nicholas returned her grin and raised his can to toast her back.

"You proud of your team, Captain?" asked Coach, winking at Harvard.

"Always," said Harvard.

The fire burned merrily on, shining bright as a trophy in the dark of the woods. Nicholas made a grab for the big bag of marsh-mallows, despite Seiji's attempts to foil him. He fought for pos-session of the bag while Harvard brought Aiden a drink from the cooler and Eugene protested loudly: "Watch the fire! Bros, I'm concerned you're gonna actually fall into the huge roaring fire."

"Would you not describe it as a broaring fire, Eugene?" asked Aiden, and the sound of their laughter was louder in this shel-tered grove than the hissing of flames or the surging of the wind.

On a night like this, at a golden moment like this one, Nich-olas could almost believe his own and Coach's dreams might come true.

They might all be winners in the end.

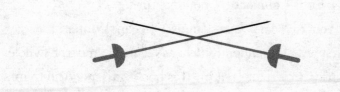

ACKNOWLEDGMENTS

A million thank-yous are in order.

A universe-size thank you to C.S. Pacat for a hundred Skype sessions, emotional calibration, heist plotting, and sorely needed aid with the fencing.

Thank you to Johanna The Mad for so many things, including the art for our gorgeous cover.

Thank you to my parents for recording all those Basil Rathbone sword-fighting scenes for me.

Thank you to Susan Connolly for the cold-steel read, and Holly Black for the climactic emotional turn!

Thank you to Mary-Kate Gaudet, Regan Winter, Lindsay Walter-Greaney, Alexander Kelleher-Nagorski, and the whole team at Little, Brown for creating this book with me. And thank you to Dafna Pleban, Shannon Watters, and Sophie Philips-Roberts, and everyone at BOOM! for welcoming me to the Kings Row universe.

Always endless thanks to my peerless agent, Suzie Townsend, and to Dani Segelbaum and the whole team at New Leaf.

And many, many thanks to the *Fence* fans, who welcomed me to Kings Row as well. Happy to be here.

Edel Kelly

SARAH REES BRENNAN is the number one *New York Times* bestselling YA author of over a dozen books, both solo and cowritten with authors including Kelly Link and Maureen Johnson. She was long-listed for the Carnegie Medal for her first novel. She was born in Ireland by the sea and lives there now in the shadow of a cathedral, where she's working on—among other things—her series of tie-in novels with the hit Netflix show *The Chilling Adventures of Sabrina*. Her most recent standalone novel, *In Other Lands*, is a tale of love, friendship, and wings, starring the crankiest boy to ever stumble into a magic land, and was a Lodestar Award, Mythopoeic Award, and World Fantasy Award finalist.